WILDWOOD
LARKWING

SHARI L. TAPSCOTT

Wildwood Larkwing
Silver and Orchids, Book 3

ISBN-13: 978-1974290963
ISBN-10: 1974290964

Editing by Z.A. Sunday
Cover Design by Shari L. Tapscott

Silver and Orchids

Moss Forest Orchid
Greybrow Serpent
Wildwood Larkwing
Lily of the Desert
Fire and Feathers: A Silver and Orchids Novelette

The Eldentimber Series

Pippa of Lauramore
Grace of Vernow: An Eldentimber Novelette
Anwen of Primewood
Seirsha of Errinton
Rosie of Triblue: An Eldentimber Novella
Audette of Brookraven

Fairy Tale Kingdoms

Puss without Boots: A Puss in Boots Retelling
Chains of Gold: A Fairy Tale Kingdoms Novelette

Contemporary Fiction

Just the Essentials
Glitter & Sparkle
Shine & Shimmer

For Zindy, Laurie, and Angie

I am so blessed to have you three as my aunts. You all mean the world to me.

CHAPTER ONE
He Thinks You're Married

Phoenixes will burn you, basiliskas go for blood, and kelpies will lead you toward your death. But a lie...a lie will haunt you every night and burn you from the inside out.

"You told him *what?*" Adeline exclaims, looking at me as if I just said I was going to adopt a baby goblin and raise it as my own.

"I didn't know what to do," I hiss at a whisper, reminding the seamstress to keep quiet so our voices won't travel through the infirmary's door. "Gregory told me not to upset him."

"But now he thinks you're married!"

That's one downside of my chosen profession—adventuress for hire. Sometimes you find yourself on a hidden island in a whirlpool, marrying the handsome captain who, only two months earlier, robbed you of one hundred and sixty thousand denat's worth of Moss Forest orchids. And then, sometimes, said captain gets stabbed in the stomach by a deranged duchess whose husband was arrested by the king, and even though he's near death, you must tell him the marriage wasn't binding because:

1. You didn't have a witness who spoke your language.

2. You had no idea what the vows you repeated were. (Again, different language.)

3. You didn't—and I quote the kindly, white-haired clergyman—"consummate the marriage."

*Or...*you don't tell the handsome captain all that—which is the path I went with one month ago here in Mesilca, and I've been paying for it ever since.

Today, Gregory has finally given us the all-clear to move Avery from the infirmary onto the Greybrow Serpent so we may sail him home. Today, the captain is going to expect his wife to stay in his cabin with him. Today, I must tell him the truth.

Therefore, today, I want to hide under a rock.

"Do you think he'll be angry?" Adeline asks, finally lowering her voice.

I shake my head. "No."

My pretty friend frowns and nibbles her bottom lip in thought. She wears her auburn hair down, and she has on a traveling gown in dove gray—her own creation. After much thought and many tears, she's decided to leave her family and come home to Reginae, with us. I never thought I'd say it at the beginning of summer, but I'm so grateful she is.

"Then why are you so worried?" she asks, genuinely confused.

"I'm not sure."

Avery's doing much better, and I know he can handle the news. I tell myself it's because I'm embarrassed, but deep down, I know the truth.

I glance at the door and frown. "Perhaps some part of me—a small, tiny part—might wish it were true."

Adeline's expression softens, and she pulls me into an embrace. She smells exactly like lace looks—floral and feminine and slightly overwhelming, but in the nicest way.

"Yes, yes," I say, gently pushing her away.

The seamstress has always been nice—in her own, snippy I-cannot-believe-you-go-in-public-in-those-rags sort of way, but she's been especially kind now that I've ended any romantic confusion with Sebastian—my business partner and the man she's over the moon for.

Of course, now Sebastian isn't speaking to me. At all. Which will likely make business difficult when we get back home.

"It will be all right," she promises. "And even if Avery's angry at first, what's he going to do? Toss you off the ship?"

Her words are meant to be reassuring, but I've said the exact same thing before and ended up floating in a dinghy in the middle of the Aelerian Sea.

CHAPTER TWO
Enjoying the Ruse

"Careful, Captain. Watch your step here," Tom says as he and five other men assist Avery onto the dinghy that will take us to the Greybrow Serpent. The crewmen fuss over their captain with the skill of a flock of hens.

Avery grits his teeth. He looks like he's about to toss them all into the cove. "I can *walk*."

Their captain's tone doesn't deter the men, and they continue to coddle Avery, which only makes him more irritated. I hang back, trying to decide if I want to laugh or cringe. Once he's in the boat and his men are satisfied, I step in and take the seat next to him.

Things are, for lack of a better word, *awkward* between the captain and me. We haven't spoken about the "marriage," and we certainly haven't mentioned it to anyone else. Well, except for Adeline, but for obvious reasons, I haven't told Avery about that.

I study him, looking for signs of exhaustion. Avery's handsome, alarmingly so. He's tall and rugged, well-muscled but lean. His hair is light brown—that particular shade that grows dark in the winter months and light in the summer. After our weeks in the tropical sun, it's more blond than brown.

He catches me looking at him, and I give him a nervous smile. He narrows his eyes slightly and smiles back. He knows something. What, I have no idea, but he's been giving me that look for weeks now. I feel I've been branded for all to see—*liar.*

It's eating me alive. I'll tell him as soon as we're on the ship.

But I can't do that because as soon as we're aboard the Serpent, Avery takes a wrong step and hisses in pain. His face goes pale, and I hold my breath along with everyone around us. Gregory, our mage and healer, frowns, and I don't like the grim concern in his expression.

Avery waves his crewmen away—more like threatens he'll keelhaul the lot of them if they don't stop hovering. His stern expression makes him look formidable and older than his twenty-three years. Though he tries to hide the pain, it's obvious this short jaunt from shore to ship was almost too taxing.

I hover on the deck as they usher him to his cabin,

but I do not dare get too close. As I bite my lip, thinking over my options, the dinghy arrives with Adeline and Sebastian. Mason and Zeb, the seventeen and sixteen-year-old ship's boys, practically trip over each other as they attempt to reach Adeline first so they may help her from the lift. At twenty, a year younger than Sebastian and me, she's too old for them, but that doesn't deter them in the slightest.

Adeline smiles, ever polite, and takes Zeb's hand. Mason scowls but continues to hover, just in case Her Loveliness should require his assistance at some point. Sebastian, behind Adeline, wears a bored look. He's pressed, polished, and combed—looking perfect in his cobalt doublet and long gray traveling jacket. His hair is teak, the darkest of cool chocolates, and every short strand is in place.

He looks past Adeline and her young entourage, and our eyes meet. I wait for that familiar catch in my breath, for my heart to stutter as it did the last time we were in Grenalda.

But there's nothing there but the memory of handing him my heart only to have him respectfully, perhaps even regretfully, hand it back. Our relationship changed in that moment, or maybe it went back to the way it was before, when we were friends, oblivious to love. But we're not quite friends now, not quite business partners, not quite acquaintances if appearances mean anything.

I miss him—not for what I wanted him to be—but for what he was. We've had our disagreements—we've had flat-out fights. But never this silence. Our arguments were loud, passionate. This is...different.

Sad.

And much, much too cordial.

Sebastian doesn't look away this time, and I stare back, refusing to be the first to relent. I know what he wants. He wants me to turn away from Avery, come back to him, trail after him like the perfect pet I used to be. He came after me to Mesilca; I know he cares. But there are too many things keeping us apart. One of those things happens to be the man who is currently snarling at the crew in his captain's cabin.

If Sebastian were to choose me, if he were to tell his grandfather he's willing to walk away from his deceased father's rightful title, estates, and inheritance, then it would all go to his third cousin—his third cousin who just happens to be Avery.

And there is no one in Kalae who Sebastian dislikes more than Avery.

Shaking his head, Sebastian finally looks away and walks briskly through the door that leads below deck. Adeline stares at him, lips parted, confused by his sudden departure. She wears her heart on her sleeve for all to see. I wonder if I was quite so obvious before I became jaded.

She looks at me, wanting me to explain Sebastian's mood, but I only shrug.

"Lucia," Gregory says behind me, drawing me from my brooding. He nods toward the captain's cabin. "Captain Greybrow wants to see you."

I look at the door, wary. "Did he say why?"

The mage shakes his head and gives me a strange look. Though we've told no one what happened on that island, Gregory suspects something. For all I know, Avery muttered about it when he was delirious with pain-relieving teas.

"Thank you, Gregory."

Adeline steps to my side and gives me a bolstering smile. "Go on then."

"Maybe now's not the time..." I cringe because I know I'm just avoiding it.

"It's like cauterizing a wound," she says. "The pain is horrible, but you have to get it done and over with."

"What do you know about cauterizing wounds?"

She shrugs cryptically and wanders after Sebastian.

I open the door slowly, hoping I dawdled long enough that Avery will be asleep. No luck.

He looks up from his desk, his hair ruffled and his eyes tired behind the spectacles he uses to read. Sitting back, he clasps his hands on the map in front of him.

"You should be resting," I say, distracted. I love those glasses.

He raises an eyebrow, and even in his current state, my knees go soft. He removes the spectacles and settles deeper into the chair, silently showing me he's not moving.

Stubborn. I never knew *how* stubborn the captain was until he took a knife in the stomach. He's the worst patient—he never listens, tries to move too quickly, and doesn't give himself the chance to heal. It's that wretched Thane blood in him.

"You summoned me?" I ask, clasping my hands at my waist.

"And why do you think I did that?" His eyes find mine, and his eyebrow tilts knowingly.

"I'm assuming because you wanted to speak with me." I am fully prepared to play it as cool as he is— even if my heart skitters with nerves.

"Why are you avoiding me, Lucia?"

The captain's too tired for this conversation—*I'm* too tired for this conversation. Surely it can wait until tomorrow. Or better, next week. Maybe when we return to Kalae.

"I have no idea what you're talking about."

Avery stands. He walks toward me, taking his time—not because of his wound but to make me sweat.

IO

I gulp but stand my ground. Even barely on the right side of death's door, Avery makes me feel things I'm not sure I should feel.

He stops right in front of me, too close yet too far. "I think it's time we tell the crew."

I panic. I can't tell him yet, not when he's already had such a taxing day.

"I don't think that's a good idea. We just got on the ship...and..."

Chuckling under his breath, Avery brushes my hair behind my shoulder and grazes his lips over my ear. It's the first contact of this kind we've had since we returned to Mesilca, and it muddles my brain. I sigh when his hands find my sides.

"Oh, but I think we must," he says. "Imagine what they'll say when I have your things brought to my cabin if we don't inform them that you're my *wife*."

I shiver when he whispers the last word.

"Avery..." I close my eyes, tilting toward him. "There's something we should discuss..."

His lips move to the edge of my jaw, and he whispers in a deep, dark, ever-so-alluring voice, "Like the fact that we're not actually married?"

Startled, I gasp and push him away. "You knew!"

Avery sucks in a harsh breath, and I realize I've hurt him. I leap forward, grasping his arms. "Oh, I'm *sorry*. Are you all right? Here, sit."

Gently as I'm able—which apparently isn't very gentle at all—I lead him to the edge of his bed. I sit next to him with my arm wrapped around his back, feeling like a cow. For once, why can't I be soft and sweet like Adeline?

The captain takes several moments to collect himself, and then he meets my eyes again. We're close enough I could kiss him if I angled my head just slightly.

"The ceremony wasn't binding," I admit as I look away to avoid temptation.

This is too much for today—he didn't need this. It's exactly what Gregory's been lecturing me to avoid.

"I know."

"How did you find out?"

He gives me a wry smile. "You've been abnormally pleasant. It didn't take me long to figure out something was amiss."

"You almost died—of course, I've been pleasant."

Ignoring me, he continues, "And whenever I attempted to broach the subject, you would suddenly have something 'pressing' to take care of. I spoke with the man from the church a few weeks ago."

"Weeks?" I demand, looking back. "You let me carry on this charade for *weeks*?"

His smile goes all the way to his light brown eyes, making the edges crinkle in a way I haven't seen for at least a month. "I didn't mind you fawning over me. Besides, you were enjoying the ruse. I didn't know how to let you down gently."

I glare at him and tell myself that I should not want to kiss a man this cocky. "Let me down gently? I think you're a bit confused. *I* didn't want to let *you* down."

He full-out grins. "Is that so?"

I nod, absently noting that we've drifted even closer. "This certainly wasn't about me."

Avery angles his head, and his breath tickles my lips. "Admit it, Lucia—you want me. You want my ring on your finger, your clothes in my wardrobe, and a spot in my cabin."

I suck in an offended breath, even if his words are truer than I will ever admit.

"You have some nerve—" I begin, but all rational thought leaves my brain when our lips barely brush. Getting close to Avery is like playing with fire. You know you should stop, but the flame's too mesmerizing to walk away. Still, he's just healing.

"Avery, you shouldn't—"

"Don't you start too." His nose brushes mine, and delicious tingles travel my spine.

Honestly, who am I to fight the captain? And it's been several long, long months since Avery's kissed me.

I sink into him, needing more, careful to avoid his abdomen. His hand cups the back of my neck and his other drifts to my back, but his lips don't quite meet mine. He explores my temples and my cheeks, but he never drifts where I so desperately want him to.

Just when I'm drunk on sensation and ready to demand more, Avery tilts his head back so he can look me in the eye. "Say it, Lucia. Admit that you wanted it to be real." Then, carefully enunciating every word, he adds, "*You want me.*"

Still reeling from his kiss, I move back. My old friend Pride rails at the sure way Avery's looking at me, as if he knows he's cream to a cat. "*No.*"

He leans in and brushes his lips along my jaw as he whispers, "Are you sure about that?"

I angle my head away, needing to break contact so I can *think*. The captain plays dirty.

"What happened on the island...it was..."

The captain's lips brush the sensitive skin behind my ear, and my mind goes blank. The island...I was talking about the island.

What was my point?

"Yes?" he murmurs, his breath warm against my skin. I shiver from the feel of it, and goosebumps rise on my arms.

Come on, Brain. Make yourself useful.

I clear my throat and tilt away from him. "We

were in a whole different world—our emotions were high. We were alone and—"

"We're alone now," he points out.

I'm two seconds from letting myself get carried away, so I leap out of his arms and step back to a safe distance. I try to control my breathing, but I know he can tell how flustered I am.

Amused, he rests his hands behind him on the coverlet, watching me like a wildcat about to pounce.

Gulping, I continue, "It wasn't real."

His eyebrows jump, and his eyes narrow. "*Lucia.*"

That one word tells me he can see right through my lie. Of course it was real—we both know it was.

But I'm terrified.

I cannot be in love with him; I just cannot. He thinks he cares for me now—I won't deny it. And we would have both slipped happily into each other's arms if the marriage had been binding. It would have been messy and awkward, but our future would have been set—the decision out of our hands. But he's free to leave now, and anytime he likes.

It hurt with Sebastian, but it would kill me with Avery. I'm afraid I like him too much.

I let myself begin to care for a man who's too unpredictable, too swayed by whims. It was supposed to end on the island. It wasn't supposed to follow us home.

"You have become a good friend—"

I'm cut off by Avery's groan. He falls back on the bed. "You're impossible—and stubborn and difficult." He tilts his head and looks right at me. "But if you think this is over, you have another thing coming. I will wear you down, Lucia. Day by day, week by week, year by year if that's what it takes."

My knees soften, and my resolve melts like snow doused in boiling water. Yet I somehow hold my ground. "You should get some rest."

Knowing the discussion is over at this point, Avery slowly sits up, wincing at the pain in a way that makes my heart hurt for him. "I should be at the helm."

But, of course, that's not possible—not with Avery in this condition. Arthur, the king's man who was sent in charge of the arrest of the Duke of Mesilca, has already arranged for a substitute captain. I cannot imagine how Avery will bear it.

"Goodnight, Captain. Try to sleep, all right?"

"Did you speak with Sebastian?" Avery asks before I'm through the door.

I look over my shoulder and take note of the veiled worry in his expression. Apparently, he's not as sure of himself as he pretends.

"Yes."

Playing unconcerned, he asks, "And how are... things?"

I know what he's asking, even if he won't come out and say it bluntly. But Sebastian is not the reason I have reservations, and though I cannot explain why, I need him to know that.

I directly meet his gaze. "He's not speaking with me at the moment."

A cocky, relieved smile flickers across Avery's face before fatigue wipes it away. "That's a shame."

Shaking my head and laughing under my breath because I can't help myself, I shut the door softly behind me.

CHAPTER THREE
Royal Welcoming Committee

The king's city slides into view. It promises fresh food, a change of scenery, and most importantly, the end of the most wretched month-long sea voyage I've ever been subjected to. It's been an entire season since I've seen Kalae's mainland. When Avery and I left, we were running from a passel of amateur bounty hunters. It was autumn, the height of the harvest season, and the days were still warm.

Now it's late winter. The city of Teirn never truly grows cold, not like the mountains of Reginae where Sebastian and I are from, but it's not as pleasant as it was when we left. The early morning is slightly cool, just cold enough to need a light jacket or cloak. Later, the day will be warm enough to shed outer layers, possibly even walk about in short-sleeves.

Teirn is a city of nobles and courtiers—the rich. They flock here in droves, escaping the gloomy months for sunshine by the sea. Because of that, the dock is quiet this early in the day. Most of the city's inhabitants are still in their beds, possibly just breaking their fasts on scones and other delicate pastries.

The sun peeks over the horizon as we near the pier. I spot a few couriers running about, and the restaurateurs begin to open their shoppes for the day. They toss open shutters, sweep entries, and prop doors open, welcoming patrons in.

Teirn is gorgeous, as one would expect the king's city to be. There are walkways adjacent to the main road, separated by continuous rows of flower beds and short bushes. It's too cool this time of year for most of the summer blooms, but ruffled ornamental cabbages in purples, reds, and dusky greens decorate the streets. There are benches in welcoming nooks—places encouraging people to stop and chat.

Toward the north of the city lies the castle and its grounds. It's a great gray stone palace with gleaming windows and flag-topped turrets, and it towers over Teirn. It's larger than any of the castles that belong to the dukes who rule over each of the nine provinces and far grander.

The city is for those who have all the time in the world, the ones who don't concern themselves with the harvest or how many eggs their prize hens are laying. The citizens here don't worry about stocking the cellars at just the right time so the root vegetables will not rot before they're eaten. They have people for that, people who are paid handsomely.

Even the lower-class citizens are dressed well—because who would want anything shabby marring the fair city?

Covering a yawn with her hand, Adeline shuffles up next to me. The seamstress doesn't like mornings, and she usually sleeps in much later than I do. We've shared the guest cabin for the last month. Where it seemed large and luxurious compared to the tiny sleeping quarters on the Sea Star, the ship Sebastian and I first sailed on, it's not quite large enough for the two of us. Especially considering Adeline talks in her sleep.

There's only so many times a person can hear, "*Oh, Sebastian,*" before the charm they wear to keep sea sickness at bay fails to control nausea.

When we are near the docks, a small boat makes its way toward us. Two of the king's coastal guards call their greetings to Avery, who is at the wheel—as the stubborn man has been for most of the voyage.

"His Majesty has reserved a spot for you at the royal pier," one hollers. "We're here to escort you."

Avery's words from before we arrived in Mesilca

float to my mind. He said we were going to be celebrated. Apparently, he was right. At least *he* is. I still have my doubts the king will want to fawn over the daughter of a chicken farmer from a tiny village in Reginae.

The Serpent follows the small craft, and soon we are docking at a separate pier. Flink, my wolfhound-sized lesser dragon, runs back and forth, knocking into the crew, bumping into random cargo—generally being an oversized, elemental nuisance.

"Come on." I grasp hold of the dragon's harness and wrestle him below deck, to my cabin.

He stares at me with disappointed amber eyes as I tell him to stay on his bed—an old tattered sail that Avery's boatswain gave us after Flink took up residence on a rather important coil of rope.

"Be good," I warn.

The dragon settles onto the fabric and nuzzles his solid gold ball, which is actually a very expensive gazing ball Avery finally gave him just to keep him out of his cabin. The captain collects all kinds of priceless artifacts, and Flink decided halfway through our voyage here that they were there for his amusement. Strange dragons and their pack rat tendencies.

I shut the door, hoping he doesn't destroy any more of Adeline's dresses. She likes the dragon well enough, but her patience has limits.

We are docking when I arrive back on the deck.

If a pier can be grand, this one is. Men in the king's scarlet and gold mill about, waiting to assist us. Some are here to help with our luggage; others hold trays of pastries and fruits and steaming silver pots filled with what I hope is coffee. I lean far over the railing. Adeline yanks me back, possibly fearing I'm going to topple right over the edge.

The gangplank is lowered, and the serving men, along with several official-looking types, flood onto the Serpent, overwhelming us all. Several men set out for Avery first. They surround him, shaking his hand and congratulating him on his successful mission.

Some find Sebastian, asking him how they might be of service. Adeline and I watch them, slightly overwhelmed.

"They are handsome, aren't they? Perhaps one of *them* will notice me," Adeline says after a few moments, her voice slightly bitter as her eyes linger on my business partner.

She's wrong about Sebastian. He notices her, even if he's careful not to let her catch him. I think it makes him feel guilty—an emotion I am intimately familiar with. But, still, he notices all the same.

And how do I feel about that? I'm undecided. It would be a lie to say I'm not affected by the glances that last a hair too long, to not feel betrayed by the kind way he speaks to her. But I have an aching suspicion it's for the wrong reason.

Avery's been right all along. Sebastian and I have a twisted sort of relationship, one we need to sort out. I want him in my life; I know that much. I think even Sebastian will admit that. Born a day apart in our little village, together constantly since birth, we're practically family. Now we need to learn to give each other a bit of breathing room, space to live our own lives without walking completely out of the other's.

"If it isn't Lucia of Reginae, adventuress extraordinaire," a masculine voice says from beside me.

I turn, startled to find a familiar, blond-haired man bowing in front of me. He straightens and smiles, obviously amused by the incredulous look on my face. "I'm part of your welcoming committee."

His name is Gerard, and he's somehow connected to the royal family, but I've never quite figured out how.

"An improvement over my last position as a human shield, don't you think?" he adds, letting a grin slide over his face as he hints to our last meeting.

The last time I saw him, Avery and I were fighting bounty hunters. I might have ducked behind him while aiming my bow. Of course, he's the one who loudly announced our presence to the entire pier, so it's not like he didn't deserve it.

If first, and second, impressions are anything to

go off, I don't really care for the man. Adeline, though, sidles in closer, hoping for an introduction.

Gerard's eyes widen in appreciation when he sees the pretty seamstress.

"Adeline this is..." I motion toward Gerard, pausing as if I'm at a loss for words. "I'm sorry, sir. I cannot quite remember..." I intentionally let my words trail off and wince in an exaggerated manner.

The handsome young man chuckles, knowing full-well I'm lying through my teeth. Bowing over Adeline's hand, he says, "I'm Gerard of the family Render, and I'm very pleased to make your acquaintance."

Her lips part in surprise when he says his surname.

"Adeline of the family Daughtra, from Grenalda," I fill in since she's a bit starstruck.

Adeline blushes when Gerard brushes a kiss over her knuckles. Though she looks bemused, her eyes dart to Sebastian to see if he's watching the exchange.

Sebastian continues his conversation, pretending he doesn't notice. Adeline's shoulders sag with disappointment. Irritated with Sebastian on Adeline's behalf, I frown at him. I know what it feels like to be snubbed by Lord Thane.

"Adeline, weren't you just saying you had hoped to stretch your legs?" I say. "I'm sure Gerard would be happy to escort you down the pier."

Gerard nods, eager to be of service. "Of course."

Adeline gives me a questioning look, but she's too much of a lady to argue. "That would be very pleasant."

There. I've done my good deed for the day.

The two certainly make a pretty couple. When they reach the pier, they're approached by a woman selling hothouse roses from a basket. Gerard pauses despite Adeline's protests and buys her a light pink blossom. Feeling a bit melancholy for reasons I don't quite understand, I watch Gerard gallantly lead Adeline down the dock.

Over my shoulder, I take a surreptitious peek at Avery. He stands with a group of the king's men. He obviously knows them well, and the group laughs at something he says.

This month at sea has been good for the rogue captain, even if it's been torture for me. Being this close to him...it's difficult. The last few weeks have been filled with lingering gazes and knowing glances...very much like the one he's giving me now that he's noticed me watching him.

I meet his eyes and give him a tiny smile before I disappear below deck. But after the door is closed behind me, I lean against it and close my eyes.

Avery swears he cares for me, but almost the entire time we've known each other, we've either been trapped on his ship or an island. The rest of the world is about to get in the way, and his world is so very different from mine.

Sebastian's a regular reminder of that. The largest obstacle in our friendship has been the great cavern of nobility separating us, and Sebastian isn't even quite as high on the social ladder as Avery. The captain's father is an earl—he's not going to want Avery with me any more than the senior Lord Thane wants me with Sebastian.

Shaking off my fears, knowing there's nothing I can do about them right now, I make my way to the storage cubby/temporary infirmary/personal cabin of Yancey Edelmyer, displaced son of the former Duke of Mesilca.

"Yancey!" I holler as I knock on the wooden door. "Time to join the world!"

Not a bit put out that I'm answered with silence, I knock several more times until the great beast of a man tosses the door open.

Grinning at his surly expression, I cross my arms and angle my head up to look at him. "Hello, Starshine. Did you sleep well in your personal princess cabana? Is there anything you require? Tea? Hot towel?"

We turned the storage cubby into an infirmary when Yancey was attacked by a vampiric siren on our way back from our last voyage. Even though the wounds on his neck healed nicely some time ago, he adopted the space as his own.

Since I was the one to save him from the siren, we've developed a bit of a friendly bond. And by friendly, I mean he no longer knocks me off my feet with the wind charm that's a specialty of his. Well, not often anyway.

Yancey grunts—as friendly a greeting as you'll ever get out of him—and turns back to his room. I, of course, follow him in.

"I really like what you've done with the place," I say, nodding toward the stacked crates that take up half of the space. "Very homey."

He rolls his eyes.

"So...there's a little detail I thought you might like to be made aware of before you head up to the deck..."

"Do you have a point?" he growls.

Like Adeline, Yancey's not much of a morning person.

"Half the king's men have boarded the ship, and they're making themselves cozy with our captain."

Yancey growls and rubs a meaty palm over his forehead.

Since Yancey's father isn't on the greatest of terms with King Harold at the moment—and we're not sure what that means for the man we've reluctantly be-friended even though he has the personality of a bad-ger who has repeatedly been poked with a stick—our plan was to introduce Yancey into Kalae without any fanfare.

And by introduce, I mean sneak.

Which might be difficult now.

"I'll lie low for a day or two," Yancey grumbles.

I purse my lips, knowing he's not going to like the next part.

"What now?" he asks, noticing my expression.

"We were intercepted on the way in and are currently docked at the king's personal pier."

Yancey curses under his breath. "Your pirate companion is chummy with the king. Perhaps he can arrange something—he's certainly slick enough, isn't he?"

Where Yancey and I are doing better, he and Avery are...not. Their already tenuous relationship was bound to be further strained considering it was Avery who conspired with the king to arrest the duke. Still, if Duke Edelmyer hadn't attempted to illegally charter ships to sail into forbidden water, he wouldn't have gotten himself into trouble.

"I'll speak with him. You just stay..." I wrinkle my nose at the dark, small room. "Stay here for a bit."

I wander back to the deck, hoping to find Avery alone for a moment, but I don't see Avery at all. The ship is still abuzz with activity, so I find a spot against the rail and look out over the city.

As I stand here, a weird sensation settles over me. It very much feels as if I'm being watched. I scan the growing crowd—people eager to see what important person has arrived in the city—and my eyes meet the gaze of a thin man in a fine jacket and simple black doublet. Normally, a person would look away, avoid the awkward moment, but the man continues to watch me. I narrow my eyes.

"There you are," Avery says behind me.

I turn, dismissing the strange man from my mind. Leaning close, I ask, "What are we going to do with Yancey?"

Avery frowns. "I forgot he was down there, hiding like a groundhog."

"Avery," I warn.

The captain shrugs, not terribly repentant. "This chaos will die down eventually. We'll figure it out when it does."

"What about Flink?"

Avery glances around the deck, looking for the beast.

"I took him to my cabin," I explain before he can ask.

"Leave him here with Mason and Zeb for now, just until we work everything out."

I glance at the ship's boys, who already appear to have their hands full. But Flink likes them, and they like Flink—which is more than can be said about most of Avery's crew. Frankly put, the dragon's not going to become the ship mascot anytime soon.

More men in the king's colors board the ship, and now there are more of them than crew.

"Why all this fuss?" I ask.

Avery leans against the rail, looking weary. Though the captain's better now, he still tires quickly. Gregory says time and the healing charms have done their job, and now he only needs to regain his strength.

I study him, wondering if he's overexerting himself. Distracted, my eyes lower to the bow of his top lip, to the shadow of stubble on his jaw. Realizing where my thoughts have drifted, I snap my attention back to the chaos.

"No one has sailed past the siren islands in over eighty years," Avery says. "We're the newest novelty in a city of bored nobles. You have no idea how much attention you'll receive once the king learns it was you who slew the beasts. Already, he sent a courier demanding details. By tonight, everyone in Teirn will know of your prowess with a bow."

A strange mix of emotions pass through me—excitement, apprehension, curiosity.

"His Majesty has sent a carriage to take us to the castle," Avery continues. "That's why I was looking for you."

"What about your ship?" I ask.

"My crew will look after it. It's not the first time I've had to leave it."

We're interrupted by one of the visiting men. "Captain, are you ready?"

Avery looks at me, silently asking me if there's anything else I need to attend to. I already have my trunk packed—as long as Adeline didn't try to shove anything else in there, I should be set.

I track down Zeb and Mason and ask them to watch Flink. The boys nod earnestly, happy to take on the task.

"Don't feed him scraps," I remind them. "No matter how he begs. Meat only, everything else gives him indigestion. And don't play too roughly with him after he eats."

"Lucia, we know," Zeb says, rolling his eyes.

I stand there staring at them, wondering if it would be better if I stayed as well.

"We've lived with him for months," Mason reminds me. "We know how to take care of him."

They're good young men—they are. But they're also young. What if they decide to leave with the crew for a night at the tavern? All it would take is a pretty girl, and they'd forget all about their responsibility to Flink.

And he hates the dark.

"It will be fine," Mason reassures me, though I can tell they both think I'm worrying too much.

"Yes, I know," I say after a moment. "Thank you."

"Everything all right?" Avery asks when I return.

I nod, and we make our way to the gangplank, toward the carriage.

As we walk down the pier, I notice the man I saw earlier. He watches me again, his gaze still disturbingly intent. I frown and turn toward Avery.

"Look to your right," I hiss. "That man has been watching us all morning."

Casually, Avery looks that way. "Who?"

When I look back, the man is gone.

I frown at the masses of people as we make our way to a carriage just beyond the pier. The crowd has picked up now, but I have no idea why. The king's guards have gathered, and they usher us through the streets. We're led to a grand carriage, one with King Harold's crest on the back, and my heart flutters in my chest.

This cannot be happening, not to me.

More guards surround the carriage, controlling the crowd. The people who have gathered are casual onlookers, not nobility but a collection of wealthy people who fit well enough into Teirn that they're allowed to stay.

"Where's Adeline?" I ask Avery as we near the carriage.

"Gerard has already escorted Miss Daughtra to the castle," our guard says, answering for the captain.

I look around. "And Sebastian?"

"Sebastian had business in the city," Avery answers this time. "He said he'd meet us later."

Shocked, I turn to Avery. "The two of you had a civilized conversation?"

Avery gives me a wry smile. "Astounding, isn't it?"

When we are very near the carriage, the footman tosses the door open, gives me a respectful, crisp nod, and offers his hand to assist me inside.

"All right then," I murmur under my breath, feeling as if I've stumbled into someone else's life.

The carriage is gilded. As in, with gold.

Gold.

The seats are made of plush, heavy velvet in the deepest of rich purples, and the seats are upholstered in a coordinating fabric. The ceiling is lined with embroidered satin, and tiny tassels hang from decorative swags. I stare at it all, astonished. But what really has me dumbfounded is the lovely, dark-haired woman who lounges on the left-side bench, smiling like a cat who just caught a canary.

Avery bumps into my back and comes to an abrupt stop.

"Hello, Avery," the woman says, and before I can

make sense of the situation, she rises from the seat and throws herself into the captain's arms. "Miss me?"

CHAPTER FOUR

More Like a Doll than a Slayer

I stumble onto one of the benches, astonished. It takes me all of five seconds to realize who this woman is. Her gold circlet gives it away, but when Avery says her name, that's the clincher.

"Minerva." He sounds nearly as surprised as I am that the Queen of Kalae is hanging from his neck. "What are you doing here?"

He awkwardly pats her back, and though I want to look away, I can't drag my eyes from his fingers, which rest on the fine fabric of her bodice.

"I'm here to welcome you back to Teirn." The woman finally pulls away, holding him at arm's length even though he's much taller than she is, and the angle is awkward in the carriage. "You look awful."

A hesitant smile crosses Avery's face. "I've been

better."

Her hair is sable, the color of mink's fur—cooler than my brown, somehow more sophisticated. The front pieces are twisted around her circlet, creating a complicated half updo. It's beautiful.

She's beautiful.

After the queen smiles at Avery for several more moments, she seems to remember I exist. Her eyes drift to me, and she wears a perplexed smile. "And who is this?"

Avery takes a seat next to me. "Minerva, may I introduce to you Lucia Linnon of Reginae, the girl who single-handedly slew three sirens."

"It wasn't single-handedly," I murmur.

Her Majesty's smile isn't quite as warm as it was for Avery, but it's cordial and only one degree off friendly. "That's quite an accomplishment for someone so...young." She raises an incredulous eyebrow as her eyes skim over me. "And *petite*."

I am not petite. In fact, I am quite an average height. No, I might not be as long and lithe as most adventuresses, and perhaps my curves are a bit soft, but I am strong and capable, and vaguely insulted by her words. Which I believe was her intention.

Because I have no idea how to answer, I attempt a smile.

"Your Majesty," the footman says, half entering

the carriage and bowing his head. "May we leave? Or would you care for more time?"

"Yes, please. I am eager to return home."

The queen returns to her seat, watching us with those sharp, almost feline eyes. "How old are you, Lucia?"

I squirm, thoroughly unprepared for an inquisition. "Twenty-one, Your Majesty."

She studies me, thoughtful. "Yes, so young."

That's odd, coming from someone who cannot be a day over twenty-four.

"And when is your birthday?"

"Early spring, Your Majesty."

She shakes her head, mock benevolent. "Please, we are friends now. You must call me Minerva."

I swallow and nod.

"And your parents, what do they do?" She tilts her head slightly, waiting for my answer.

Licking my lips, I glance at Avery. He watches the exchange, as uncomfortable as I've ever seen the captain.

"They are chicken farmers, Your—Minerva."

The woman's eyebrows shoot up with surprise. "How darling! My husband will love the story—an adorable little chicken maiden, slaying sirens. I'm sure your parents will be so proud of you. Tell me, when do you plan to return home?"

I don't like her.

"I am a scout, Your Majesty. My business partner and I do not have plans to return to Reginae anytime soon." My words are voiced as sweet as can be, but from the slight hardening of the queen's eyes, I believe I get my point across.

"You have a business partner? Is he a fellow chicken farmer?"

"He is Lord Sebastian Thane, of Reginae."

The smug look falls from her face. "Ah. Related to the duke, I presume?"

"His cousin."

Never mind that Sebastian and I have barely spoken two words in the last month. The extent of our conversations aboard the Serpent went something like, *"Please pass that hard, crumbly biscuit, Sebastian"* and *"Don't stand so close to the edge, Lucia. You'll fall overboard."*

But he's still my partner, whether he likes it or not, and I'll toss around his name if I want to.

The carriage slows, and I assume we're almost to the castle. When I glance outside, however, I find a crowd of people and a great commotion in the street.

A group of the king's guards gathers outside a shoppe. One of the windows is busted. Shattered glass lies on the ground, and sunlight glints off the sharp edges of what's left in the sill. The shopkeeper stands with the guards. He has a bandage wrapped around his head. The fabric is tinged with pink, and the man looks disoriented. It's a surreal sight in picturesque Teirn.

"The city has seen an unfortunate increase in thievery as of late," Minerva says, dropping her faux snobby voice, sounding truly distraught. "We're still unsure of the cause, but alchemy and herbal supply shoppes have been targeted."

It's not uncommon in the seedier cities, like the port city of Fermall in the province of Colrain. Supply shoppes carry a great many treasures, some exceedingly rare and nearly priceless. But it's a shock in Teirn, whose pristine beauty makes it appear to be above such things.

People loiter in the street—gawkers trying to get a closer look. They block our path, and I can hear the queen's driver shouting at them to move out of the way.

"I've sold to that man before," I say quietly.

I'm not familiar with the city, so it takes me a moment to recognize the shopkeeper.

"He's the man who bought the hippogriff feather," I tell Avery, speaking of the rare item that started Sebastian and me on our scouting journey.

Minerva glances at me. "He specializes in animal ingredients."

Scales, quills, feathers—it seems morbid, but they're all needed for certain recipes. And while pigeon down might not be worth much, items from greater elemental beasts, like dragon belly scales or chimera hide, are worth a small fortune.

"I wonder what they were after?" Avery asks.

"Hard to say." With a sigh, the queen looks away.

The crowds finally clear, and the carriage rolls on, leaving the broken shoppe behind us.

The ride to the castle takes both forever and not nearly long enough. My anxiety grows the closer we get. Though he seemed hesitant at first, Avery has no trouble slipping into conversation with Minerva. He laughs beside me now, a low rumbling sound of real amusement, as she tells him about something her young brother did last week. The sound grates on my nerves for the first time ever.

I'm not jealous, mind you. The queen is just that—the queen. But it's clear the two are more than casual acquaintances—and old ones at that. From the tidbits I've picked up, it seems Avery's no stranger to the castle. He was there often as a youth.

I bet young Avery was a sight to behold. I'm sure he was charming, even back then. Probably perfected his crooked grin on all the maids.

Fortunately, I don't have time to dwell on it because the carriage rolls to a stop, and a plethora of guards waits for us just outside the door. Minerva stands first and is efficiently swept into the castle court-yard. To my surprise, Gerard sticks his head in the doorway next. "May I escort you, Lucia?"

"I have that covered," Avery says in a smooth voice, one that makes me glance at him in surprise. He sounds just possessive enough it makes me warm and tingly, but not so much that I want to smack him.

Gerard has the audacity to wink at me, and then he moves out of the way.

The captain steps from the carriage and then offers his hand. I take it, feeling a bit like royalty when I see all the eager eyes waiting for us. Half the castle must be out here. Not only are there maids and gardeners and a bevy of other workers, but the courtiers have gathered as well. Perhaps starved for excitement in this last month of winter, they watch us eagerly, whispering amongst themselves.

I'm so flabbergasted, I end up tripping on the step and careening to the ground. Well, I would careen to the ground if it weren't for the solid arms and chest that catch me.

I look up at Avery, blinking in embarrassment. He doesn't quite smile, but his eyes are bright. I back up quickly, afraid I might have hurt him.

"I'm fine," he says under his breath, so only I will hear.

"Sorry." I can feel the heat rising to my cheeks,

and I know I'm as red as a tomato.

Avery places my arm in his, tucking me close, and we turn toward the castle. I know I'm staring like the wide-eyed chicken maid I used to be, but I simply cannot help it. I've never seen anything like His Royal Majesty's palace. Huge doesn't even describe it. It's four times as large as my village, at least.

There are towers on top of towers, and flags flap in the warm breeze of midday. We're inside the outer walls, standing right outside the main entrance. And it's not just a set of double doors as Duke Thane's castle is—oh no. This castle has a long stone entry, like a longhouse attached to the front, and there are dozens of arching windows lining the rail along the side. It's open to the air like a gazebo and as tall as a two-story house. At the front, for all to see, is a ten-foot pennant with the king's stag crest. It's the grandest thing I've ever seen, and this is just the outdoor entry.

And there, waiting for us, stands King Harold himself.

I clasp my free hand at my waist, nervous. I've never seen the king before, not so much as a glimpse, and now I'm going to be expected to carry on a conversation.

His Majesty is younger than I expected, twenty-six, maybe twenty-seven years old. He's handsome in a rugged way, and he stands with the strength of a noble knight of old. But his eyes are bright, and he wears an eager look that I find terrifying.

Avery pulls me along, oblivious to my nerves. When we are a bare fifteen feet away, Avery releases me and gives the king a formal bow, bending low with his arm held stiff at his waist. I stumble into a curtsy, awkwardly holding out my skirts as I dip, feeling very much like a cow at a ball.

"Rise," King Harold says.

I'm out of breath from nerves, and I think my heart might come out of my chest when I stand. His Majesty takes me in, studying me.

Finally, after several long moments, he nods, almost smiling. "Captain Greybrow, bring my siren slayer forward."

The courtyard is deathly silent, everyone taking in the spectacle. I swallow and resist the urge to wipe my palms on my ornate skirt.

I'm having an audience with *the king*.

Minerva stands at her husband's side, smiling for the masses. The smile, however, does not reach her eyes. She's as poised as a queen should be, as lovely as they come. Her hands are softly folded at her waist, and her posture is perfect—nothing like her cat-like lounging in the carriage. She plays her part well.

King Harold steps forward. Unlike his wife, he looks genuinely pleased to meet me. He holds out his hands, taking me from Avery, and looks me right in the eye. "It's a pleasure to meet you, Lucia Linnon. Had I known my siren slayer was so lovely, the weeks I waited for the Greybrow Serpent's return would have been torturous indeed."

I smile, nodding like a fool, unable to find words. The king just said I was lovely—wait until I tell Sebastian! And then my mood falls because we're not speaking.

Smiling, Harold's eyes drift over my gown. "You look more like a doll than a slayer." He glances at Avery. "And I can see why the captain's kept you to himself."

The king looks at me so directly, I want to squirm away from his attention.

"Thank you, Your Majesty," I manage to say, knowing I have to speak. "You are lovely...as well..."

Unable to stop myself, I cringe. I've been at the castle for less than five minutes, and I've already made a fool of myself.

"I mean..." I clear my throat. "Thank you, Sir. Er, King Harold, Majesty...Sire."

Stop talking, Lucia!

Avery snorts from next to me, amused.

I glance his way, ready to shoot him a glare that would make ice shiver, but I falter. The queen stands next to her husband, the picture of royal beauty, but her eyes are on Avery. Because no one is paying her any attention, she's dropped the facade, and there's a wistfulness in her gaze. I know that look; I've worn it myself.

I snap my attention back to the king, but my mind is reeling because I am quite certain that at one point or another, no matter how impossible it might seem, Avery has had a romantic relationship with Her Royal Majesty, the Queen of Kalae.

CHAPTER FIVE

Skip Over the Best Parts

"We have much to discuss, but there's no reason to linger outside," King Harold says, still holding my hands. He looks at Avery, a strangely mischievous look on his face. "Besides, you have company, and I don't believe you'll want to keep them waiting."

Avery looks taken aback. "Company?"

King Harold twitches his nose in a funny way—a way that makes him seem rather normal and human. His cheeks work as if he's holding back a grin. "I might have let it slip that you were wounded in the act of service..."

Avery groans out loud and clenches his eyes shut as he tilts his head toward the sky. "You didn't."

"I did."

My gaze flickers between them. Though I'm curious what they're speaking about, I'm mostly over-whelmed by their relationship. It's as if they're... friends. Which I find very strange. Does a king have friends? I mean, is that generally allowed? Aren't they supposed to sit on their thrones, looking down at the rest of us with vague disinterest?

Much to my horror, King Harold slides my hand on his arm, obviously planning on escorting me into the castle. I glance at Avery, wondering if I'll be tossed into the dungeon if I protest. But the captain has his hands full. Minerva sidles up next to him, sliding her hand along his arm before he even offers. Avery frowns at the contact, but he doesn't make a fuss.

I snap my gaze forward, trying not to think of the two of them together. Luckily, I can only focus on so many things at once, and the castle demands my entire attention. There are grand things everywhere—ancient, shining shields on the walls, glistening suits of armor, tapestries, rugs, statues, art galore, and an abso-lutely massive charmed fountain inside the four-story foyer.

A minstrel stands in front of the water feature, quietly plucking away on his lute. Remembering Min-erva's snide chicken maid comment, I try to appear very cultured and disinterested, but I find myself gap-ing. There's simply too much to take in.

The king leads us past the fountain, through a tall

pair of doors, right into what appears to be the royal throne room. The courtiers who loitered in the court-yard follow us in, making it seem as if we are leading a great parade.

We leave the multitudes behind when we pass through another set of doors, these ones the size doors should be. The room beyond is welcoming with lots of soft places to sit. There's even a crackling fire in the hearth, though it's too warm for one. The room is a pleasant temperature, however, which makes me think the flames might be charmed to add ambiance only.

A young woman leaps up from a settee the moment we walk into the room, a huge grin spreading across her very lovely face. "Avery!"

I'm certain she'd fly right across the room, assaulting the captain, if it weren't for the elderly woman next to her, who grabs hold of the back of the girl's bodice, keeping her in place. The woman is stately, tall and elegant. Her eyes are sharp, and she vaguely reminds me of someone, though I cannot place whom.

"Hello, Grandmother," Avery says as soon as he enters the room, and it all snaps into place. This is Sebastian's great aunt, and judging from the hawkish look on her face, she's not going to like me any more than Lord Thane. Avery turns his eyes on the girl and grins. "Elizabetta."

She bounces on her toes, making her long, blond

curls sway, and shoots her grandmother a pleading look. Sighing in the most refined way, the woman releases Elizabetta, but not before she gives the girl a sharp look, reminding her to mind her manners.

On the island, Avery told me his sister was thirteen, but she looks closer to fourteen now. Nodding to her grandmother, Elizabetta smooths her skirts and gives the king and queen a polite curtsy before hurrying to her brother. She stares at him for several seconds before she tosses her arms around him, holding him tightly. "You didn't say goodbye," she says, sobbing into his tunic.

Avery loops his arms around her, smiling in a brotherly way. "There wasn't time, Betta."

"You could have left a note!" Then she pulls back and, just like younger sisters are prone to do, smacks him in the stomach.

Avery doubles over, his face etched with pain from the ever-healing stab wound. Everyone of us but the baffled Elizabetta leaps forward to see if he's all right.

"What's wrong with him?" she says, her voice small and terrified. "*Avery?*"

The captain shoos us all away and takes a moment to breathe deep before he turns back to his sister. "I'm fine."

Elizabetta blinks back her previous tears, but it

looks like she's about to start a whole new batch. "What happened?"

"Nothing."

"*Avery.*" Worry shadows her pretty face. "Tell me."

"It was just a dagger—"

"A *dagger!*" She takes a step back, looking like she's about to lose her composure again.

Avery clears his throat. "It's nothing, Betta. It's almost healed."

Not believing her brother, Elizabetta turns to her grandmother. "Did you know? Is that the reason we came to greet him? Because he's injured?"

"Calm yourself, Elizabetta," Lady Claire says, clearly uncomfortable with the scene.

Elizabetta sucks in a breath and stares at the bottom of her skirts.

Like a sweet mother hen, Minerva tucks the girl to her side and escorts her back to the settee like they are dear friends. I watch them, not liking that one bit.

I step next to Avery and ask him under my breath, "Are you all right?"

"It was just a twinge," he whispers.

"Liar."

He grins at me, stealing my breath away. And it hits me as I take in our surroundings—who is this man I exchanged vows with on that solitary island a world away? Surely this is not his life.

And if it is, what could he possibly see in me? Now more than ever, I realize it's very dangerous to let myself have feelings for the captain.

But that's easier said than done when he looks at me like that.

Before I can ponder it longer, a guard clears his throat from the doorway. "Gerard has arrived with Captain Greybrow's companions."

It's funny how the addition of a few people you know can put you at ease in a crowd of strangers. All it takes is one look at Sebastian and Adeline, and I don't feel as out of place. My relief must show on my face because it takes Sebastian off guard. He falters for a moment, and he raises a questioning brow. I offer him a tiny smile. It's the most heartfelt interaction we've had in a month.

Adeline sweeps into the room, a vision in her frothy sea-green gown, and immediately drops into a curtsy in front of the king and queen. It is so beautifully executed, I can't help but wonder if she's been waiting for this moment all her life.

"Your Majesties," Sebastian says, bowing in greeting just as Avery did earlier. "We are honored."

After watching how comfortable they seem, I can't help but question how it came to be that all my friends instinctively know how to address royalty.

Minerva smiles at the pair. Her eyes linger for a

moment on Sebastian, and I know what she's thinking.

When Sebastian and Avery are side-by-side as they are now, it's easy to tell they're related, even if their coloring is very different. If Avery is a golden morning in summer, Sebastian is twilight in autumn. But they're both strong and tall—each intimidating in their own way. Even their expressions are similar, though Avery's most often smirking and Sebastian usually tries very hard to keep his features blank.

"Aunt Claire?" Sebastian says in surprise when he straightens. His eyes widen in shock, and his gaze darts to Avery.

And possibly for the first time since I made the great announcement that he and Avery are kin in Mesilca, Sebastian truly *believes*. His jaw tightens as he looks at Lady Claire, and the color drains from his cheeks. But, ever the gentleman, he shakes his head to free himself of his shock and dons a cordial, if some-what distant, expression.

Adeline walks across the room, the picture of grace, and takes Lady Claire's hand. With the sweetest smile, in the most heartfelt way, she says, "It's such a pleasure to see you again, Lady Claire." Then she beams at Avery's sister. "And Elizabetta, too."

It doesn't bother me the way it did when Minerva was doting on her—but Adeline doesn't do it in a way that makes me think she's demonstrating the natural order of things.

"You all know each other then?" Lady Claire asks.

Adeline nods. "Oh, yes. We just sailed back from Mesilca on Captain Greybrow's ship."

"You were together?" The lady looks genuinely surprised. She turns to Avery. "I wasn't aware you are well-acquainted with your cousin."

"It was a shock to us all," Sebastian deadpans.

To others, he sounds friendly enough, but to me... well, I know. Sebastian catches me pressing my lips together, trying to hide my amusement, and a ghost of a smile crosses his face.

Harold waves a hand in the air. "Please, sit. There's no reason for us to hover."

We all turn about, looking for a spot to rest. I choose the bench closest to me—probably the only hard, unupholstered seat in the room. I fully expect Minerva to find a place next to Avery, but he crosses the room and sits by my side. I am grateful for the tiny gesture, and though I tell myself he's only being polite, a few butterflies flit in my stomach.

"Now, Avery," Harold says, tossing his circlet onto a table next to his chair. "I want to hear more about this voyage of yours."

I gladly let the captain do the talking, though I do feel he embellishes a bit for entertainment purposes. Also, he omits a few key moments, such as our wedding, but he glances at me every time he slides over one.

"So, these island people were hospitable?" Harold leans forward, resting his elbows on his legs, enthralled.

Avery's knee bumps mine. "Extremely. In fact, I can honestly say it was the best twenty-four hours of my life."

A few more butterflies join their friends in my stomach.

Why does he have to go and say things like that once I've decided that I'm not going to fall in love with him? Does he have any idea how difficult he's making that task?

The captain goes on, spending a disproportionate amount of time speaking about the sirens. Sebastian watches, not saying a word, but he glances at me every so often. Because we weren't exactly chummy on the voyage back to Kalae, he's never heard the full story.

I study his face, wondering if he's horrified, hoping that he might be the tiniest bit impressed. He's never thought I could take care of myself, and I realize I want him to see I can. Worse, I want him to be proud of me.

We come to the end of the tale, to the part where Avery heroically pushed me out of the duchess's grasp and took a knife in the stomach for me. He doesn't linger—doesn't embellish or boast. In fact, he glosses over it like it was nothing. Which is probably for the best because Elizabetta looks like she's going to cry again.

I know from speaking with Avery that the girl has suffered a great deal of heartbreak even at her young age. Their mother died suddenly when Elizabetta was only ten. Their father distanced himself and left her care to Lady Claire, his children's maternal grandmother. The thought of losing her brother too must shake Elizabetta greatly.

When Avery is finished, Harold sits back, shaking his head as he grins. "You have all the fun, Captain. And here I am, stuck in my castle, surrounded by my cold riches."

"Yes, it's difficult being king," Avery says wryly.

"Speaking of an abundance of cold riches, I must take you around the shoppes," Minerva says, changing the subject. As she says it, she looks at Adeline, Lady Claire, and Elizabetta. Almost as an afterthought, she turns to me. "You may come as well, Lucia."

How kind of her.

I give her a tight smile, and Sebastian widens his eyes marginally, reminding me to play nice. For a moment, it almost feels as if things are back to normal. I stare at him, silently asking what's going on between us.

In answer, he smoothly infiltrates the conversation, saying, "Speaking of shoppes, I assume you'd like to visit them this afternoon, Lucia? Adeline said you have items the alchemists might be interested in. I will go with you if you'd like. I know the shoppe on the corner of Convill and Midtown specializes in unique ingredients. I'm sure they'll be interested."

Avery stiffens by my side; Adeline gapes. The rest of the group appear confused by our strange reaction.

I stare at Sebastian, dumbfounded. I shake my head, trying to clear it, and quickly nod before he thinks I'm saying no. "Yes, of course."

He glances at his pocket watch. "I have family business to attend to shortly. Let's say three o'clock?"

"Yes...that's fine."

"Lucia and Sebastian are business partners," Adeline explains to the group. "Scouts."

"And apparently you are very good ones since you were able to bring back a sea fire ruby," King Harold says, smiling indulgently. "Of course, it never hurts to have the captain at your disposal."

Avery glances at me, wearing that not-quite smile. "Lucia's welcome to have me at her disposal any time she wishes."

I expect Sebastian to scoff, but it's the queen who makes the low sound in her throat. When we turn to her, she schools her look of disgust and exchanges it for a patronizing one, which she bestows right on me.

"How...sweet."

Harold gives his wife a stern look, and an uncomfortable silence blankets the room. The king clears his throat, breaking the spell, and turns to Sebastian. "We've had a bit of a crime problem as of late. We believe the streets are generally safe in the light of day, but it's best to stay away from the shoppes in the evening. We've encouraged the shopkeepers to close early and head home before dark."

"And what of the goblins?" Elizabetta asks, her face etched with concern. "Are those rumors true as well?"

The king rolls his eyes, disgusted not with the girl but the situation. "Yes, I'm afraid so. We've had several sightings in the forest to the north of the city. As far as we know, none have ventured into Teirn, and our guards are working hard to ensure that they don't. But there are whispers that the beasts are behind the thievery. The crude way in which the doors and windows are broken, and the careless, almost deliberate mess the thieves have been leaving, would hint that it might be the work of goblins. Still, we don't want to jump to any conclusions in the matter."

Adeline goes pale, and Minerva, not liking the somber mood, smiles brightly. "Enough of this morbid conversation. I have good news."

The women turn to her, relieved, but I would

rather speak of the goblins.

"Madam Lavinia is in Teirn, and she's planned a performance! You all must join me as my personal guests."

Lady Claire and Adeline both look quite impressed, but I have no idea who the woman is.

Minerva turns to me, her face the picture of innocence. "I will take no offense if you do not wish to join us, Lucia. I know how you adventuresses are—all work and no play. I imagine it would be difficult to sit through a performance, while the entire time, you're dreaming of scampering off on your next adventure."

"I think I can manage."

"Wonderful," she says with a bright smile and hard eyes. "We will be glad to have the pleasure of your company, I'm sure."

After that, she turns to Adeline and Lady Claire and promptly forgets my existence. I resist the urge to look at the imposing grandfather clock in the corner and wonder how long I must stay before I can escape this royal dungeon.

CHAPTER SIX
But a Very Handsome Thorn

A knock sounds on the door of my room—my gloriously large, cannot-believe-I'm-going-to-be-sleeping-here, decked-in-all-things-feminine room. Unused to anyone hovering over me, I sent the maid away, and I'm just hanging the last of my gowns in the wardrobe by the settee.

"Come in," I call.

I have the glass doors to my own private balcony tossed open, and the gossamer curtains flutter in the warm breeze. Everything about the room is light and airy—the furniture is delicate, the fabrics are various shades of creams and whites, and the gleaming hardwood floors are covered with plush rugs.

I'm in a wing across the courtyard—in the castle but separate—and when I stand on the balcony, I can look out at the great towers and watch the flags flutter in the breeze. I stood there for a good fifteen minutes when I first arrived, marveling at the view.

The door opens. Expecting Adeline since Their Royal Majesties placed her next door and she's already come and gone a dozen times, I don't bother to turn.

"You don't have to keep knocking. Just come in next time."

"I'll take that as an open invitation," Avery says.

I whirl around, startled, and laugh when I see him lounging in the doorway. He looks so much better than he did when we left Mesilca.

"I thought you were Adeline," I explain.

He smiles and cocks a brow. "I get that a lot."

"Did you rest?"

Avery lets out a sigh that might be a grumble. "I read for a bit, but I find it difficult to sleep during the day."

That must be a good sign. Not a month ago, he could barely stay awake due to all the pain-relieving tea Gregory was pouring down his throat. Of course, anyone would want to be half-conscious for the medicines the mage plied the captain with twice a day. If they tasted half as bad as they smelled, they had to have been ghastly.

"So..." He strides into the room, hands clasped behind his back, looking at nothing in particular. "You and Sebastian are going on an outing."

"*Avery,*" I warn.

He looks back at me, raising his hands in mock innocence. "Small talk, Lucia. That's what *friends* do, isn't it?"

I narrow my eyes, trying not to smile. "You may come with us."

"Hmmm." He frowns, thinking. "An afternoon in a musty alchemy supply shoppe with my baby cousin? Hard as the decision might be, I think I must pass that up."

"The two of you need to find a way to get along."

He turns toward me, only his eyes smiling. "And why is that?"

"Because he is my business partner, at least until he decides otherwise, and you are..." Oh dear. Where was I going with that?

Avery grins and strides toward me. "Yes, go on. What am I?"

"A thorn in my side."

"The man you dream about at night? Giver of the best kiss you've ever received? Love of your life?" He grins as he steps closer. "Feel free to pick any one you wish."

I set my palm on his chest, locking my elbow to keep him at a safe distance. "I'm worried about your self-esteem, Captain. You're always so critical of yourself."

"Say it, Lucia." He smirks, so ridiculously sure of himself. "Say you love me."

I cannot deny something significant happened between us on that island in the whirlpool, and it would be a lie to try. However, at the time, I thought those days were all we had. Things are not as easy here as they were there, and previous heartbreak makes you cautious. I cannot just fall in his arms and hope for the best, no matter how much I want to.

"If you'll excuse me, I have an appointment." I brush past him, but he catches my hand before I'm out of reach.

"Believe it or not, I had a purpose for visiting you this afternoon."

"What's that?" I ask, trying not to focus on the feel of his fingers twined with mine.

"Harold gave me a peek at this curious invitation." He pulls the cream envelope from the inside pocket of his jacket and flicks it in the air, taunting me. "It's being distributed to all the nobles in Kalae as we speak."

Breathless, I demand, "What is it?"

"See for yourself." He offers me the envelope, and I swipe it from his hand like a greedy child.

I pull the parchment out—even the paper is fine— and quickly scan the document. Waves of incredulous excitement crash over me with every word.

"He's holding a soirée," I breathe.

Avery nods, chuckling at my exuberance.

"In our honor..." I whisper.

I scan the invitation over and over again. Right there, on the page, it reads, *In honor of Captain Avery Alexander Greybrow of the Greybrow Serpent and Lucia Linnon, professional adventuress and scout, slayer of sirens.*

"I cannot believe it." I shake my head, overcome. "What do I do? It's next week! How will I prepare? What will I *wear?*"

Avery laughs and plucks the invitation from me before I crush it on accident. "Take Adeline and buy yourself a new gown from Serena Hanhaust. She has a shoppe in the main district near the restaurants, and she's renowned throughout Kalae as the best. I'm sure Adeline will be more than pleased to meet her."

"I have no money." I glare at him, though there's not a lot of heat behind it. "But I would, if a certain pirate captain hadn't stolen my orchids."

He rolls his eyes. "If a subject can be beat to death, this one has been. And if you'll remember, I reimbursed you for your loss."

Yes, and Adeline informed me that practical Sebastian invested every last denat. Thank goodness he's more scrupulous about choosing a banker than I am.

"Besides," Avery says, stepping closer and lowering his voice. "I'll buy you a gown. I'll buy you whatever you want—you already know that."

Mother would question the morals of a woman who lets a man constantly shower her with beautiful things, and goodness knows Avery's already done that for me and more. But what's one more dress?

"I suppose," I say as if I'm doing him a favor. Then I give him a suspicious look. "How do you know this Serena woman?"

"Have fun shopping." He chucks me under the chin in a way that he knows will aggravate me and excuses himself from my room.

"Don't think I didn't notice that you evaded the question!" I call as he closes the door.

The captain laughs from the hall. With the safety of the door separating us, I grin like a lovesick fool, and then I catch myself and wipe the expression off my face.

CHAPTER SEVEN
A Curious Shortage of Butterflies

As we agreed, I meet Sebastian by the stables. I give him a hesitant smile, and he gives me a stiff one in return.

Well, this isn't awkward. Not at all.

While he speaks with our driver, I look around, taking in the castle grounds. The courtyard is huge, and it houses many different buildings. The stable's to the west, the armory to the east, and a beautiful chapel with dozens of long stained-glass windows stands to the south. The castle's gardeners have bedecked the winter flower beds with multitudes of purple and yellow pansies, and their cheery little faces almost seem to smile. Rose bushes tower behind the flowers, full-to-bursting with scarlet blooms. Even here in Teirn where it's warm, it's a little too early for such a display. They must be charmed to bloom year-round. Evergreen hedges with thick, glossy leaves form tidy borders, and I want to wander their rooms, get lost for the afternoon.

But first, business.

"Are you ready?" Sebastian offers me his hand to assist me into the carriage.

I give him a funny look. Since when does he treat me like a lady? Or a girl, for that matter. Unsure how to proceed, I set my hand in his. We both stare at our joined palms for several heartbeats, and then I scurry into the carriage.

It's an open top sort of trap, more like riding in Father's wagon but a bit grander with its velvet uphol- stered seats and all.

Sebastian and I sit in silence until the carriage jerks forward.

"Adeline says you are unsure how long you will be in Teirn," he finally says.

I watch him for several moments, irked by that particular statement. "Is that what we do now, speak through Adeline?"

Sebastian exhales slowly, taking his time to an- swer as he always does. He stares at the scenery for several moments before he looks back. His eyes are so familiar; they hold so many memories.

"I don't know..." He pauses, looking for the right

words, appearing both frustrated and forlorn. "*How* do we return to normal?"

His words neutralize the sharp response that was already on my tongue. Deflated, I look at my hands. "I don't know."

We pass several large and elegant houses, all nestled next to even *more* large and elegant houses, all in a coveted part of the city. Each has a small strip of flower bed directly off their pillar-flanked entries, followed by steps that lead to the walkways Teirn is known for. Past the walkways lie another strip of landscaping maintained by the king's gardeners, and then there is the fine cobblestone street. It's strange to view the city as the nobles do, from atop their grand carriages—to see things as they see them for the first time. I feel very tall.

People stroll the streets, but no one is in a hurry or seems to have a destination in mind. Many of the women carry munchkin dragons in their arms or in satchels at their sides. They wear their jeweled pets like accessories, and I notice that many women coordinate their outfits to match their dragon's scales.

I suppose I'm fortunate that Flink settled on a metallic color. He matches virtually everything. I find the thought amusing, and I smile to myself until I catch Sebastian watching me.

We're silent for a long while, but Sebastian finally

clears his throat. "Are you in love with him?"

The question settles between us, tainting the beautiful late winter day. I continue to watch the street instead of facing him. "I don't know."

"But you've forgiven him?" he asks, incredulous.

This time, I meet his eyes. "I have."

Obviously thinking I'm a fool, Sebastian shakes his head. "And what will you do when he fully recovers? Once he returns to the sea?"

His words are an ice dagger in my heart. Of all the things I've pondered, this is the one I have dared not face. My life is here, in the provinces of Kalae, with my two feet planted firmly on solid ground—I cannot even set foot on a ship without my anti-nausea charm. But the sea is Avery's home—his one true love. We have no rightful place with each other, no matter how I might wish it weren't so.

I shrug because I have no answer. Thankfully, Sebastian does not press for more, at least not now.

We are saved from further conversation when the carriage pulls up in front of the alchemy supply store. Thankfully, for the owner and us, no guards loiter outside, and the windows appear intact.

We push through the door, and a bell tinkles above us. My eyes scan the room as we wait for the shopkeeper. It's a pleasant temperature inside, just a few degrees warmer than the outside air, likely regulated with a thermocharm that shopkeepers prefer over fires.

As with most supply shoppes, all but the most common of ingredients are kept under lock and key, and you must go to the counter to ask for assistance. Like Sebastian's grandfather's shoppe in Reshire— one of Lord Thane's many investments, the counter is made of glass cases.

Because the shoppe only has a large front window, there are tiny floating orbs of light hovering at the corners of the cases, illuminating the goods. The charm serves two purposes. It makes the items easier to see, and it also casts them in an enticing, ethereal light. I lean down, already impressed with the stock up front. The shopkeeper has various dried flowers, leaves, and roots—all exotic and hard to obtain. I recognize one with an impressive name.

Unable to help myself though I have no idea where we stand, I poke Sebastian. "Look—Anubish Gramerilianor."

Sebastian leans down to read the small writing under the name. "Donated by none other than Baron Malcomny of Baywhite."

"I've heard he's quite the talk of the horticultural community," I joke. "Did you know he recently obtained a Moss Forest orchid cutting?"

Sebastian offers me a real smile, not one of the

tight-lipped fake ones he's so good at. "Impressive."

Feeling as if we are making progress, even if it's at a snail's pace, I go back to my browsing. The shoppe seems to specialize in flora for the alchemists, apothecaries, and herbologists. Yet there are gemstones, jewels, and coils of Elven chain for the magicsmiths as well. The owner has several animal ingredients—harpy and greater cockatrice feathers, will-o-wisp fluff, and scales from several different types of elemental greater basilisks, just to name a few.

One case holds nothing but crispy insects. A shiny purple beetle catches my attention, and I study it, slightly repulsed.

"Hello, there. I'm Dante," a friendly-looking brown-haired man in a sharp jacket says when he steps from the back. He has an attractive dimpled smile and is quite handsome for his late twenty or so years. "If you're looking for butterflies or moths, I'm afraid I'm all out."

I wrinkle my nose. "What are those used for?"

The man laughs at my expression. "Dandruff tinctures, mostly. Apparently, we've had an epidemic in Teirn because I cannot keep any in stock."

"We've come to sell," Sebastian says, "But I don't believe we have either butterflies or moths."

My partner looks at me for clarification. I shake my head and dig into my satchel for the pouch where

I've kept the items I gathered from the island in the whirlpool. "Sorry. I do have some rather strange mushrooms, though."

With great care, I set my items on the counter. I have a little of everything: dried flowers, lots of leaves and roots, a great amount of strange, now wrinkled, red mushrooms, and various other things that would look like rubbish a toddler collected if you weren't interested in the art and business of alchemy or herbology.

With every specimen I place, the man's expression grows more surprised. He takes a mushroom and looks at it with a magnifying glass. "Where did you find this? I've never seen one before."

I shrug. "An island past the circular archipelagos, about a month to the south of here."

The man slowly lowers the mushroom and magnifying glass and says in an awed voice, "You're *her*—the siren slayer. Scout extraordinaire. The king's new favorite swashbuckling adventuress and soon-to-be darling of the royal court."

Swashbuckling?

Never mind that. I flash Sebastian a look that says, "*See there. I'm special.*"

He looks incredulous.

"Um, yes? I'm Lucia." I do a little curtsy bob. I think I'm getting the hang of it.

The man's eyes travel to Sebastian, and he steps back, overwhelmed. "That must make you Captain Avery Greybrow." He thrusts his hand out in greeting. "It's an honor to have you in my shoppe, Captain."

"Er...no," I interrupt. "This is my business partner, Lord Sebastian Thane. Of the Reginae Thanes," I feel the need to add, just to give Sebastian's title a little boost.

Sebastian shakes the man's hand, less than amused.

"Oh." The shopkeeper nods, looking mildly disappointed. "But you must have been on the ship with them then, yes? Did you see Lucia slay the sirens?"

"No," Sebastian answers curtly.

The poor man's elation dies away, leaving him looking rather pathetic and sad.

I lean close in a conspiratorial manner. "He was in Reginae, attending to a matter that I'm afraid is still of a rather lock and key nature—if you know what I mean."

I give the shopkeeper an exaggerated look, and he slowly nods, his face lighting again as he gives me a friendly wink. "Of course." He turns back to Sebastian. "Well, it is an honor to meet you as well."

"The pleasure is mine," Sebastian answers wryly.

"So..." I wave my hand over the eclectic grouping of island paraphernalia.

"I'll take it all," Dante says immediately. "Even if it's just for my own personal experiments. But I must be honest with you. Since I have no idea what most of it is, I don't know how much to offer for it."

"It's not every day you have the darling of the king's court offering you first choice of her bounty," Sebastian says, his voice terribly serious.

The shopkeeper sighs and nods. "True. A thousand denats?"

Sebastian frowns.

"One and a half—" Dante stops when he sees the look on Sebastian's face. "No? No, of course not. Two... yes? Two thousand denats?"

I try to hide my glee. I would have happily accepted seven hundred and fifty and run out the door, squealing like a pig in a fresh bog of mud.

"That sounds reasonable," Sebastian finally agrees, nodding.

"Again," Dante says, catching my hand in a debonair way that would make me blush if I were the blushing sort. "It was a pleasure to meet you."

"You too," I say, grinning. There's something immensely likable about this man, and the fact that Sebastian doesn't care for him is a happy bonus.

Content with the success of the outing, I leave with enough money in my satchel to buy my choice of Serena Whatever's gowns without using Avery's money. As we're leaving the shoppe, I turn, about to ask Sebastian a question, and accidentally plow right into a man as he enters.

"I'm sorry..." The words die off when I take in the stranger's face.

"Quite all right," the man who watched me from the pier assures us. Without so much as a backward glance, he steps around me and makes his way to the counter.

Sebastian touches the small of my back, helping guide me out of the shoppe, and I jump as if stabbed.

"Are you all right?" he asks, genuinely concerned.

I mumble something, but my attention is on the man.

"Afternoon, Sam," Dante says, friendly in a familiar way. "What brings you by?"

The man lowers his voice, but I can just hear him as we're walking out of the shoppe. "I'm looking for a wildwood larkwing. Do you know anyone who has one in their stock?"

"Hmmm," Dante hums with thought. "Remind me again—is it a dragonfly? Moth?"

Before the man answers, he shoots me a look over his shoulder and then leans close to the shopkeeper. "Butterfly."

My mind is still on the man in the alchemy shoppe

when we step out on the street. I'm rational enough to know it was a coincidence, but the meeting was still unsettling.

I'm so deep in thought, I don't notice the commotion ahead of us.

"Let's go this way," Sebastian says quietly as he steers me in the opposite direction.

I look up, taking in our surroundings. A man in ratty clothing shakes his fist at a pair of guards. He's almost incoherent, but a few phrases stand out—goblins near the city, larks singing from trees, underground masquerades. It's all gibberish, but he's adamant they listen to him.

Pulling out of Sebastian's grasp, I linger for a moment longer.

"Come on, Lucia. You don't need to watch this."

"What do you think is wrong with him?" I whisper.

Sebastian shakes his head and frowns.

"I didn't think they allowed beggars in Teirn," I add, keeping my voice low. "I thought they shipped them off to Fermall."

I'm only partially joking.

One of the guards clasps the man's shoulder, trying to calm his tirade. I watch the scene for a few more moments.

"They have the larkwings! Why do you think the goblins are here? They're going to attack during one of

75

the masquerades!" The man yells at the guards, louder now, "Why won't you believe me? Don't you care about the city?"

"We've been over this. There are no tunnels under the streets, Giacomo," one of the guards says, losing patience. "The goblins aren't getting into the city, and there are no masquerades." But he doesn't seem so sure about that last part.

Giacomo grabs the man's jacket. "I've been there. I've *seen* them."

When he sees the guards aren't going to help him, he begins yelling at random people. Left with no choice, the guards arrest him and drag him toward the castle. The man's hollers fill the street long after the trio turns the corner.

Sebastian whistles low.

"Sounds like someone should stay away from the night floss," he says, speaking of an illegal stimulating elixir that can be found at the caravans if you know the right people to ask. It does seem something has addled the man's mind.

I take one last glance over my shoulder at the now empty street as Sebastian steers me to our waiting carriage.

CHAPTER EIGHT
When Good Dragons Go Bad

Courtiers overwintering in Teirn do strange things. For example, because they have nothing better to do, they eat six tiny meals dispersed throughout the day—which means they're eating all day long. The queen insists we have breakfast, morning tea, luncheon, afternoon tea, an early evening sampling of wine, cheese, and various fruits, and finally a late evening supper that isn't served until almost nine. After that, we retire for several hours of "spirited" conversation and eventually wander to bed around midnight. No one bothers rising before nine in the morning.

It's a strange schedule for a girl who grew up on a farm—even one who spent the first lean years of scouting by playing barmaid in local taverns as she traveled.

We're in the middle of our fifth meal now, and

I'm gorging myself on little cubes of a yellow tropical fruit that wouldn't be available right now anywhere but here. It's exceptionally good, and I continue to sneak pieces, but only when no one is looking—I don't want to look like a glutton, after all.

Adeline, Elizabetta, and Minerva discuss whether lightweight velvets are appropriate for spring couture. Elizabetta absently strokes the queen's darling amethyst munchkin dragon on her lap. The beast is named Mirabella, and she's the tiniest thing, the size of a petite female cat. Her eyes are emerald, and the scales on her snout are a darker purple, giving her an adorable little nose stripe like a horse.

She's not fond of strangers, which is a shame because I want nothing more than to whisk her from Avery's sister and carry her about the room.

Sebastian sits in the corner, reading to avoid being drawn into conversation, and Lady Claire badgers Avery about his health. The captain sits on an upholstered bench, looking as if he's about to go out of his mind from boredom. We've been in Teirn for three days, and the captain is already growing restless. Sebastian's words come back to haunt me, but I try not to think about them.

As I idly listen to the conversations and sneak more of the fruit, I wander the room. Her Majesty has a lovely collection of antiques, including a Milindrian vase that's several hundred years old. I pause in front of it, admiring the design's careful brush strokes. It must be worth ten thousand denats, at the very least.

"All I'm saying is that you need to see a proper physician, not a jack-of-all-trades ship's mage," Lady Claire insists.

She's been harping on the captain for the last half hour, and it's not the first time it's come up.

"And I'm saying that I politely, and firmly, decline," Avery answers.

"I do not think—"

Avery stands abruptly, drawing my attention from the vase. "We're done with this conversation, Grandmother."

The entire room goes silent. Lady Claire purses her lips, looking as if it's taking a great deal of effort not to argue further. She flicks her hand in the air. "Fine. If you are content with subpar care, then I suppose there is nothing more to discuss."

And there isn't, at least not at the moment, because a fidgety looking serving man knocks on the frame of the open door. We all turn, some of us more thankful for the intrusion than others.

"Captain Greybrow, my lord, a...er...delivery has been sent from your ship."

Avery cocks his head to the side. "What is it? And who sent it?"

The man doesn't answer. Instead, he gestures for a boy to step forward from behind him. Unfortunately for the boy, he's pulling a familiar lesser dragon who refuses to come into the room. Flink stands outside the door, haunches lowered like an obstinate donkey, and he digs his talons into the carpet runner.

Because I've just stuffed a few more squares of fruit into my mouth, I'm forced to chew and swallow a little too quickly.

"Flink!" I manage after a moment. "He's supposed to be on the ship!"

Flink immediately softens his stance upon hearing my voice and trots merrily into the room.

Mirabella takes one look at my dragon, leaps onto Minerva's lap, useless wings all aflutter, and hisses through her tiny, sharp teeth. Flink focuses on Mirabella, lowers his head, readying for the chase, and barrels into the room, dragging the startled handler behind him. The poor boy is probably used to well-behaved wolfhounds, not lesser dragons.

"Flink, no!" I holler as I lunge for him.

The queen screams as the two-hundred-pound dragon gallops toward her, full-speed. Luckily for Minerva, Flink's top speed isn't terribly impressive, as he's still a bit young and clumsy. He slips on the hardwood floor, legs splaying out in all directions. Before we can catch him, however, he rights himself.

Mirabella lets out a horrid noise and begins to claw her way up Minerva's shoulder, onto the queen's perfectly coiffed hair.

The boy, who possibly weighs eighty pounds soaking wet, tries to hold Flink back, but he's barely able to keep his feet on the floor. Flink reaches Mirabella before I can grasp his tether.

The tiny amethyst dragon shrieks again, leaps off Minerva's head—thank goodness, and races across the back of the settee. Like a cat, she makes a great leap for a nearby bookcase. The tiny dragon almost misses, and her taloned back feet work furiously as she pulls herself up.

Avery, who's also in pursuit of my horrid pet, changes direction at the same time as I do. I go left, and he makes to cut the dragon off by going right, behind the bench. We crash into each other and knock into a vase. *The* vase. In horrifying slow motion, it rocks back and forth. Just as I'm grasping for it, it crashes to the ground and breaks into shards.

Avery grabs Flink just before the dragon leaps up on the bookcase. The sounds of chaos fade, soaking into the rugs and drapes and upholstered finery, and all is silent except Mirabella's low, warning hisses.

I stare at what used to be the vase when someone loudly clears his throat from the room's entrance.

Lord Selden Thane, Sebastian's one and only

grandfather, stands by the door. His eyes are trained solely on me, and he wears his usual disdainful expression. "Creating pandemonium, Lucia? I suppose some things never change."

A ball of lead settles into my stomach. What's he doing here? And he had to arrive just *now*?

The man's timing is impeccable, as always.

Adeline leaps to her feet and curtsies. "Lord Thane! What a pleasure to see you!"

"Yes, Selden. A pleasure." Lady Claire pulls her eyes away from the remains of the priceless treasure on the floor and looks at the man who's still lingering near the doorway.

Lord Thane bows to the queen, keeping his balance despite his cane. "Your Majesty."

"Welcome, Lord Thane." Minerva appears quite harried. She'll probably have to spend the next day in bed, just to recover from the scene. Breathless, she turns to the waiting servant. "Fetch someone to clean the mess."

He bows and disappears into the hall.

"To what do we owe the honor?" Lady Claire asks her brother.

The older man eyes his sister and then moves his steely gaze to his grandson. "I was along the coast, and I received word Sebastian had returned from his hastily-executed holiday."

82

To Sebastian's credit, he doesn't even flinch. "Hello, Grandfather."

"Imagine my surprise when I learned you greeted my sister before notifying me of your return. And I have been so concerned for your safely these last months."

"I sent a message when we arrived, but seeing as how you're not in Silverleaf, it's understandable how it did not make it to you."

I gawk at the exchange. The two are obviously at odds, and Sebastian isn't leaping to smooth Lord Thane's ruffled feathers like he usually does.

"Yes, well," Lord Selden says, tapping his walking stick on the floor twice. "I am returning to Reginae this afternoon, and you may ride with me."

Adeline, who's still standing after her greeting, very slowly sinks into her seat next to Elizabetta, trying not to draw attention to herself.

Sebastian clasps his hands behind his back. "I'm afraid I still have business in Teirn. I will return to Reginae when I've settled it."

The elder lord's jaw twitches, and the room grows quiet enough Mirabella's low growls are audible again.

Avery ends up breaking the silence. He strides forward, hand extended. "Uncle Selden. Good to see you."

Lord Thane's eyes light up with genuine surprise.

83

"Surely you are not young Avery?"

"I am, sir."

"Your grandmother says you are a captain now, like your father. Impressive, especially for one your age." He glances at Sebastian before he looks back to Avery. "It's good to see a young man with direction."

They shake hands, and Sebastian leans against the back of Adeline's settee, looking about ready to murder something.

Avery, too, glances Sebastian's way and bites back a rotten smirk as he looks back at Lord Thane. "I think it's important to have direction in one's life. A plan, a purpose."

Lord Thane nods heartily, as if finding a kindred spirit.

Oh, if you only knew, Lord Thane.

"I could not agree more. Sebastian, you could learn a thing or two from your cousin."

Sebastian grips the back of the couch, and his knuckles turn white. Adeline covers his hand with her own and puts on a pained smile.

"Once you figure out what you want in life," Avery says as he slowly pins me with his eyes. "You must not let anything, or anyone, stand in your way. Isn't that right, Lucia?"

The room goes up at least ten degrees. I gulp and resist the urge to snatch Adeline's fan from the side table.

"Lucia never lets people, rules, or consequences stand in her way." Lord Thane laughs like my only purpose in life is to entertain those higher in social ranking with my misadventures. "Do you, Lucia?"

I force a smile.

Avery narrows his eyes, not caring for the exchange. "I suppose that's why King Harold is holding a soirée in her honor this Saturday."

"*Our* honor, Captain Greybrow," I murmur as I watch Lord Selden's eyes grow large. He looks like he was smacked across the face with a week-old fish.

It's rather satisfying.

"News hasn't traveled to you yet, Lord Thane?" the queen asks, her expression perfectly friendly but her voice tinged with irritation. "Lucia is a siren slayer—my husband's new favorite adventuress. She and Captain Greybrow are being honored for their service to the crown. It's all anyone in Teirn can talk about."

That's not entirely true, but the look on Lord Thane's face is priceless.

"Oh, Selden," Lady Claire says after several long moments, steering the conversation to a more neutral subject. "Madam Lavinia is in Teirn. She's performing tomorrow."

"You must come," Minerva says, brightening considerably.

Beside me, Avery grimaces. I give him a curious look, and he leans close. "If there were a good time to contract food poisoning, it would be tomorrow."

Before I can ask him what he means, the serving man returns with a maid. She makes quick work of the broken vase with a simple levitation spell. With the wave of her hand, the mess rises off the floor and settles into a dustpan. Easy as can be.

That's a clever trick.

"Frederick?" Avery asks the man when he is finished supervising the cleanup. "Why was the dragon sent?"

I almost forgot about Flink, but my eyes move to him now. Avery's still holding him by his lead. Given no choice, Flink lies on the floor, his head resting between his two front feet, looking mopey. Mirabella continues to glare at him from her perch atop the bookcase, but at least she's stopped hissing.

Frederick glances about the room, unsure how to answer. "He was said to be causing havoc, Captain."

"Havoc?"

Frederick clears his throat. "If I understand correctly, the beast barricaded himself in your cabin, pilfered every piece of gold from your private collections, piled them on the bed, and claimed the area as his own. With the snarling and snapping and breathing of elemental fire, the crew became uneasy and thought it best if he were returned to his..." He looks at me and clears his throat again. "Lucia."

Without a word, Avery flicks me the beast's lead.

I take it and attempt a smile, but I probably look like I have indigestion. "I'm sure he was just...lonely."

Avery raises a brow, both amused and irritated. I'm not sure which emotion is winning.

The room goes quiet, and I feel as if every set of eyes is on me.

I clear my throat and look toward Queen Minerva—but not quite at her as I can't seem to meet her eyes. "I'll replace your vase."

CHAPTER NINE
Quite the Catch

I wince as Madame Lavinia hits a note that could shatter glass. A quick glance around me confirms that I am not the only one less than impressed with the performance. My companions and the royal entourage watch the songstress with varying degrees of polite, intrigued expressions. Elizabetta, however, keeps glancing at Sebastian's pocket watch, which he finally let the girl borrow after she asked for the time one too many times.

She looks bored to tears.

I cringe again at another loud, shrill note. This must surely be the woman's finale. *Please let it be over.*

She's going to hurt herself.

The note cuts off, and the open-air auditorium goes blissfully silent. My ears still ring. Around me, the intimate crowd—the elite of Teirn's elite—leap to their feet, bursting into riotous applause. I follow suit, grateful the ordeal is over.

But to my great horror, the woman sweeps back onstage, curtsying and throwing kisses at the audience. Then her stringed players begin anew.

No.

Avery leans close. "It's called an encore."

"It's called torture of a cruel and unusual nature," I whisper back.

He grins and then makes a face as the woman reaches heights that have, until this point, never been attained by anything other than a tea kettle. It's the worst thing I've ever heard, and I'm familiar with the distress call made by rabbits.

And then the song ends, and this time, the songstress doesn't return to the stage. I could cry tears of joy, but I must hide my relief from the other members of our party.

Minerva dabs her eyes with the tips of her long white gloves, as overcome as I am, but for completely different reasons. "It was beautiful, wasn't it?" she says to no one in particular.

Adeline agrees, sighing. "I've never experienced anything like it."

Neither have I.

The queen grasps Adeline's hand. "I will never forget the first time I heard Madame Lavinia sing."

I'm certain they were only two seats down. Did they perhaps hear a different performance?

Other members of the party join the conversation as we make our way down our row of stone seats. Serving staff wait patiently by, ready to collect the cushions they brought to line the royal rumps. I can't complain about that—they brought me one too.

We are the first to leave. The rest of the courtiers wait for the queen's party. Our progress is slowed dramatically because Minerva feels the need to stop often and speak with people. Right now, she's clasping the hands of an elderly woman, beaming at her as they talk about the performance. I take a moment to get a better look at the amphitheater. Mages have cast orbs of light into the sky, and they form a softly glowing canopy that competes with the stars.

The open-air auditorium is impressive, built entirely from gray stone on a hill that lies to the north east of the city. The structure is sunk into the ground, so the top row of seats is flush with the earth. The rows form an arc around the stage. The whole structure is at the heart of Teirn's botanical gardens, and it feels older than Teirn. There is history here, and many of the trees feel ancient. They embrace the theater, protecting it. Other nearby structures dot the gardens—statues and gazebos and stone benches. It's a maze of hedge rooms and secret nooks.

I think of the king's talk of goblins lurking nearby, and I glance at the overgrown perimeter of the theater. Guards line the edges, looking stoic in their scarlet and gold tabards, armed with their gleaming swords. It does seem like an awful lot of protection for an evening performance.

I'd like to visit again in summer when the gardens are in full bloom. For now, they are asleep, and the mages seem hesitant to tamper with the flora here. There are a few earthen pots of flowers, more pansies that enjoy the cool weather, but the great stretches of beds are untouched.

We reach the top of the amphitheater and step into the courtyard that surrounds it. More lights have been cast into the sky, and waitstaff hold silver trays of refreshments. I take it all in, sure I'll never be invited to something like this again. As I'm looking about, movement in the trees catches my attention. I narrow my eyes and take a step forward. Whatever it was is either gone now or has hidden itself very well. But maybe I'll take a look.

Adeline nudges me in the side just as I'm about to step away and hisses quietly, "Pay attention."

I turn back and find a waiter in front of me, patiently waiting for me to accept a drink from his tray. I thank him and then glance over my shoulder at the trees.

Queen Minerva accepts a silver flute from another waiter, and with a smile and a soft word of thanks, she turns to us. "I would like to propose a toast to new friends" —she first nods to Adeline, Sebastian, and me, and then, in turn, nods toward the rest of our group, lingering on Avery and grinning in a familiar way that makes me a bit uncomfortable— "and old friends."

Watching the rest of the group for clues, I raise my flute.

"I am so pleased you could all join me this evening." She directs her charming smile right at Avery.

He nods in response—not in an overly friendly way…but not distant either.

"Cheers!" She bobs her drink in the air and then takes a demure sip. We all follow her lead.

"Lucia," Gerard says, turning toward me. "You mustn't divulge too many details, or Harold will be sorely disappointed that we didn't wait until his soirée, but you must tell us—did you truly slay three sirens?"

I clear my throat, uncomfortable to be put on the spot. "I did."

Minerva leans in. "Using enchanted arrows, correct? No doubt from Avery's illicit stash."

The group laughs when the young queen gives the captain a mock chastising look, none of them shocked. She knows of Avery's illegal weapons collection? Of course she does.

I only smile, growing increasingly uncomfortable.

"Oh! There she is!" Minerva says, losing interest in our conversation. She waves a gloved hand in the air. "Madame Lavinia!"

The group hurries toward the songstress, accosting her with praise. I hang back, nursing my drink. Avery steps up next to me, looking uncomfortable enough to confirm my growing suspicions.

"Tell me, Captain Greybrow. Did you engage in a romantic relationship with the Queen of Kalae before or after she married King Harold?"

He smiles in a disconcerted way that does nothing to soothe my nerves, and he looks at our group instead of me. "Before."

I knew it.

"And what happened?"

After letting out a resigned sigh, Avery turns toward me and relieves me of my drink—as if he's worried I'm going to toss it in his face after he answers.

"Well?" I ask, bracing myself.

"She broke our engagement."

There is no preparing for that answer. I stare at the captain, not blinking, beyond incredulous. "You were engaged to the *Queen of Kalae*?"

He shakes his head, laughing a little. "Now let's put this in perspective. She wasn't the queen then."

"Who was she?"

Thank goodness for the crisp night air. I take in a deep lungful, rip my flute back from Avery, and drain the drink in one long gulp.

Almost amused, Avery answers, "She's the daughter of the Marquis of Brigend, a good match, and her father is a friend of the family. We were companions at court—when I was present, which wasn't very often. Mother thought we'd be happy."

She's the queen. She's beautiful and poised and charming. And he's probably held her hand, whispered into her ear, kissed her in the same perfect way he's kissed me.

I feel ill.

If I thought I wasn't good enough for Sebastian, it's nothing compared to picturing myself with a man who was engaged to the Queen of Kalae.

"She also happened to be madly in love with Harold, a man who was like an older brother to us," Avery continues, either oblivious to my dismay or ignoring it. "Well, apparently not much of a brother to her seeing as how she married him."

"How? I mean, *why* did she break the engagement?"

Avery takes a sip from his own drink. "Mother died. I realized life was too short to be with someone who didn't love me. I gave her the option to leave, and she gladly accepted it. She was engaged to Harold within the month."

That had to have stung. Avery can be as flippant as he wants—that sort of thing leaves a mark.

"She seems to like you well enough now."

A real smile plays on his lips. "Well, I'm quite a catch now."

I narrow my eyes. "And you weren't then?"

He moves in closer, almost too close in this crowd. "I was too wholesome, too naive and youthful. I needed to lose some of that shine before women started to look my way." His next words brush my ear. "And before you argue, I will point out that you like the pirate as well."

I shiver, shaking my head, and take a safe step to the side.

Though she's deep in conversation with Madam Lavinia, Minerva looks our way. Her eyes linger on Avery for a moment too long. Now that I know their history, I can see the regret in her actions. She sees Avery now, the Avery I've known from the beginning, and she wonders what it would have been like if she hadn't left him. I glance at the captain.

I don't want to have those same regrets.

Minerva pulls her gaze away and returns to her conversation, laughing joyously even though she's emotionally conflicted.

My head hurts, and I want to leave. This crowd is

exhausting. Everyone's so mannered, but no one says what they mean. Everyone's connected somehow, and if you're not born into it, it's a tricky spider web to maneuver. I don't belong here, and honestly, I don't want to. I'd rather raid caves, face dragons, slay nasty lesser basiliskas in the bottom of an apothecary's shoppe. Eating on a regular schedule is nice, but I don't think I can do this.

"Avery—"

He catches my hand, suddenly serious. He gives me a stern look, a gentle warning. "Don't."

"But this isn't my world," I mutter, exasperated.

"It's not mine either. I'd rather be anywhere but here."

"Then why are we?"

I'd give anything to be back on his ship—better yet, back on the island where things were simple and easy and honest.

"Because the king is throwing a soirée in your honor, Lucia, proving that you are, like it or not, *someone*. I want you to see that—not for them. I don't care about them." His thumb brushes my knuckles. "For you."

Tired of discussing it, feeling flutters I'd rather suppress, I tip my flute over. Sadly, it's empty. "Have you always been this charming, Captain? Or was it a learned trait?"

He drapes his arm over my shoulder. "Always, I'm afraid. It's simply a burden I'm forced to carry."

"You have a very difficult life," I tease as I swipe his flute and take a sip.

Mock serious, he shakes his head and lets out a long sigh. "Don't I know it."

CHAPTER TEN
Pastels are all the Rage

-or-

The Dressmaker and Her Hobgoblins

Adeline and I arrive at Serena Hanhaust's shoppe at
half past ten in the morning. It's a warm day, one that
feels more like spring than early winter. The shoppe
sits to the east of the city, near the elite part of town.
A spire from one of the guild buildings towers in the
distance, glistening in the late morning light.

The dressmaker's shoppe is constructed of stone
with large windows at the front. Black iron sconces
flank the doors, and cheerful flowers grow in baskets
that hang from the decorative beams of dark wood.
Adeline's eager but nervous, and she fidgets with her
gown as we walk toward the entrance, less confident
in her skills than usual.

Dreading the outing, worried the woman will be a snob, I give one of the double doors a tug just to be jolted when they don't open.

"Are they closed?" I ask Adeline, peering at the welcome sign nestled in the shrubs next to the doors. It would be a lie to say I'm not relieved. I've been dreading coming here, and I'll take any excuse to leave.

Looking heartbroken, Adeline peers at the sign. She shakes her head, and her auburn curls softly follow the movement. "She should be in."

I shrug as if to say, *"What can you do?"* Then I turn on my heel and try not to skip back to the carriage.

Adeline, not as eager to leave as I, knocks on the door. Frowning, I study an alabaster doe statue near the door. When no one answers, she knocks again, a little more insistent.

This time, the door swings open, and a pretty, petite woman stands on the other side. She purses her lips as she scans us. "I do not believe you have an appointment."

Adeline blinks. "Appointment?"

The woman looks at her as if she's daft. "You think Serena Hanhaust has the time to attend to people who simply walk in off the street?"

"Uh..." Adeline stutters, and her cheeks turn red. "I didn't think—"

"No, I suppose you didn't."

Irritated with the woman's attitude, I step forward and take Adeline's arm. Narrowing my eyes, knowing that this hoity-toity woman probably caters to the upper class every single day—knowing my next words won't make a bit of difference—I say, "We'll find someone else to make us gowns for the king's soirée."

The woman turns to me, ready to say something snide, but falters. Her entire demeanor changes, and she asks, "Are you Lucia of Reginae?" Incredulous, she adds, "The siren slayer?"

All right then.

Adeline turns to me, just as surprised as I am.

"Yes?" I say, unsure and a little disconcerted. The infamy is losing its appeal. Sure, it was enjoyable enough at first, but it's uncomfortable. Perhaps I'll learn how to deal with it graciously, but now, I'm itching to leave the city, scout in the wilderness. I can't help but think all these people are scrutinizing me, sizing me up, wondering if I really slew the sirens or if perhaps a man did it for me and we're not fessing up.

I don't measure up to some of the women scouts—I know that. I've seen them myself, tried not to envy their strong frames. Some are hardened to the world, but many, the ones I admire, are beautiful and respected. They can take down a full grown woodland lion as easily as other women churn butter.

But that's not me, not exactly. I'm strong enough,

but my curves are soft. Adeline's taller than I am, and my features could only be described as sweet. Not beautiful like Adeline, not willowy like the queen. Sweet.

And "sweet" unfortunately, is not exactly what you think of when you picture an adventuress renowned for slaying sirens.

Looking torn, the woman glances over her shoulder, into the shoppe. "Serena is indisposed at the moment, but I do believe she'd like to make you both gowns. Come inside; I'll take your measurements."

At the same time I'm declining, Adeline clasps my arm, digging her fingers into my flesh and yanks me forward. "That would be lovely!"

The inside of the shoppe doesn't look much different than Adeline's little boutique she owned in Mesilca, except it's larger and only a few gowns hang on elevated forms dispersed throughout the room, giving it an upscale sort of look.

Adeline looks around, enraptured. She hovers her hand over the delicate silk of the turquoise and gold gown closest to us, not daring to lay a finger on the fabric.

Serena's assistant quickly and efficiently takes my measurements. When she's finished, she stands back and studies me, eyes narrowed. I fidget, unsure what she's doing.

"Since you are the belle of the ball, I'm going to recommend scarlet for your gown. You have the skin tone and hair for it, and you'll stand out."

Adeline opens her mouth, obviously wanting to add her opinion but not brave enough to second guess the woman who works for the most renowned seamstress in Kalae.

"What do you think, Adeline?"

My friend's eyes go wide, and she looks as if she's going to scold me as soon as we leave. "Scarlet would be lovely."

"But?"

She gives me a stern look, but when I don't relent, she sighs. "But pastels are still so popular this season, especially that light coral I've seen so many girls wearing. Lucia would stand out, but the dress might clash and look...unfashionable." Her voice softens on the last word, especially when the assistant raises a haughty eyebrow at her.

"What color would you recommend?" a second voice says from behind us.

We turn abruptly, and the assistant stands a smidgen straighter. "Hello, Madam. I wasn't aware you were finished with your...meeting."

The woman in front of us is gorgeous, the kind of gorgeous that makes even Adeline look like a young girl in comparison. She's a smidgen taller than Adeline, and her hair is the color of pale honey. It tumbles down her back in glossy, sleek waves that are so perfect, they should be unattainable for a mere mortal. Her gown is long and sleek, and it just happens to be the exact color of coral Adeline was talking about.

She's a real life, human siren. And she's as intimidating as all oblivion.

"I'm so sorry, Madam Serena," Adeline says, sounding almost near tears. "I wasn't saying—"

Serena holds up her hand, brushing away the apology. "What color?"

Adeline bites her bottom lip and looks at me for courage. I widen my eyes, telling her to spit it out. After looking at the gowns on display, I have no doubt my friend is every bit as talented as this woman.

"Steel gray, perhaps with a black brocade skirt. It wouldn't clash with the pastels, but it would make her stand out."

The dressmaker wears an enigmatic look. "And what cut would suit her, do you think?"

"She looks lovely in a full skirt, and since her shoulders are delicate, I like to put her in a sweetheart neckline."

Serena finally smiles, still studying me. "Yes, we'll leave her shoulders bare but add detached sleeves. And maybe a feminine tapering A-line to juxtapose the dark fabric. She looks too young, too innocent to be a siren slayer, let's play that up whilst making her appear mysterious. She'll wear her hair down, and we'll darken it to a rich chocolate for the evening."

Darken my hair? What's wrong with it the way it is?

Adeline beams, and she looks at me as if I'm already wearing it. "It sounds stunning."

Serena nods at me as if approving the idea, and then she turns to Adeline. "Are you a seamstress?"

"I am." Adeline's almost breathless, and she nods, slightly too eager but in her usual enchanting way.

"You have a good eye."

It's a simple statement, but Adeline looks as if she's about to float away. "Thank you," she gushes.

The dressmaker's eyes return to me. She studies me, almost frowning. "You're not what I expected."

You and the rest of Kalae.

I shrug, because what are you supposed to say to that?

"If rumor is to be trusted, you can track down anything. After all, if you can bring back a sea fire ruby, what is beyond your grasp?" Her words are light, but there's steel behind them, and I don't quite understand why. She watches me carefully, intent on what my answer will be.

"I didn't bring it back alone."

A quick smile flashes across her face. "No, you've

partnered with Avery, haven't you?"

Two things: First...*Avery*? She practically purrs his name. And why not refer to him as Captain Greybrow? Surely—*surely*—he didn't have an affair with this woman too. She's at least eight years his senior, but she's... well.

Secondly, it sounds as if she's assumed Avery and I have formed a business alliance and not a...

What are we, anyway? I need to figure that out; I really do.

"Captain Greybrow and I are friends. Lord Sebastian Thane, of the Reginae Thanes, is my business partner."

Serena turns to Adeline. "And how do you fit in with this tidy little fellowship?"

Adeline blanches, unsure how to answer. What is she anyway? In the beginning, she was sort of a reluctant companion. Now...I suppose she's a willing companion?

"She's a friend as well," I say.

The dressmaker eyes me for one more long minute. "Are friends important to you, Lucia? Loyalty? *Trust?*"

"Yes," I answer slowly, wondering if this is a trick question.

There's a long moment of silence. Finally, Serena says, "Good. I'll send your gowns to the castle this evening."

"This evening?" I ask, surprised. Adeline's fast, but even she can't work like that.

Serena's already heading toward the back, but she looks over her shoulder before she disappears through the door. "I employ hobgoblins."

Adeline sucks in a breath, obviously shocked at the admission.

"Obviously, I don't want word of that to spread," the dressmaker says. "I trust you'll use discretion."

"All right..." I honestly couldn't care less. She could employ trolls for all I care.

"Friends are important to you, Lucia, just as discretion is important to me." The woman's gray-blue eyes bore into me. "Do you understand?"

It's the strangest thing, but I do not think we're talking about her miniature, pointy-eared seamstresses.

"Yes?" I answer.

She nods once, making her long, glistening hair sway, and disappears through the door without another word.

Adeline and I share a mystified look, and then Serena's assistant, who was silent throughout the whole exchange, shows us to the door. She doesn't look terribly friendly. I don't think she cares for us much, to be honest.

"That was odd," I whisper as we walk down the steps.

"Very odd," Adeline agrees.

I glance back at the shoppe as I'm stepping into the carriage, and I find a familiar face—black hair, somewhat bushy sideburns, intense expression. The man who I swear is stalking me leans against the lamppost, and our eyes meet. This time, I return his gaze, hoping to convey that I am not someone to trifle with.

His lips crook in a bare smile, and he doesn't look away until we've rounded the corner.

"Did you see that man?" I demand as soon as we're out of sight.

"What man?" Adeline asks, startled by my tone.

"He was—" I take in her bewildered gaze and shake my head. "Never mind."

There's no way it's a coincidence. But what does he want?

CHAPTER ELEVEN
Work on Your Technique

I wander the entire castle, looking for Sebastian. Eventually, I find him outside the armory, sparring with a few of the royal guards. He's shed most of his layers, and he stands shirtless, rapier extended, as he waits for the man across from him to prepare himself for the duel.

It's quite a sight—one I haven't had the pleasure of witnessing before. Flink's tied to a post at the corner of the seats in the shade, content to rub his face on his golden ball. It's good that Sebastian remembered to bring it, or the dragon would find something else to distract himself with—probably trying to pull the wooden seats down. Without drawing attention to myself, I climb the stairs and find a spot to watch.

Sebastian's good, better than I would have thought

my once-awkward friend could ever be. But he's grown into himself, gained muscle and confidence, and now he's quite the figure. And I'm not the only one who thinks so. A trio of laundry maids loiters at the edge of the yard, heads bent together as they giggle amongst themselves.

With one last parry and a lunge, Sebastian bests the guard opposite him. The day is pleasant, not overly warm, but sweat rolls off them. They wipe their brows, laughing.

"Who challenges the winner?" I yell, happy to take Sebastian by surprise.

His head jerks my way, and his gaze meets mine. I smile, cocky. I could always beat him when we were children. Of course, back then we were playing with sticks. Something tells me he's graduated past that level.

"You think you can best me, Lucy?" he hollers up, using my mother's nickname for me that I hate—that he *knows* I hate.

It's as close to our banter as we've gotten in ages, and I give him a wicked smile. "It's never been a problem before."

The guards exchange glances, curious, and step back. The girls who were ogling my business partner watch with avid interest, perhaps hoping they can have a turn as well.

I jog down the steps and pat Flink's head as I pass.

"May I borrow your blade?" I ask the guard nearest me. He grins and extends it toward me, hilt first. "Thank you."

"Do you have any idea what you're doing?" Sebastian asks as he takes his place across from me. "Last time I remember, you were doing this with twigs."

"Last time I remember, I poked you in the belly, and you cried."

He narrows his eyes. "That's not quite how I remember it."

Technically, I pushed him back, right into a camouflaged hornets' nest. The two of us booked it out of there as fast as we were able. There might have been a few stoic tears on both our parts. We were thirteen at the time, and it was right before Sebastian decided I was too female to duel with.

Sebastian lowers himself into his stance. "Since these are real blades, here are the rules: no stabbing, slicing, or kneeing in the groin—"

"That was *one* time. Let it go." I lunge forward, making him begin because if I do not, he'll talk for ages.

His blade meets mine with a satisfying metallic twang, and we dance around each other. I'm barely keeping up, but it's clear he's going easy on me.

"You got rather good at this," I pant after several

long minutes. This must be what a mouse feels like when a cat decides to give it a sporting chance.

"And you should stick with a bow." He feints an attack, catching me off guard, and then he knocks the rapier clean out of my hand. With bright eyes, he slides his blade in its sheath. "Looks like I won."

I double over, not ashamed to be exhausted. I glance up at Sebastian, trying very hard to look at his face and not his ridged abdomen. Then I straighten and set my hands on my waist. "Again?"

"Maybe you should practice first," a deep voice says from behind me. Before I can swirl around to face Avery, the captain steps closer, pressing his chest against my back, and places another rapier in my hand. With Sebastian glaring, he practically purrs in my ear, "I'll be happy to help you with your technique anytime."

My body hums with pleasure, and I try not to giggle like one of Sebastian's trio of admirers.

Sebastian all but snarls as he steps forward, "Perhaps we should test your skill first—see if you're qualified to teach."

"I think that was a challenge," Avery whispers against my neck. Delicious tingles run down my spine, and my common-sense excuses itself. Sadly, the captain steps away and holds out his hand, silently asking for his sword back.

"Avery, no," I whisper, not wanting to embarrass him in front of the king's men and Sebastian, but knowing he's not ready to fight.

"I'm fine—I swear," he promises, his words tickling my ear. Then he turns to Sebastian. "All right, little cousin. Let's see what you can do."

Sebastian's eyes flash, but he's smart enough to keep his wits about him when someone's baiting him. Unless that someone is me, but I've had a lifetime to learn what specifically riles him up.

With a bare smile, Avery strips off his jacket, then his doublet...then his shirt. Sebastian's girls giggle again, but my eyes land on the scar on the captain's abdomen. Just seeing it marring his tanned flesh brings back that horrible day. But at the same time, it is *just* a scar. Gregory's right—Avery's healed.

Slowly, I exhale and back into the post where Flink's currently residing. The two begin their duel. Before long, they've gathered a fair amount of attention. Soon, they've got quite the crowd—and a good three-quarters of the spectators are female. Which I'm sure has little to do with the display of rippling muscles and more for the women's obvious love of the sport.

Early in the duel, it becomes clear they are evenly matched, though I think Avery might be the better of the two once he fully recovers his strength. Relentless, the two keep going, waiting for the other to make a foolish mistake.

My hand drifts down so I might mindlessly pet Flink, but my fingers find nothing but air. I glance at the ground, wondering if he managed to squeeze himself under the bench. He's gone.

I lean down, a little concerned. "Flink?"

His golden ball is missing as well, but his lead is still tied to the post. His harness lies on the ground, still attached to the lead. He must have squeezed out of it.

Growing quite nervous, I look around for him.

"Stop!" I yell to Sebastian and Avery.

Startled by my tone, they both freeze mid-parry and turn to look at me.

"Flink's missing."

Sebastian lowers his blade first. "I tied him to—" his words die abruptly when he sees the abandoned lead and harness.

"You must help me find him."

The thought of him on the streets of Teirn, wandering wherever he pleases, causing unimaginable havoc—it terrifies me. Sebastian and Avery are both still breathing deeply, but they nod and sheath their blades. The female population of the crowd murmurs their disapproval when the pair slip their shirts back on, but my glare must be intimidating because the audience breaks up, leaving us be.

We search for hours, and there is no sign of Flink. We try all the butchers, thinking the smell might have attracted him, all the gold and silversmiths, the king's guarded treasury rooms—everywhere. But no dragon.

Disheartened and sick with worry, I allow Avery and Sebastian to escort me back to the castle. The day is done, and night settles over the city. The first few stars prick the sky, and a fat moon rises from the east.

As soon as we're in the entry, a young man pushes away from the wall, where it appears he waited for quite some time.

"Captain Greybrow," Jeb says, his face relieved. "Master Gregory sent me. He wanted me to tell you that Flink wandered back to the ship this afternoon."

We find the Greybrow Serpent engulfed in snow—which is unusual considering it was a reasonably warm, sunny day. Avery gapes, and people on the pier gawk. A perfect soap-bubble-like film of magic surrounds the ship, locking the blizzard inside. Stars shine from overhead, making the scene very surreal indeed.

"What in the world," Avery mutters as he jogs up the gangplank. Sebastian and I follow right on his heels.

To my surprise, we walk right into the whirling snow. The crewmen all wear heavy jackets and woolen cloaks, and they shiver from the perimeter of the deck. Gregory stands in the middle, scowling at something in his hand.

"What happened?" Avery demands.

The mage turns, not terribly concerned with the blizzard-like conditions. "Oh, hello, Captain. Since we're not sailing for a while, I thought I'd experiment with a few new enchantments."

"Did you mean to turn the Serpent into a giant snow globe?" I ask, bewildered.

"Not exactly." Gregory again studies the charm in his hands. "But when you're working from scratch, you can't expect to create a functioning enchantment the first time."

Avery stares at him for a moment, and then he shakes his head, dismissing it all. "Fine just...clean it up."

"Yes, Captain. Oh—the dragon's in your cabin."

That's not good. I reach the cabin first and stop in the doorway. Flink stares at me from atop his golden perch, his snout twitching like he's happy to see me. I gape into Avery's quarters, horrified. Half his priceless collections are on the ground, and the dragon sits on them like they are a great nest. Anything made of gold or silver, anything adorned with jewels, lies in the pile.

Avery goes completely still, and I very slowly turn toward him, hesitant to meet his eyes. "I'd like to remind you that it's your fault I have the dragon in the first place."

The captain meets my eyes. He doesn't look mad, not exactly. Perhaps a bit frustrated. "Do me a favor, Lucia?"

I glance at Flink, who has now snuggled even deeper into the captain's treasures. "Yes...?"

"Do you think you can remove your dragon from my cabin?"

Easier said than done, especially when there's a blizzard outside. Flink likes to be warm.

Sebastian stands behind us, probably more amused than he should be. He insisted he come, even after we found out my dragon was safe in Gregory's care. And I'm pretty sure he's happy with his decision to join us.

"Come here, Flink," I call.

The dragon rolls onto his back, getting comfortable.

"Flink," I warn. "Don't make me come get you."

It sounds like an empty threat, even to my own ears.

"You might try to be a bit sterner, Lucia," Sebastian supplies, ever so helpfully.

I glare at him and then walk toward Flink. "This is very bad, Flink. You shouldn't have done this."

The dragon yawns.

"Mason," I holler at the young man lingering outside. "Bring me a bit of cheese."

"You told us to never give him cheese—you said it gives him indigestion."

I roll my eyes. "I know. Just *do* it."

It takes several minutes, but the boy finally returns. I take the cheese from him and step into the room. Once I have Flink's attention, I wave the treat in front of his snout. Immediately, the dragon rights himself, and then he rises to all fours.

"There's a good boy," I sing as I back out of the cabin. "Do you want the cheese?"

Flink makes pathetic snuffling noises as he follows me from the room. Only once Avery slams the door shut do I give the dragon the treat.

Sebastian frowns. "I'm not sure you should reward him for wandering away."

"I'm not rewarding him for wandering away—I'm rewarding him for leaving the room."

Avery looks like he might agree more with Sebastian than me—and that doesn't settle well with him. It doesn't settle particularly well with me either.

"I just think you might spoil him," Sebastian adds because he doesn't know when to let things go.

"He's young," I argue, glaring at the pair. "Just past a baby."

Avery steps forward, his manner soothing. "Of

course he is. But it might be a good idea to work with him—teach him some manners. That's all Sebastian is saying."

Since when are they on the same side?

I put Flink's harness back on him and turn on my heel, ready to leave the two of them behind.

"Lucia, wait," Avery says. To make peace, he rolls the golden ball through the thick layer of snow, right to the dragon. "The king's soirée is in a few days—why don't you try leaving him here again. I'll have Gregory keep an extra eye on him this time."

I frown, but it does seem like the dragon is happier here on the Serpent than he is at the castle. After a few moments of deliberation, I reluctantly agree.

Before we leave, I kneel and look Flink in the eyes. "Be good."

In response, the dragon head-butts me, takes the ball in his mouth, and wanders away to find somewhere warm to sleep.

"That's a good sign," Sebastian mutters, and Avery snorts.

I glare at the two men and then leave them on the snowy deck.

CHAPTER TWELVE
Royal Order of the Stag

"A dagger under your skirts, Lucia? Truly? For a soirée in the king's castle?"

I glance at the dagger and bite back a wicked smirk. "It wasn't comfortable in my bodice."

"Fine," she mutters, letting out a dramatic sigh. "Do whatever you like—you always do."

"I'll let you darken my hair a little more," I offer, trying to cheer her as I pull up my skirts and slide the blade into the sheath secured to my thigh. It's just a little dagger, nothing noticeable. And really, it's just a precaution. You see, every time I leave it behind—especially when it's only because the dress won't allow for it—I get attacked. Therefore, I'm simply ensuring the evening will go smoothly.

After the dagger is in place, I stand and smooth

the skirts back into place. Waves of nervousness run over me, and I'm never quite sure when the next bout is going to hit. One moment, I'm fine—ready for the evening. The next I'm half sick to my stomach with nerves.

We're in a mirror-covered powder room just off the main hall, "adding a few last touches" as Adeline said. An orchestra plays in the room just past the door. It's a soft, gentle tune that reminds me I'm out of my element. The smell of roasted lamb, pork, and venison wafts through the air, mingled with the scent of peppercorn, bay leaves, and sage. Flink would love to be here, raiding the tables, but it's probably good I left the dragon on Avery's ship. Hopefully, Mason and Jeb can keep track of him for one more evening.

Serena's gown fits me like a glove. It's soft and sleek, and the fabric drapes in an elegant way that would make me want to spin in circles if I were eight years old, just so I could watch it twirl out around me. As Adeline suggested, the bodice is steely gray, and the skirt is made of a delicate black brocade that shimmers like onyx in the evening's lighting—a mix of candlelight and magic. My shoulders are bare, and my arms are bedecked in tight, detached sleeves.

It's gorgeous, and I feel beautiful and a bit mysterious, just as Serena promised. If only I felt like I belonged.

Adeline gives her turquoise bodice a good final tug, wiggling her shoulders as she secures her gown into place. Serena made her a vision, choosing fabric that sets Adeline's dark auburn hair on fire. She's going to turn heads tonight, but there's only one she's interested in.

If Sebastian is half as smart as he thinks he is, he'll pay attention to her. With Adeline looking as lovely as she does, he's going to have plenty of competition. Especially when she's a new face in the crowd.

It's strange to think of Sebastian this way again, as nothing more than a friend. It's going to take time for it to feel natural; I know that. But right now, it's so awkward. Part of me still wants to claim to him—demand that he is mine although I don't necessarily want him.

But it's wrong of me to begrudge him happiness, especially when I like Adeline well enough. I think she might even be good for him—she simply must convince him of that.

When Adeline is done fussing with her gown, she stands in front of me, frowning at my hair in her familiar, thoughtful way. "Just a touch darker."

I shrug, past caring. Adeline promised the charm would fade by morning, so what does it matter? She can make me raven-haired if she likes.

After several moments, she nods, satisfied, and then she propels me toward one of the numerous mirrors. "What do you think?"

I don't look all that different, not really. My usually medium-toned chocolate hair is the color of rich coffee, but there are still a few lighter streaks here and there, making it look sun-kissed. Earlier, Adeline lined my eyes with kohl and shaded the lids with sparkling micas, but the effect is nowhere near as startling as the makeup I wore on the island in the whirlpool.

All in all, I look like myself, but more polished. Serena's very good—the girl staring back at me could be a siren-slayer. With the expert cut of the gown, I look strong but feminine, and I know I will stand out in the crowd.

Our room is invaded by a gaggle of noblewomen. Their conversation stops short, and they stare at me. I feel like a trained owl griffin, the ones the wanderers of the caravans keep around to entertain and draw in the crowds. These women all watch me as if expecting me to perform, all waiting for me to entertain them.

Adeline gives them a soft smile, correctly interpreting the flustered look on my face, and escorts me from the tiny room.

Sebastian and Avery stand just inside the huge ballroom, attempting to make small talk. They face each other, Avery leaning against a pillar and Sebastian with his arms crossed. My steps falter when I see them.

"Oh my," Adeline says, her eyes straying to the

pair.

Oh my is right. They are handsome apart, but together...

Well.

And we're not the only ones who think so. Clusters of young women hover near the pair, glancing their way often and giggling to themselves. If the men's expressions were not so stern, I'm sure they would have company.

"Are you ready, Mademoiselle Siren Hunter?" Adeline asks, trying to ease my fears. I haven't told her I'm terrified, but she knows.

"I suppose."

She links her arm with mine, and we make our way into the large room.

A room full of elemental wyverns? No problem.

A den of basiliskas? That's nothing more than a walk by the sea.

But this ballroom full of courtiers? Most terrifying thing imaginable.

I paste a smile on my face and match Adeline's pace. People watch us, and they aren't subtle about it. Several couples stop to congratulate me. They all insist on touching me. Women briefly place a hand on my arm or shoulder, and men brush chaste kisses over my knuckles. It's all very genteel and smothering.

The ballroom is massive, and it must hold half

of Teirn. Just as Adeline predicted, it's a sea of pastels. Pinks, periwinkles, lavenders, and corals mingle in front of us, making me feel very conspicuous in my silver gown. There will be no blending in tonight.

Very well then. If I must do this, I will do it well. I straighten my shoulders, toss my hair behind me, and beckon over a server carrying crystal flutes of sparkling cider. I take a drink, decide it's good, and then drain it before I exchange the empty flute for another.

"Feeling better?" Adeline whispers, her eyes twinkling.

I shrug. "Sometimes real confidence doesn't show up until after you pretend for a bit."

Adeline takes a sip of her own cider and holds it up in a toast. "Wise words. And with that said, let's find Sebastian. I have some pretending to do."

The crowds are thick, and we are constantly stopped. There are plenty of people who only treat me as a novelty—the evening's scheduled amusement, but there's admiration in many of their expressions, and I feed off it.

Avery glances our way, and then he does a subtle, but very satisfying, double take. The handsome captain is as at ease in this ornate ballroom as he is on his ship, always comfortable in his own skin. Still leaning against the pillar, he loosely crosses his arms, and a promising smile plays at his lips. He's like a panther, a lion—all sinewy muscle and grace. And his eyes are on mine, his smile for me alone.

I'm not immune to him, and I doubt I ever will be. My stomach flutters; my mouth goes dry. I want to check my hair, check my makeup, find something to do with my fidgety hands. But mostly, I want to quell the memories which insist on playing in a constant loop through my head.

So, I do the only thing I know to do—I give him a feline smirk of my own, playing coy because I know it will make his smile grow. It works, and his response is enough to take my breath away.

Sebastian glances at the ceiling when he notices the exchange, perhaps asking for strength to make it through this evening where Avery and I will be praised, but there's no anger in his expression. When he looks down, he smiles briefly at me. Then he lets his eyes wander to Adeline.

He gives away nothing, but I have a feeling there's something there, something he's hiding.

Adeline tugs me back and says quietly enough no one will overhear her, "Let them come to us."

"But..." I glance at the women hovering near the pair of cousins. The bejeweled nobles might as well be harpies for how they leer at Avery and Sebastian.

But before I can argue, His Semi-royal, High and Mighty Handsomeness himself steps up to us, blocking our path. Gerard bows low, looking dashing in his masculine finery. "Do you have a need for a shield again? I am here, gladly offering my services."

He smiles cheekily, raising his blond brows with good humor.

"You have excellent timing," Adeline tell Gerard as she peeks over his shoulder.

Sebastian and Avery are already making their way toward us.

Gerard narrows his eyes with good humor and glances behind him before he turns back to face me. "I see how this is. Tell me, which one have you set your sights on?"

I didn't like the man when we first met—especially after he assumed I was Sebastian's maid the first time we first came to Teirn. But he's growing on me— much like a barnacle on the hull of a ship.

"The captain," Adeline supplies for me. I shoot her a murderous look, but she only smiles.

"It's always Avery." Gerard chuckles darkly and shifts his weight, getting comfortable. "There's no competing against a captain. The title alone sends girls all aflutter, and then you add in Avery's roguish, devil-may-care attitude." He lets out a lingering mock-sigh. "It's a lost cause."

I glance away, trying not to think of how many girls Avery's "set aflutter."

From across the room, our young queen catches my eye. She's mingling with the crowd, waiting for her husband to make his appearance. And wouldn't you know it—she's wearing a silver gown. It's almost identical to mine.

Trying to ignore Minerva, I look back at Gerard. Then, thinking it might help to know—perhaps help me quell this inconvenient infatuation, I give him a wry smile. "And just *how many* girls have you lost to Avery?"

The man gives me a knowing look. "Do numbers really matter?"

"That many?" I ask, laughing though the thought makes me queasy.

"Well, let me tell you about this time in Bay-white—"

"I'm quite sure Lucia doesn't want to be bored with tales from our past," Avery interrupts as he joins us.

"Lucia's quite sure she does," I say to him sweetly.

The captain chuckles under his breath and expertly directs Gerard's attention to the current price of silver. Gerard, who apparently owns several mines, is immediately diverted, and just like that, I've lost my informant.

Avery glances at me with a smug sort of look as Gerard speaks of the fluctuating market. Before I can draw the conversation back to Avery's numerous past exploits, a pair of trumpets cries out from the front of the hall, announcing the king's arrival.

Harold steps into the room from behind the crests hanging behind the thrones. Immediately, the room goes silent. Respectful of our monarch, the men bow and women dip into deep curtsies. I must be getting the hang of it because Adeline doesn't shoot me a reproachful look.

"Rise," the king says, already smiling. Wasting no time, he begins, "Tonight, we celebrate. For the first time in eighty years, a captain has successfully sailed a ship through the forbidden waters and returned unscathed. And, for the first time in history, Kalae may claim their very own siren slayer. Captain Greybrow, Lucia Linnon, please come forward."

The crowd parts like a curtain being drawn. They sweep out of the path in front of us, every eye on Avery and me. Without a moment's hesitation, Avery takes my arm and escorts me forward.

Oddly, I'm reminded of our peculiar wedding, of the way the people of the island watched us so intently as we exchanged those unknown vows. My heart begins to pound, and my breath quickens.

We reach Harold, and he gives me a quick wink. The simple, familiar gesture eases my nerves, even if only slightly. Minerva stands next to Harold, eying my gown. She looks as pleased about our near-matching as I am.

"Captain, for your bravery and steadfast loyalty to the crown." Harold extends his hand to Minerva, and she places a huge gold medallion in his palm. He hands the token to Avery, and the captain bows again. The two look almost bored of the process, as if they've both been through it numerous times.

Then Harold turns to me, and a large smile grows across his face. "Lucia Linnon, daughter of William and Marta Linnon of Reginae, for your service to Kalae—for the protection of our people and your prowess with a bow, I hereby induct you into the Royal Order of the Stag. Henceforth, you will be addressed as Lady Lucia and you shall receive all the honor and respect the title is due."

I stare at him, dumbfounded.

His Majesty leans close. "You should probably curtsy now."

"Oh, yes." I snap out of my stupor and sink in front of him, only stumbling slightly. When I rise, Harold sets a golden arrow in my palms. I stare at the token, unable to fully comprehend the events of the last few moments.

To me, since Avery obviously has done all this before, Harold whispers, "You'll turn now. Stand for a moment while the crowd basks in your glory, and then you may join your companions."

Still numb, I nod.

As one, we turn. I search for a familiar face, someone I can rest my gaze on. As they have for the last twenty-one years, my eyes find Sebastian. He stares back, an odd expression on his face. It's not cloaked as it usually is—it mirrors my own shock. And there's something else there, something that makes me remember an imagined future from not so long ago.

To show polite respect, the men in our audience bow their heads and the women once again dip in curtsies—though these are not as low or sweeping as the ones they graced the king with. Sebastian, though, doesn't move. He stares at me as if in a trance.

Avery stiffens beside me, obviously noticing. Then he puts on a carefree smile, takes me by the arm again, and escorts me into our crowd of admirers. But instead of taking me to Adeline and the rest of our group, he steers me to the left, toward the back of the throng.

I recognize Lord Thane's gray head first, but then I blink several times because with him is a group I cannot believe is standing in the king's hall.

My brother Anderson, who towers a head above most in the crowd, grins when he sees me coming, and then the rest of my family looks my way. I gape at them as Avery sweeps me along, right to their tight little cluster.

"Little duck!" Father bellows as soon as I'm near, and he crushes me against his chest in a bear hug. "Or I suppose I should say Lady Duck now!"

"What are you doing here?" I manage as I'm passed to Anderson and Erik, the eldest of my brothers, and they too try to squeeze the air from my lungs. George and Hansel join them, wrapping themselves around my back, and little Kiersten joins the fray.

"Let her breathe," Mother chastises as she steals me from my exuberant siblings. Someone has done her hair, twisted it up into a beautiful updo, and she wears a simple gown in midnight blue. She's gorgeous, more beautiful than any of the courtiers in attendance.

The last words we spoke were not friendly. I stare at her as she stands there, an expression on her face that's as hesitant as my own. And then she offers a small smile. "I'm proud of you, Lucy."

And just like that, to my great horror, I burst into tears.

CHAPTER THIRTEEN
Stalker in the Castle

I dab at my eyes, thoroughly humiliated, and Mother wraps her arms around me like she used to do, laughing like she hasn't a care in the world.

"Who's watching the farm?" I ask.

"Connor's family volunteered," Mother says, speaking of the man who I've declined marriage offers from twice. She was especially angry with me the second time, and that's what created the rift between us. But her tone carries no chastisement now.

"I just don't understand—how did you find out?" I blink quickly, thankful the tears are ebbing. "I didn't even know what was going to transpire this evening. I thought I'd get a small purse of gold and be sent on my way."

Father turns to Avery, who I almost forgot was

standing behind me. "Captain Greybrow sent us a personal invitation. We wouldn't miss this for anything, Lucia."

And my poor, poor heart—it cannot take this. I turn to Avery, overwhelmed with gratitude and something else I cannot put my finger on. He sent for my family? Knew me well enough to know I would want them here?

"How? There was no time."

"I sent the message by pigeon."

"Thank you," I murmur because there is no way I'll be able to manage anything else without crying again.

It's very embarrassing.

Avery simply nods, his eyes warm with understanding.

Oh, this man. He's going to be the death of me. Just when I convince myself our time on the island, on his ship, was fleeting, he does something like this.

"Tell us how you killed the sirens," young George demands, tugging on my arm. "I want to hear everything."

The rest of them chime in, pouring out more questions all at once. I end up regaling them with the tale more times than I can count.

Lord Thane stands quietly by, ever watchful. My eyes meet his once, and he nods, *thinking*. I've seen that look before—but it was directed at Adeline.

My stomach knots with confusion. What I would have given for him to look at me that way last autumn. I glance at Avery. Oblivious to his uncle's thoughts, the captain gives me his cocky smile, the one that tells me I'm doomed.

After my brothers have properly stuffed themselves with enough food to last them a week, and my sister finishes her fifth icing-ladened petit four, we say our goodbyes. Though the night is nowhere close to finished, Father says they want to make Clear Creek before nightfall. It's a week's ride back to Reginae, longer if you take your time.

I hug them all and thank them for coming at least a dozen times.

"Visit as soon as you're able," Father says before he leaves.

"Thank you for convincing Mother to come," I whisper.

He gives me a knowing smile, and then he follows the rest of them out of the castle.

When they are gone, I feel as if my heart has been mended. I didn't realize how the disagreement between Mother and me weighed on my shoulders.

Soon after their departure, Avery and I are swept apart by admirers. By the time the evening is nearing its end, I'm so sick of the story of our adventure, I feel

I'll never want to speak of it again. Every time I'm free, someone else corners me, wanting to talk with me, wanting me to entertain them. It's exhausting.

"Lady Lucia!" someone exclaims just as I'm attempting to make my way toward Avery. The captain is deep in conversation with Gerard and the queen, and the sight makes my stomach squirm in the most uncomfortable sort of way.

I turn, holding back a sigh.

Dante, the apothecary from the alchemy shoppe Sebastian and I visited, stands in front of me. He gives me a crisp bow, his eyes sparkling. "Good evening, Lady Lucia."

Grateful for a familiar face, even one who's only an acquaintance, I relax. "Hello, Dante. How's your shoppe?"

"Happily intact, thank you for asking." He glances around the room. "My congratulations are due—this is quite the party."

"Thank you." Exhausted, I look around as well.

Dante cocks his head to the side, studying me. "You're looking a bit weary."

"I am," I admit. "I'm unused to this glitter and extravagance."

He steps forward, leaning closer. With a teasing quality to his voice, he asks, "So I don't suppose we'll hear rumors of our favorite siren slayer attending one

135

of the dark masquerades this evening?"

I turn to Dante sharply, taking him by surprise. "What masquerades? A beggar in the street outside your shoppe was hollering about them when we left, but we assumed he was on night floss."

Dante's eyebrows rise. "That's all you've heard about them?"

I nod.

Glancing around us, he steps in closer and lowers his voice. "If the rumors are to be believed, they're taking place under the city. Apparently, it's all very secretive, and you must have an invitation to attend."

"Have you been to one?"

"Me?" He chuckles like the thought is very humorous. "Oh no. I'm not quite noble enough. It's said the masquerades are for certain courtiers, the rich, the notable. Do not be surprised if you find yourself an invitation at some point."

"I'm not noble or rich," I point out, and then I pause. Am I noble now?

Dante angles a bit closer, giving me a good whiff of the subtle earthy, musky scent of his cologne. "Lady Lucia, you are more than just noble—you're famous, and that might be even better."

I'm not sure how to answer that, but it doesn't matter because Avery has broken away from his conversation, and he finally joins us.

"Ah, the real Captain Greybrow," Dante says, taking a subtle step away from me. "What an honor it is to meet you."

Avery nods and settles next to me, tucking me against his side like it's the only place I could possibly belong. My breath catches, and I work to keep it even.

The men exchange pleasantries, and soon the shopkeeper excuses himself, leaving me with thoughts of dark masquerades swirling in my head.

"How much longer must we stay?" I ask Avery quietly.

"Avery!" Minerva calls from across the room, waving her hand in the air to get the captain's attention.

I pull away. "It appears you're being summoned."

Avery groans low, but his face is a perfectly pleasant mask.

"Go on," I say, nudging him. "Your admirers need you."

He gives me a wry look and brushes a chaste kiss over the top of my head before he casually walks their way. The sweet gesture startles me, and my eyes linger on him as he mingles with the crowd.

"Why, hello there, *Lady* Lucia."

I jump at Adeline's voice, and I whip around, feeling as if I've been caught doing something wrong. Adeline's eyes narrow with concern. "You look almost dead on your feet."

Sebastian's with her as well, and he crosses his arms. I can feel his gaze on me, but I purposely avoid his eyes.

"I'm exhausted," I admit.

"Did you tell Avery you're ready to leave?" Sebastian asks, his tone giving away nothing after the look we shared earlier.

I shake my head. "No. He's very popular this evening. I've barely had a chance to speak with him after the..."

"The ceremony?" he supplies, and his dark green eyes lock on mine when I make the mistake of looking up.

I clear my throat and nod. The air grows thick, and Adeline's gaze flickers between us. Her bright expression dims.

"I noticed the shopkeeper from Convill and Midtown visited with you for a few minutes," Sebastian says, ending the awkward silence.

"Dante."

Sebastian nods. "Is his shoppe well?"

"Yes, he said it's fine." I lean closer to the pair. "He also spoke of the masquerades the beggar was going on about. Do you remember that?"

"It would be difficult to forget." Sebastian frowns. "What did he say?"

"Only that they're by invitation only, and it's all

very secretive and elite."

Sebastian shakes his head. "There aren't any cat-acombs underneath Teirn. They're rumor, that's all. The city has been searched dozens of times."

I nod, still intrigued, and then I cover a yawn with my hand.

"It's late. Fetch your cloaks," Sebastian says to Adeline and me. "I'll say our goodbyes and escort you across the courtyard to your rooms."

Before he can turn, I catch his arm. "Thank you."

He glances at my hand and then nods.

As we're walking to the coat room, Adeline stops to chat with someone she met earlier in the night. I go on without her, telling her I'll fetch her cloak.

The attendant is just slipping mine around my shoulders when I notice my stalker's face in the hall-way. I hurry away, forgetting all about Adeline's cloak, and race after the man. By the time I've turned down the hall I'm sure he disappeared into, I've already pulled my dagger from its sheath.

This time, I'm going to catch him, and he's going to tell me why he's been following me.

Several people call out my name, but I rush past them as I hurry after the man, intent on my mission. The crowds thin as I go farther into the halls. Just ahead, I see the man dart into a room. Holding my dagger at my side, hidden under my long black cloak,

I throw the door open.

The room is pitch black. Before I can step back into the light of the hall, perhaps find a candelabra or wall torch, a hand closes around my arm, and I'm yanked into the black room.

CHAPTER FOURTEEN
A Secret Meeting

I struggle against my attacker, but just as quickly as I am grabbed, I am released. A spark of light springs to life, and then it spreads, illuminating the room. It appears we're in some sort of storage cubby. My stalker stands in front of me, holding the charmed ball of light that's casting a blueish glow on the walls.

Undaunted, I hold out my dagger. "Who are you, and why have you been following me?"

The man's close to forty years of age, and he's not much taller than I am. He doesn't seem to be armed, and he watches my dagger, uneasy. "I have no intention of bringing you harm, my lady."

I jab the blade a bit closer and repeat, "Who are you?"

"My name is Sam, and I am a steward."

"All right, Sam the Steward. Why are you following me?"

The man swallows and finally pulls his eyes from the blade to meet my gaze. "My employer would like to hire you."

I frown. "Hire me? For what?"

"A scouting job, something rather covert. I trailed you this week, hoping to ascertain your character."

Not seeing this squirrelly man as much of a threat, I slowly lower my dagger, but I keep it in my hand. "And what did you discover?"

The man shrugs, cryptic.

"What sort of job is it?"

"Item retrieval. Nothing you aren't capable of."

"What item?"

"You'll have to discuss that with my employer."

"And the pay?" I ask.

"You'll have to discuss that as well."

"Why not speak to me the first time I saw you on the docks, why all this subterfuge? You realize I could have killed you?"

The light flickers. "It crossed my mind, yes."

"So now what?"

Sam shifts, nervous. "Now you come with me, if you're interested in the job."

This is reeking of trouble, but my curiosity wins, as it usually does. "Fine. But I'm going to bring my business partner."

The man doesn't seem to like that idea, but I won't budge if he refuses. I might be curious, but I'm not a fool.

"Fine," Sam finally says.

"And Captain Greybrow?" I ask.

Sam winces. "I don't think that's a good—"

"I bring Avery as well, or you can consider your-self less one adventuress."

The man rubs his forehead. "Fine, but you must come tonight. We're running out of time."

My feet are killing me, and I'm dying to take off this awful corset. But, despite all that, I find myself saying, "All right. Tonight."

CHAPTER FIFTEEN
Thane Scouting, Inc.

"You met with this man in a storage closet?" Sebastian demands. "*Alone?* Without telling anyone?"

"Yes, Sebastian." I glance at Avery, hoping he'll come to my rescue with one of his flippant remarks. That hope dies when I meet his eyes. He doesn't look angry like my business partner, but there is definitely concern in his expression.

We're standing in an alcove just outside the castle courtyard. I finally rounded up our group, feeling as if I was herding chickens. Avery's far too popular, and Adeline's only been here a week, and she seems to already know everyone. Every time I had one, I'd lose the other. It was ridiculous.

"What was I to do?" I demand. "He would have gotten away."

Sebastian growls under his breath. "It didn't occur to you that he might have been hoping to lure you into a dark corner—"

"Technically, that's exactly what he did—"

"Lucia!"

"She's fine. It's all fine." Adeline adjusts her cloak and hides a kitten yawn with the back of her hand. "Lucia's not exactly helpless."

Adeline's the last person I expect to come to my rescue, but I shoot her a grateful look.

The seamstress turns to me. "Unless we're talking about her fashion choices, but that's what I'm here for."

I roll my eyes and look back at Sebastian. My business partner doesn't seem to be swayed by Adeline's light conversation, and Avery looks far too serious as well.

"Are you coming with me or not?" I set my hands on my hips and stare the pair down.

"If we don't, you'll go alone," Avery points out.

I don't even bother to agree because it's a given.

Sebastian runs a hand through his hair, messing it up. Adeline watches him, lips pressed together, eyes focused on the wayward strands. I know she wants to brush it back into place. It's killing her.

"Fine," my business partner finally says, not wanting me to go on my own but obviously exasperated with my choices.

It's nice to know some things never change.

"We'll take Adeline home, and then—"

"Why can't I come?" Adeline demands.

"Well, I..." Sebastian frowns, confused. "I didn't expect you'd want to."

"But you didn't even ask." She tilts her nose in the air, disdain dripping from her voice.

Sebastian turns to me with a look that suggests Adeline is my fault, like some of my temperament has rubbed off on the once docile seamstress.

I smile, and Avery covers a chuckle with a cough. My eyes stray to the captain, as they are wont to do, and my amusement fades. He looks tired—not sickly, just wiped out. "You're exhausted."

Avery scoffs, though I know I'm right. "I'm fine."

"You're still healing. You should—"

"Don't say it," he warns.

A loud and quite likely inebriated group of noble-men stumbles from the gates, either forgetting their carriage or deciding it's a nice night for a walk. As one, we step a little deeper into the shadows. A cool breeze blows through the trees, gently lifting my hair from my neck, reminding me I need to pull it up.

"Listen, we're running out of time," I tell them as I poke the ground with my toe, looking for two semi-straight twigs. "I'm going now. Whoever wants to tag along is welcome."

I spot a long, thin stick that looks strong enough. I snap it in half, wind my hair into a loose bun, and jam the sticks into the rope-like coil to hold it in place.

"That's a clever trick," Avery says.

"Never wear your—"

"Hair down," Adeline finishes for me. "We *know*."

"Good." I flick her updo. "Lucky for you, you're all set."

"Adeline isn't going with us," Sebastian says in that tone that riles me up when he uses it on me. Now I sit back and watch the show.

Adeline turns toward Sebastian. "Yes, I am. If Lucia can go, then I can too."

"Weren't you paying attention? Lucia slays sirens. She's got wicked good aim with her dagger, and she's not above biting when push comes to shove."

I raise my eyebrows, nodding toward Avery. The captain shakes his head, probably thinking my ego doesn't need inflating.

Adeline doesn't argue with Sebastian, doesn't try to sway him with wit and reasoning. No, she pulls a completely different weapon from her arsenal. The seamstress steps forward, all soft doe eyes, and gently rests her hand on his chest. "Please... I want to go with you."

Sebastian frowns, but I can already tell she's won. "I...fine."

She grins. "Thank you, Sebastian."

He nods, but I know he thinks it's a terrible idea. In his mind, business transactions should not take place after dark, in secret locations given to you by a man who has stalked you around the city.

Come to think of it, that might be sound reasoning.

No matter Sebastian's reservations, an hour later, the four of us find ourselves in front of what looks like a gardener's cottage on the scholars' guild grounds.

"Are you sure this is the right place?" Sebastian asks, frowning at the dark building.

"It's the right address," I say, though I too am wondering if I got my directions confused.

"Only one way to find out." Avery strides to the door and knocks three times, then he turns back and gives me a roguish smirk. "I should have asked; were you given a secret code? Several long knocks followed by a brisk one?"

"That's ridiculous," Sebastian says, shaking his head. "How do you 'knock long?'"

Avery angles toward him. "Well, little cousin, it's all a matter of—"

Before the two can get into it, the door cracks open, and Sam sticks his head out. His eyes fall on Adeline, and he scowls at me. "You said the captain and your business partner."

"She's with us. Take it or leave it."

Sam frowns at me, probably thinking that I'm horrible at following simple instructions. Reluctant, he ushers us inside.

Though the room looks dark from the grounds, it's only because there are makeshift drapes pinned over the shuttered windows. A fire burns in a hearth so sooty, my mother would faint dead away just to look at it. The small house isn't much more than a hut, and the interior has a disheveled, somewhat ominous feel—especially with the years of dust coating the ground and furniture. I'm fairly certain no one's lived here for quite some time.

The setting isn't instilling confidence in my friends—or in me, for that matter.

Sam shoots me one more disgruntled look, and then he grabs a candelabra and walks toward the kitchen, beckoning us to follow him. Sebastian takes a step closer to Adeline, and Avery sets his hand on the hilt of his favorite ancient broadsword. In the dim light, the blade lets off the slightest blue gleam, betraying the fact that it's enchanted—which is quite illegal in Kalae.

Without looking back, Sam tosses open the larder and steps inside. We stare at him, bewildered. Even I'm growing uneasy. Before Sebastian can quickly and efficiently usher us out of this mad man's abode, Sam disappears.

Adeline gapes after him, looking as if she's re-thinking her decision to join us.

"Uh, Sam?" I take a few steps closer to the larder.

"Hurry up," he calls gruffly. "There's no time to dawdle."

The four of us exchange questioning looks, and then I step toward the cupboard. Just before I'm in, Avery gently pulls me back. "I'll go first."

"That's very chivalrous of you," I hiss quietly. "But you're not exactly at the pinnacle of your health, now are you?"

Before Avery can argue, Sebastian pushes in front of us. "I'll go first. Avery, take the rear."

Avery looks like he's going to argue, but Sebastian is already stepping into the cupboard—and going down. I follow and find there are narrow stone stairs, leading into what I assume is a hidden basement.

But it's not a basement we follow Sam into, but a large tunnel. He continues ahead of us, his candelabra flickering on the tight stone walls. We go straight for a while, and then we begin to climb.

"I've heard this tale," Avery whispers to me as we go deeper and deeper into the tunnel under the groundkeeper's cottage.

I shoot the captain a warning look.

He leans in closer, his breath warm on my cheek. "In case you're wondering, the pretty, helpless one usually dies first. Keep an eye on Adeline."

I'm already on edge, and though he's only teasing, my nerves are wound tight as it is. I'm just turning to tell him to keep his thoughts to himself when Sam's light illuminates a plain wooden door at the end of the tunnel.

Our possibly-insane guide stops at the dead end, and then, ever so quietly, taps on the door three times and then raps once, letting the sound vibrate through the wood.

"That's how you knock long," Avery murmurs, just for Sebastian's benefit.

Sebastian scowls at his cousin but doesn't bother with a retort because the door opens a sliver, and Sam speaks with someone.

"I'm sorry. I didn't know what to do. You said you had to have the girl." Sam nods, looking contrite. "I know. Yes."

I try to peer at the person on the other side, but the shadows are too heavy, and the flickering flame distorts the light.

After several more moments, the door closes, and Sam turns toward us. He peers at our group like we are the largest inconvenience known to man, and then his gaze settles on Avery. "You three may go in. The captain will wait in the hall with me."

"No, I'm afraid that won't work for us," Sebastian

says bluntly. Then, as if we're walking away from a normal business deal, he places his hand on Adeline's shoulder and steers her back the way we came. "Come along. We've wasted enough of our evening as it is."

"Wait!" Sam says, desperate. "Just...wait."

He turns back to the door and knocks again, repeating the same ridiculous pattern. Exactly who else would be standing in the tunnel? It's not like they didn't just speak to him seconds ago.

The door opens, and there is another discussion. This time, Sam looks quite worked up. We wait about five or so minutes, and then a parchment ledger and quill are shoved into Sam's hands. The door slams shut yet again.

Sam turns toward us, writing utensils in hand. "The captain may come, but my employer insists you sign a confidentiality agreement."

"Is this really necessary?" Avery asks. He leans against the wall, his hand absently held over the doublet that hides the long scar on his abdomen.

"Yes."

"Fine. Whatever." I step forward and take the quill from his hand. I scan the hastily written up document, frowning. "Business name?"

"Just fill in the blanks," Sam snips, as if it is my fault we're standing here at nearly one in the morning, filling out contracts.

"We don't have a business name—"

"How about The Greybrow Company of Scouts Most Extraordinary?" Avery says, his voice dry. "I'll pop over to the stationary shoppe on Vine and Bounds tomorrow and request letterhead."

"Avery—"

"Captain Greybrow and his Band of Peppy Pirates? Lucia's Luscious—"

"For heaven's sake, shut up, man," Sebastian says, taking the quill from me. I peer over his shoulder, wondering what he's going to write.

Thane Scouting, Inc.

"Why Thane?" I demand. "Why not *Linnon and Thane, Inc*? Or *L & T, Inc*?"

"What does 'incorporated' mean, anyway?" Adeline asks, joining the conversation. "I've always wondere—"

"Just sign the ledger!" Sam bellows, apparently at the end of his patience.

We four turn to him, mildly surprised.

"Someone's crabby," Avery mutters under his breath as we pass the book around, signing our names in the correct spaces. We leave *Thane Scouting, Inc.* for now, but we will return to this subject later.

The last to sign, I hand the ledger back to Sam. "Are we allowed to go in now?"

Sam nods, and then he knocks one more time

before he opens the door himself and leads us into a circular room that takes me completely by surprise. There are heavy velvet drapes covering what I assume are several windows. Lanterns burn on the walls, washing the area in pleasant light. There's a dark wooden desk in the middle of the room, topped with all kinds of delicate metal contraptions. A glass tank of fish stands in the corner, and a dim light charm hovers just beyond the glass toward the back, illuminating the exotic contents.

But it's not the tiny desktop pendulums or the fish or even the floor-to-ceiling cases of insect specimens lining the walls that take me by surprise. No, it's Sam's employer, who stands behind the desk, looking particularly lovely for the wee hours of the morning.

"Madame Serena?" Adeline asks, baffled.

The dressmaker watches us with sharp eyes, apparently not liking the crowd I've brought with me. When her gaze falls on Avery, her frown deepens. "Captain."

Avery looks as baffled as we are, but he collects himself and nods in her direction. "Serena."

Serena looks at Sam and holds out her hand. "They all signed, correct?"

"All four of them."

She accepts the ledger and confirms Sam's words. Then she looks at Avery. "You will not utter a word of this. Do you understand?"

"I signed, didn't I?" The captain looks around, taking in the room. "This is your husband's quarters. How's marriage treating you?"

The woman purses her lips and blinks far too quickly. "Not well, I'm afraid. And that's why you're here."

CHAPTER SIXTEEN
Wildwood Larkwing

I hold up my hand, asking permission to speak though I have no idea why. "Just so we're clear, we don't hide dead bodies. Or create them."

Serena narrows her eyes at me, and I take a subtle step back. She stares at me for several moments, and then she looks away, again blinking quickly. Her blond hair hangs in a perfect, glossy sheet down her back, and it sways when she turns from us.

"I've done something…awful." Her voice breaks, and her shoulders begin to quiver. Sam is at her side in an instant.

My apprehension grows.

As if she cannot bear to look at us as she explains herself, she keeps her back toward us and continues, "It wasn't completely my fault, not really. Bib had been acting so strange, so odd—"

"I'm sorry," I interrupt, earning a sharp look from Sebastian. "Who's *Bib*?"

Serena turns. One glistening tear runs down her perfect cheek. "Bib is my husband—Master Head of the scholars' guild. Surely you know that?"

I shrug, feeling awkward. When I think of scholars, I think of old, stuffy men with soft bellies and thinning hair. Judging from his wife, this Bib fellow must be an entirely different sort.

"Sorry," I murmur. "Please go on."

She takes a deep breath, bolstering herself. "I believe he was having an affair. He's been working late, going away for weeks on business. My assistant saw him herself in a back alley with some harlot."

As she says the words, she chokes back more tears. "You must understand, I love him. The idea—it *destroyed* me. And I was angry... After only two years of marriage—*How could he?* You understand, don't you?" She's almost shaking with anger, just at the thought. "Two years!"

She killed him. I know it. Oh, and now we're conspirators... No problem. Not an issue.

I glance at all the dead insects in their cases and grow quite nervous. If she pulls back a curtain, displaying her husband...

"We had an argument." She shakes her head, freely crying now. "It was awful. We were both yelling...it got out of hand."

Here it comes.

"I begged him not to leave on another expedition, demanded he stay so we could resolve this. But he told me I was being foolish, could not believe I didn't trust him." She pauses to control herself.

We could leave now—right now. We don't know anything, not really. As of this moment, it's all our own conclusions.

Adeline's eyes are huge, and she looks like she's going to pass out—she does that sometimes. Someone will have to carry her as we make a break for it.

"He left our home, and I...I..." Serena inhales sharply. "I came here, to his quarters in the guild, and—"

I cringe, knowing I don't want to hear her next words.

She steels herself for the last bit and then blurts out, "I stole his wildwood larkwing and sold it to an eccentric collector in Fermall." And with that, Serena collapses into a chair, hiding her sobs behind her hands.

Wait. What?

"What, Madame, is a wildwood larkwing?" Sebastian asks, looking as relieved and confused as I feel.

I'm positive we all had her pegged for a murderess.

Serena looks up. Even though she has tears running down her face, and her eyes are watery, she looks gorgeous. It's quite unfair.

"A butterfly," she whispers. "An incredibly rare butterfly—their numbers have suddenly started dwindling. It was the prize of Bib's collection, his pride and joy." Her expression turns hard, almost ugly with its anger. "When he left, off to find more of the horrid creatures, I wanted to hurt him as badly as he hurt me. I know it was childish and petty, but at the time, I wasn't thinking straight. Once he finds out what I've done—we'll never resolve things."

Sebastian, ever level-headed, nods and clasps his hands behind his back. "And you would like us to retrieve another one."

The dressmaker dries her tears on the tiny towel Sam offers, and stands up, collected once again. "No, that would be impossible. As I said, they're near extinction. Bib was taking care of it, protecting it from the dangers of the world while trying to find it a mate. He's been on a wild goose chase for months now, looking for a pair. He just recently procured this one. They only live for a few months...so..."

I glance around the room, inspecting the collection of crispy insects. "So, this butterfly...it's not *dead*?"

"Oh no, it's very much alive. Or at least it was when I sold it." Her lip trembles, but she controls herself. "I need you to buy it back, bring it to me before Bib realizes what I've done."

It sounds easy enough, and it explains what Sam was doing at Dante's shoppe, asking about butterflies of all things. But why is there suddenly so much interest in them? Insects have never been a hot commodity, at least not as long as I've been scouting.

Sebastian looks at me, silently asking if I want to take the job. I shrug. Why not? It's not like we have anything better to do.

Nodding once we're agreed, Sebastian turns back toward Serena. "We'll track down your butterfly for you, though we cannot promise what state it will be in when we find it."

Serena bites her bottom lip, probably stopping herself before she can argue, and then she agrees. "I'll pay you six thousand denats if you bring the larkwing back alive, three if it's dead. No matter what, I must have it back."

We agree to the price, and then Sebastian works out all the details. Serena reluctantly hands over her husband's notes, which will be necessary to correctly identify the butterfly when we find it. She points out similar species in the cases, and I squint, trying to spot the differences between them. These ones are fairly small compared to a few of the hand-sized monster moths. They're olive green and have brown spots.

Serena says the wildwood larkwing will look just like them, except it's larger than these butterflies and has eye-like markings on the lower wings.

"The man I sold it to—he's a collector in Fermall," Serena says. "You'll find him there."

I look away from the butterflies in the case, startled. "Fermall?"

"I don't know much about him, only that he specializes in…oddities. Rare things. He's had his eye on the wildwood larkwing since Bib captured it. He's eccentric, but the scholars' guild has regular dealings with him. Somehow, he stumbles on things no one else can find."

Groaning, I rub my temples. "Things like lesser dragon eggs?"

Serena looks confused, but Sebastian grimaces. "You don't think—"

He's quickly cut off by Avery. "Even if it's not the same man, I need to pay the shopkeeper a visit anyway. He owes us several thousand denats."

Long story short, both Sebastian and Avery managed to pay the shopkeeper for Flink, which makes the dragon a very expensive glitter-breathing nuisance. Thankfully, Flink's element is rare—it neutralizes magic.

"You mustn't tell him I sent you," Serena says, ignoring Sebastian and Avery. "I already sent Sam, and the man tried to charge me three times what he paid for it. Just pretend you're collectors—he deals with them often."

I glance at Avery, giving him a look. If the shopkeeper is one in the same, he's the man Avery buys his illegal daggers from.

Avery's lips tilt up in a ghost of a smile.

"Bib will return soon," Serena says. "I must have the butterfly returned to me before he gets back, and you must not breathe a word of this to anyone. He will never forgive me for this if he were to find out."

"And if you find out he was cheating on you?" I can't help but ask.

Adeline and Sebastian both shoot me chastising looks, but I brush them off.

Serena sets a hand on her stomach and takes a deep breath. "I'll deal with it at the time."

I nod, satisfied.

"We'll do our best," Sebastian promises.

He's ready to shoo us out the door, but I have one more question for the seamstress. "Why us?"

"Baron Malcomny of Baywhite was here not a month ago for an herbology seminar, bragging about the scouting team who retrieved a Moss Forest orchid cutting for him. Imagine my surprise when I found out that you, Lucia, were one of the scouts he was referring to. If you can track down orchids in the wildlands and procure the rarest ruby in the world, while slaying a few sirens on the side, surely you can retrieve one little butterfly."

When she puts it like that...

We start toward the door, but Sam stops us. "You'll have to take the tunnel. No one can know you were here."

I glance back at Serena as we slip through the door, which is hidden by a large tapestry map of Kalae. She stands in front of the cases, staring at the pinned butterflies. Her hair falls in front of her face like a sheet of silk. She looks fragile—a woman broken.

If a man could grow bored of a woman who looks like that, what does that mean for the rest of us?

"Tired?" Avery's hand drifts to my lower back. It doesn't seem like a purposeful move, more like a magnetic need to stay close.

Sam closes the door behind us. It's an ominous sound in the dark, seldom used tunnel.

"I'm fine," I assure him, though I'm not sure if that's entirely true.

CHAPTER SEVENTEEN
On a Wild Butterfly Chase

The city of Fermall isn't pleasant like Teirn. It's located in Colrain, a province that's to the east of Tanrith, and farther north. It takes about a week to get there, and we travel along the coast. The farther north we go, the cooler it gets. We arrive on an overcast day, one where the clouds lie low to the ground, hugging the water's edge and masking the dingy, weathered buildings. Our carriage plods along, and the sounds of our horses' steady gait is a rhythmic melody that makes you tired even if you're well-rested. In the distance, a bell clangs from atop a buoy as it rocks in the shallow water just off the shore. The metallic toll adds a rather forlorn note to the already melancholy day.

Ahead of us, the city appears to be leached of color. The dirt roads are gray; the weathered wood buildings are gray; the ropes and fishing nets that decorate the shoppes and houses are gray.

With the constant smell of fish in the air and the questionable nature of many of its inhabitants, Fermall's not a particularly welcoming city.

But it just so happens to be the one I first met Avery in, the one where I obtained the egg that would hatch to be Flink, and the port in which I embarked from on my very first sea journey. I wouldn't go as far as to say I'm harboring warm, fuzzy feelings toward Fermall, but there is a bit of nostalgia here.

We make our way toward The Dappled Mare Inn, the only place in town that's nice enough to consider staying in. Dirty patches of snow dot the streets. What were once fluffy mounds have hardened into chunks of solid ice. Occasionally, a wheel catches the ice, and it jars us as we bump over it. Every time, Flink lifts his head from his spot between us all on the floor, looking disgruntled.

Finally, the carriage stops in front of the inn. As soon as the door opens, Flink barges past Sebastian, almost knocking him over. I, too, push Sebastian aside as I leap from the carriage, hoping to catch my wayward pet before he causes turmoil in the streets.

Sebastian shakes his head, giving me that *look* as I clip the leather lead to Flink's harness.

I kneel in front of the dragon and look him right

in his amber eyes. "That was bad. Bad, Flink."

He stares back, not a smidgen of remorse in his expression. Golden, sparkling flames wisp from his nostrils.

My mother says I was tiresome in my younger years, but nothing could be worse than an adolescent dragon.

We make our way up the worn steps of the inn, and I hold Flink's lead tightly. He stays right by my side, behaving for the moment, but I know all it will take is a stray cat or munchkin dragon to send him into a tizzy.

"Four rooms for the night," Sebastian says to the young woman behind the front desk.

She glances up from her book, and her eyes widen when they settle on Avery and Sebastian. Understandably, she blinks, overwhelmed by the sight of them standing side by side. A slow smile builds on her lips, betraying the fact that not a lot of nobles linger long enough in Fermall to need a room. She leans forward, her gaze going between the cousins. "We only have three available."

Then she smiles at my business partner, perhaps deciding he's the one she's taken a fancy to, and begins to twirl a loose strand of hair in her fingers.

"That's a shame," Avery says, and then he steps close to me and lowers his voice. "What do you think?

Should we bunk together, Lucia?"

I shoot the captain a look and step a safe distance away before I point to Adeline and tell the woman, "We'll share a room."

Adeline nods in agreement.

As we sign our names to the ledger and the woman pulls our keys from the pegboard behind her, she flirts with Sebastian—tossing her hair, batting her eyelashes, putting a little extra sway in her hips when she returns with the keys. Sebastian, oblivious like the daft man I know and love, asks her about Fermall and makes small talk for the sake of manners. Encouraged, the woman turns up the flirting until I almost feel sorry for her.

By the time we're finished, Adeline's cheeks are red, and her eyes flash. She doesn't say a word—not one word—but she flounces out of the sitting area the moment she has our key, off to find our shared room.

Sebastian watches her leave, bewildered. I shake my head and turn toward the driver from Avery's coach. The man stands near the entrance of the inn, eying the place as if it were about to crash down on his head. It's not that bad, not really.

The carpets are threadbare, but they're clean. The windows are filthy with smudges and weather stains, but at least they're glass. Several upholstered benches and settees are placed in the entry room, surrounding a fire that crackles in the ancient stone hearth, and though they are patched and faded, they make the room look rather friendly.

"Are you sure you want me to bring in your bags, Captain?" the man asks.

Avery's eyes brighten with amusement. "I think we'll manage for the night."

The man raises his eyebrows as if to say, *"Suit yourself."*

Avery turns to me and tosses his key in his hand. "There's still time to change your mind..." He glances at Sebastian, and then a horrible smirk crosses his face. "Lady Greybrow."

Sebastian's eyes snap to us immediately. "Excuse me?"

Avery locks his gaze on mine. I give him a subtle shake of my head, but he ignores it. "Didn't Lucia tell you, Sebastian? We were married while we were at sea."

Without another word, the captain grins and turns down the hall. I gape after him, imagining all the fun ways I could maim him.

Seething, I turn back to Sebastian and demand, "*What?*"

My friend looks ashen, almost as if someone struck him in the gut. "Tell me he's not serious."

"Well..." I think with my hands, holding them up and moving them in a chaotic fashion as I try to figure out what to say.

"Lucia…"

"The ceremony wasn't binding," I finally spit out. "It's really not a big—"

"*Ceremony?*"

"What does it matter?"

He shakes his head, at a loss for words. "I'd like to think if you were to get married, you would invite me. Or, I don't know—*your family.*"

I give him a frustrated smile. "You are my family. And what do you mean 'if?'"

Wrinkling his nose as if the notion is truly distasteful, he corrects, "*When.*"

Rolling my eyes, I shove past him and set out on my own to find Adeline.

A light drizzle has started, chasing people out of the streets. Later in the evening, the rain might become snow. The air has that sort of smell. A few stubborn villagers sit on covered porches—mostly old, sea-wrinkled men crafting their fishing nets—but most of the sane people are inside.

It's cold, and the damp clouds permeate the air, creating a thick fog of shifting moisture. It's beautiful in its own quiet, muted way. Different from the chaotic rainstorms that I love, more somber somehow.

I could enjoy it if Flink weren't squealing like a

stuck pig in the middle of the street.

"What is wrong with your dragon?" Sebastian demands.

Adeline shivers under her cloak, her auburn curls peeking from her white-fur-lined hood. We told her to stay in the inn, but she said it was dirty and dark, and she knew she'd be murdered the moment we left her alone. Avery stands next to her, with his hands shoved into the pockets of the long jacket he wears under his own cloak. He's watching me struggle with the dragon, trying not to smile. I know he wants me to ask him for help, but I do still have a scrap of pride left, and I can control this beast.

"He's just...young." I give the lead another yank, but Flink digs his talons into the dirt street, braying like a donkey.

"He's spoiled," Sebastian says, feeling the need to point it out yet again.

"He's a *baby*," I snarl back.

The problem is that this "baby" outweighs me by a good seventy-five pounds. And sometime in the last month, he's come to realize it.

Sebastian sighs in an exaggerated manner, rolling his eyes heavenward, making me wonder what kind of fool I was to fall in love with him before. Because he's driving me insane now.

"You want me to help?" Avery says, still smiling.

I meet his eyes. "No."

Adeline groans in an overwhelmingly feminine, wilting sort of way.

"He's just cold," I say, justifying the dragon's behavior. "And he doesn't like to be wet."

"Just leave him here." Sebastian shifts, ready to move. "Once he realizes you're going without him, he'll panic and follow you."

"That's mad. He'll wander away and get himself lost."

Sebastian stares me down, his eyes brightening like he just had an idea—one I won't like. "It will work. See?"

My business partner begins to walk away, dragging Avery and Adeline with him.

"Where are you going?" I demand.

"To the shoppe," Sebastian yells, grinning over his shoulder. "Are you coming?"

I look at them and then back at Flink. I know what Sebastian's doing, and I do understand the irony of it.

"Fine!" I growl as I toss Flink's lead on the ground. "You want to stay here in the rain? Have it your way."

Flink stops his cries, cocks his reptilian head in confusion, and watches me walk away. As if stuck in the street, he lets out a mewling yelp.

"Well, come on," I holler back at him as I hurry to catch up with my group.

And what does that wretched dragon do? He watches us until we turn the corner, lets out an awful shriek, and then comes barreling after me.

"I told you it would work," Sebastian says, not bothering to contain his smug smirk.

"I hate you," I tell him sincerely, even if I don't really mean it.

He grins—he's horrible to be around when he's right—and offers his arm to Adeline. "Shall we?"

She lights up like she wasn't just whining moments ago about her hair growing frizzy in the moisture and smiles at him like he's King Harold himself.

I shake my head and grab Flink's lead once he's caught up to us.

"Shall we?" Avery parrots as he offers me his arm as well, his tone lowered enough that it's downright dark and delicious.

Butterflies stir in my stomach, coaxing me to accept. It's been two months and three days since the last time he kissed me, not that I've been counting, and I do believe I'm going through withdrawals.

That's when it dawns on me, brightening my mood. This turmoil I'm in—it's not love. No.

No.

I'm infatuated. In fact, if we kissed again, perhaps it would get all this out of my head. And then I could think again.

And after that, I'll swear off men altogether because they are far more trouble than they're worth.

Even ones who look so dashing in their captain's uniforms. Or ones who smirk in that cocky way, making your blood rush through your veins just a little bit faster. Ones who—

"Are your snubbing me or not?" Avery dips his head a little closer to better look at me under my cloak's hood, his voice thick with amusement. He moves his arm a little, reminding me he's still standing here, waiting for me to take it. "Because I can't tell."

I slide my arm next to his, and he tugs me close—so, so close. The faint scent of the dark, masculine cologne he wears envelops me, and his heat reaches me even through our combined layers. I almost close my eyes and purr like a cat—just from the decadent rightness of it.

Get a hold of yourself, Lucia.

He is a cad, a scoundrel, a womanizing pirate who's had a romantic affair with half of Teirn, including the queen and possibly the woman we're working for.

Oh, but I want him.

And that's bad! my common-sense yells at me. It's a shame I'm not listening.

Sebastian and Adeline are ahead of us, heads bent to together in conversation, and they almost walk right past the shoppe they're so preoccupied. It's sweet—a little revolting, but sweet.

Avery brings his hand to his mouth and lets out a loud whistle that makes my ears ring. When Sebastian and Adeline turn back, startled, Avery nods toward the dingy shoppe next to them. The painted window letters faded long ago, and the door looks like it might collapse at any moment.

We're in the criminal district, a place where the poor congregate during the nicer weather, gathering around fires and sharing drinks and quite possibly night floss. I have no idea where they are now. Apparently, they must find shelter during the winter. Either that or the constable finally chased them away.

Still, even in their absence, the street has an ominous feel.

Sebastian frowns at the door. Realizing something is wrong, we hurry to catch up.

I read the sign and groan. It says the shoppe is closed for the winter.

"Oh well," Adeline says, trying to hide her glee. "I suppose we'll have to go back to Teirn. Can't say we didn't try."

She's already turning back the way we came when Avery lets out a low, deep chuckle and yanks the door open, almost pulling it from its hinges.

We gape at the captain, even Sebastian, as he

storms into the dilapidated shoppe, stepping over bric-a-brac and avoiding a strange and chaotic assortment of old junk and priceless artifacts.

"Mueller!" he calls out, his voice loud and authoritative. "Get out here, old man, or so help me I will come find you myself."

I stare at him, my mouth hanging open. I've never seen this side of him. He's so commanding, so *noble*.

Still, I can't imagine the shopkeeper will greet us now. Who knows if he's even here? The shoppe always has a deserted, maybe-there's-a-dead-body-languishing-in-the-back sort of feel to it, so it's impossible to know.

To my great surprise, the shopkeeper shuffles from the back room, muttering under his breath. He's just as I remember him from when we were here last. His hair is white and wild, and though he is clean shaven, he has wrinkles aplenty. He also has a fondness for clothing that is too large—almost as if he were taller and broader at some point in time.

And he's as crazy as a day-flying bat.

The man turns his eyes on us, his gaze surprisingly sharp. "Ah, if it's not the infamous young Captain Greybrow. What could I have possibly done to earn the pleasure of a personal visit?"

He's different this time—more coherent, less bumbling.

The shopkeeper's eyes travel to me. "And Delivery Girl as well. Hurry, we must set the tea. If only I had scones." He finishes in a deadpan voice, "Oh, visitors. Oh, joy. Oh, bliss."

Avery wears a wry smile, one that's half grim and half amused. "Hello, Mueller. I understand you swindled me out of three thousand denats."

"Actually, I believe I swindled that man." The shopkeeper gestures toward Sebastian and smiles, thoroughly amused.

"You will repay him," Avery warns.

The shopkeeper—Mueller—lets out an exaggerated sort of sigh, as if this commotion is beneath him. "Yes, fine. But I assure you, the dragon is worth every denat. It's me you're cheating, asking me to give him away for so cheap."

Flink, who's been behind the piles of rubbish, sniffs up a nose-full of dust and promptly sneezes a shower of golden sparkles right over me.

"Ech!" Adeline shrieks, jumping away from the sparkling cloud.

I grimace, trying not to dwell on the droplets of dragon mucus dotting my cloak, and step away. When I glance back at Mueller, I find the man frozen in place, staring at Flink. With awe, he declares in a low voice, "He's a nullifier."

Adeline and I exchange a look. Never mind; he's

still mad.

The man snaps out of his trance and turns to Avery. In a crisp, no-nonsense voice he says, "No refund."

I step forward before Avery or Sebastian can argue. "What's a nullifier?"

The man removes his spectacles and begins to clean them on the edge of his undershirt. It was probably white at some point, but like everything else in this wretched city, it's now gray. "Approximately one in every thousand dragons is born with the nullifying element, but it's more common in the lesser variety. They neutralize magic."

"We noticed," Avery says, meeting my eyes. His expression is slightly haunted, though he tries to hide it.

Memories of that awful night on the ship come back to me, of Avery coming after me, enchanted by the sirens' songs, sword raised, ready to fight. Flink leaped in front of him, breathed out the strange, harmless flame. It broke the trance.

People celebrate me for slaying those three sirens, but it was Flink who truly saved us that night.

I peer at Flink for several moments, and then I look at Mueller. "It's an unusual element then. Could some *unusual* personality quirks accompany it?"

"What kind of quirks, Delivery Girl?"

Ignoring the jab, I cock my head to the side and

rub my neck. "Flink can be a bit stubborn. He doesn't listen well—"

"At all," Sebastian mutters, but he steps back when I shoot him a scathing look over my shoulder.

"He can be a mite unruly at times," I continue then hastily add, "Not all the time."

"Most of the time," Sebastian feels the need to add.

I glare at my partner then turn back to Mueller. The shopkeeper nods, very serious. "I see. There is a reason for that behavior."

"Yes...?"

"You've spoiled him."

Sebastian lets out a loud, abrupt laugh, and I suck in an offended breath. Before I can argue, Mueller turns to Avery. "As I'm sure you're well aware, for a creature with such a unique element, you owe me for the difference in price. Ten thousand denats will suffice—Kalaen currency only. I don't want my money in shields again."

Avery chuckles, exasperated as if this is something that's been discussed before. "First—absolutely not. Second, that was a good investment. Tell me you didn't make back your money and more."

"That's beside the point. I had fifty of the blasted things, all lying about, disrupting the order of my shoppe."

Still irritated, I raise an eyebrow and glance around the disarray. Adeline, looking perplexed, lifts a finger, about to question that statement, but I cut her off. "This isn't a social call. We're looking for a wildwood larkwing butterfly, and we've been led to believe you have one for sale."

"Serena sent you, did she?" Mueller says, unsurprised. "I told her steward I would be happy to sell it back—as long as she was willing to pay the price I requested."

"You swindled her," Avery points out.

"Swindled is such a nasty word. I prefer to think of it as having good business savvy."

I nudge Avery and quietly say, "Sounds familiar."

He grins, perhaps remembering the conversation we shared on our "wedding" night. Just the thought of it makes my pulse quicken, and my thoughts get all muddled.

"We're here to buy the insect," Sebastian says, ready to leave. "How much is this going to cost?"

Mueller turns to my business partner. "I have no idea how much Ivan wants for it. You'll have to ask him."

"Who's Ivan?" I ask, though there is something tickling the back of my mind. Why does that name sound familiar?

"A business associate."

"And why would we speak with him?" I ask, dreading his answer.

Mueller tosses his hand in the air dismissively. "Because he bought the larkwing from me two days ago. Haven't you heard? Lepidoptera are in terrible demand right now in Teirn."

Something very strange is going on in the king's city.

"And why is that?" Sebastian asks. "Why the demand for moths and butterflies?"

The man shrugs, but I can tell he knows more. "Word on the street is that there is a dandruff epidemic."

He's lying, no doubt about it. Oddly enough, that's exactly what Dante said.

Adeline steps forward, smiling like the delicate flower she is. "Is there no other use for them? No obscure alchemy recipe they're required for?"

Mueller, like any man, is not immune to Adeline's charm. He smiles at her in a grandfatherly sort of way. "I'm not an alchemist, so I'm afraid I wouldn't know. I obtain things for customers, and then I sell them. Nothing more."

She glances at me, giving me a subtle apology. At least she tried. I have a feeling if anyone could get the old man to talk, it would have been her.

"This Ivan, do I know him?" Avery asks, glancing

at me from the corner of his eye. "Have I done business with him?"

"Pirate," I mutter under my breath.

Though still facing the shopkeeper, a quick smile crosses Avery's face.

Ignoring Avery, Mueller offers Adeline a sweet from a jar of hard candy that must be at least thirty years old—the candy, not the jar. She backs away, shaking her head gently, declining with a smile and a look of terror in her gray-blue eyes.

"You're sure?" he says before he sets the jar back on the table, next to a ripped doublet that looks to be about fifty years old and an iron paperweight in the shape of a rat. Then he finally turns back to the captain. "I don't believe so. He doesn't run in your usual circles."

That sounds ominous. Shadier than Avery's illegal-dagger-pawning associates? That's not good at all.

"Delivery Girl, though. She's done business with him."

My attention snaps to the loony old man. "I have?"

"You made a delivery for me this summer. Don't you remember?"

Oh no.

Sebastian rubs his hands over his face, remembering the shifty fellow I delivered a suspicious-looking box to. It rattled and emitted red smoke. I never learned what it was, but it couldn't have been good.

"Where can we find him?" Avery asks.

The shopkeeper writes down an address and bids us farewell. We maneuver around piles of books, old armor, and a six-foot statue of Victor of Tanrith that I'm quite sure was swiped from the king's palace. But before we are out the door, Mueller calls Avery's name, stopping him.

There's a greedy glint in the shopkeeper's eyes. "I have a blade you're sure to be interested in. I had promised it to the Duke of Eromoore...but seeing as how you're here..."

Sebastian gives the captain a pointed look, reminding him we're in the middle of a job and that illicit business deals should wait.

"What is it?" Avery asks, reluctant to leave.

"Five hundred years old, dragon enchanted."

"Dragon enchanted? Is it Eldish?" the captain demands, speaking of a continent far across the ocean, a three-month's sea voyage from Kalae. We have no history of the great dragons here in Kalae, the ones who history books say spoke like men. Many argue they are fables, so it's hard to say if the dagger is genuine.

The shopkeeper smiles, knowing he's snared him. "Errintonian drachite. It was said to have been crafted by the warrior king himself for his beloved queen."

Avery swallows. "You can't sell that to Devon. He

won't even know what to do with it."

Mueller shrugs as if it's out of his hands.

"Oh, go on," I tell Avery. "Tuck it in your cloak on the way out. There's no one in the streets to see you leave with it anyway. And it's not like the queen herself doesn't know about your illegal infatuation."

Smiling because he must be able to tell I'm a wee bit jealous, Avery turns back toward the man and yet again traverses the dangerous path that is Mueller's shoppe. "Let's talk price."

Sebastian shakes his head and escorts Adeline out the door, into the street.

Having no desire to wait outside in the rain myself, I wait for Avery by the door. A few minutes later, the captain returns with a sleek black dagger with intricate scrollwork on the fine blade. It doesn't glow blue, so I doubt it's actually enchanted, but it's a beautiful weapon, no doubt Errintonian drachite. I have no idea how much Avery paid for it, but it must have been a small fortune.

Finished with business, Mueller shuffles into his back rooms, calling over his shoulder, "Until next time Captain Greybrow, Delivery Girl."

I toss my hands in the air, but the man is already gone.

"Try it," Avery says, handing me the dagger. "It's perfectly balanced."

Sure enough, it lies on the palm of my hand, the hilt weighted heavier than the blade so it doesn't tumble to the ground. It's not a hard feat for our modern blacksmiths, but for a weapon five hundred years old, it's impressive.

"Keep it," he says when I try to hand it back to him. He's smiling, but he has a hesitant look in his eyes as if he's not quite sure I'll accept the gift. It's a vulnerable expression, one that's not doing my resolve any good. It makes my knees weak, and my heart all *melty*. I'm afraid I'm going to turn into a puddle of Lucia, right at the captain's feet.

"Avery," I whisper.

"It's time you replace that cheap thing you've been carrying around."

It's true my dagger is bulk forged, nothing special. But this...this is too much.

"Just take the gift, Lucia." About to step into the street, he raises my hood, fingering a loose strand of hair as he does. With a teasing gleam in his eyes, he leans close. "It's very fashionable."

Then, without asking permission, he tugs my dagger from its sheath and then takes the drachite one from my hands and slides it in place. Without so much as a look behind him, he tosses the old blade on the floor, amidst the hodgepodge of random things.

Trying not to smile, I nod toward the discarded

weapon. "Do you think he'll even notice it?"

Avery grins, letting his hands rest on my shoulders. "Not a chance."

CHAPTER EIGHTEEN
Aren't You a Shifty Fellow

Ivan's farm is not a farm at all, but a shack in a meadow. A sad-looking brown vegetable patch sits withered by the dilapidated front gate, betraying the fact that it likely went wild long before the first freeze of the season. It looks as if someone cared about the cottage at some point, but it's fallen into a sad state of disrepair.

Yesterday's rain turned to sleet overnight, and the damp chill seeps through my cloak. I'm so busy studying the shack that I don't watch where I'm going and step in an ankle-deep puddle. The water soaks right through my thin boot, which was designed more for fashion than function. Now that my stocking is wet, it clings to my foot, and the frigid water squelches between my toes with every step I take.

I glare at the puddle.

For a moment, I wish I were with Adeline, back in the inn, where Sebastian instructed her to stay. The weather is miserable enough this morning she didn't bother to argue this time. Not surprisingly since he seems to hate the cold, Flink stayed to keep her company.

Avery gingerly climbs the rickety porch stairs and raps on the door. As we wait, he crosses his arms under his cloak, attempting to stay warm. The first real snowflakes mix with the sleet, gracefully wisping to the ground.

After several moments, the door swings open, creaking on its hinges, and a familiar, twitchy-looking man pokes his head out. He narrows his eyes at us, apparently not liking what he sees.

"What do you want?" he demands.

"Only a moment of your time," Avery says smoothly. "We understand you're in possession of a wildwood larkwing butterfly, and we would like to buy the insect from you."

Ivan's eyes move to each of us in turn, lingering a little longer on Avery. "Come inside."

Avery glances over his shoulder, questioning whether this is the greatest idea. It's probably a bad sign if the pirate is leery. Yet, we find ourselves following the man anyway.

The interior isn't any nicer than the exterior, and

I find myself hovering near the door, not sure where to stand. Leftover chicken bones languish on a pewter plate on the table, remnants from last night's dinner. A gray and white cat stares at us from beside the plate, unblinking. He rises to his feet when we enter, his long tail twitching. The creature is polydactyl—has too many toes. The extra digits make his furry white feet look huge compared to his body. When he decides we aren't going to fight him for his dinner, he yawns wide and settles to his belly to continue licking the bones clean.

Sebastian wrinkles his nose at the mess, repulsed. I've seen goblins with better manners.

A fire crackles from the sooty hearth—the merry sound misleading. Ivan stands next to it and crosses his arms. His hair is a common brown, his eyes slightly too small for his long face, and his lips thin. He reminds me of a weasel.

Finished, the cat leaps from his perch and winds around his master's legs. Ivan picks the feline up and strokes the soft fur between his ears. "So, you're here for the larkwing?"

"That's right," Avery says smoothly.

Neither Sebastian or I mind the captain taking charge this time. I'm confident he's had more experience dealing with Ivan's type than we have.

Ivan jerks his chin toward me. "Why does the girl

look familiar?"

He's not exactly the trusting type, now is he?

"She occasionally runs errands for Mueller." Avery dismisses Ivan's concern with a wave of his hand, and continues, "But that doesn't matter. Do you still have the butterfly?"

Ivan scratches his chin in a musing matter. "I might."

"You either do or you don't," I say, losing my patience. "Which one is it?"

"I have a contract to fulfill, but if you're prepared to make me a better offer, I am all ears."

Avery shifts. "Who wants the larkwing?"

"That's not any of your business."

In a subtle move that's anything but, Avery brushes back his cloak and jacket, revealing his blade. "And if we make it our business?"

The shifty man smiles, obviously amused. He's tall and gangly, as stout as a beanpole, yet he doesn't look the slightest bit leery. Which means he's hiding something, something he carries in his favor. I think of the delivery I made for him last summer. Who knows what he has hidden away.

"I want to see the butterfly," I say, interrupting the conversation before this gets ugly. "It's worth more to us alive than dead, and I want to see for myself that all this disruption hasn't killed it."

Ivan turns his eyes on me. He strokes the cat for several more moments and then gently sets him on the ground. "Fair enough."

He turns toward a small table in the corner. On it, there appears to be a covered birdcage. With a flourish, he whips the thin fabric away, revealing a small insect habitat. The cage is made of the finest of mesh, and there are live plants flourishing within.

I take a closer look, trying to spot the butterfly. I study it for several moments, losing hope that the creature is actually in there. And then she stretches her wings, breaking the spell of her camouflage.

Startled, I suck in a breath. The butterfly is huge, larger than my hand. Her wings are gossamer, almost translucent, and the color of summer moss. As she moves, she lets off a faint glow, almost like that of a—

"It's elemental?" Sebastian says, leaning down beside me to get a better look. He sounds as shocked as I am. "I've never heard of such a thing."

But there's no denying it. She glows green, and as she moves, a shimmering cloud follows in her wake.

Avery nudges his way in and frowns, unimpressed. "It's...pretty?"

Sebastian rolls his eyes and stands. He turns toward Ivan. "How much do you want?"

"Twenty thousand," Ivan replies, his tone firm.

"Twenty...*thousand*?" I choke out, nearly falling

over. Twenty thousand denats? For a glowing insect?

Ivan flicks the sheet over the cage. "We all know what you want it for. Do not pretend you won't make your money back and more. I am only being this generous because I have no talent for the alchemy myself." He laughs under his breath. "I certainly have no scruples."

Avery narrows his eyes, a bare smile growing on his lips as he decides to play along. "How certain are you of this investment? How much do you estimate we'll make back?"

Ivan shrugs. "That, of course, depends on pricing. I believe, in the current market, you could easily make several hundred thousand before the guards learn of the masquerade's location."

Masquerade under the city. Larks singing in trees? Could the beggar have meant the larkwing?

The captain raises his eyebrows, clearly intrigued for real. "Really? And tell me, where might I find an alchemist keen for this sort of project?"

"Avery," I hiss under my breath.

A grin flashes across his face—the kind that says there's no harm in asking. I give him a pointed look, but he only chuckles.

"I am not at liberty to disclose names of my contacts." The man examines his nails. "Unless you have the money on you."

"We do not," Sebastian says before this goes any further. "We must be going."

I agree with my business partner. Something extremely shady is going on, and we need more information.

"But if we did," Avery goes on. "Would you be willing to half the investment with us? Fifty-fifty? Surely you don't want to miss the chance to make that kind of money."

"Avery!" I tug on his sleeve, not quite sure he's concerned with Madame Serena's request anymore. "*Come on.*"

"Fine," the captain says, holding his hands up in surrender. "We'll go."

"This is a once in a lifetime opportunity," Ivan warns Avery. "Do you have the money? Because you would be wise to invest now. The butterflies are near extinction. It's a dying market."

"He doesn't have it," Sebastian says, possibly lying. Luckily, neither of us knows how much money the captain carries on him. Far too much, I'd be willing to bet.

Avery takes a step closer to me and whispers near my ear. "I'm going to buy it."

I give him a look—one that's not terribly friendly.

"For Serena," he insists. "There's something strange afoot. If we don't buy it back now, we may never get another chance."

"He's asking too much."

Avery nods. "I know. But Serena has the money—she'll pay when she knows she has no choice. But she'll never forgive you for letting the chance slip through your fingers. The butterfly is here; it's alive. Lucia—we must take it."

I'm still not convinced he wants it for the right reasons, but I can't argue. Something tells me if we leave today without the larkwing, we'll never see it again.

"All right," I finally agree.

"Lucia!" Sebastian starts, but it's too late. Avery's already pulling two silver-laced bills from an inside pocket of his jacket.

I gape at the bills—each worth ten thousand denats.

Ivan's eyes light up with greedy glee. Just before Avery hands over the money, he points to the butterfly cage.

Nodding eagerly, Ivan takes the cage in his hands and then nods toward the bills. "Show me they're real."

Avery holds the bills to the firelight. The silver thread glows, and the enchanted fabric parchment sparkles in the light.

I've never seen a real bill before—have only dealt in common gold coins. The spelled money is mesmerizing. And it makes me ill to see it pass from Avery's hands to Ivan's.

Avery takes the cage as Ivan tucks the money away.

"Good doing business with you," Ivan says, dismissing us.

The captain turns toward the door, butterfly in hand. Sebastian shakes his head, clearly thinking Avery's a fool for paying twenty thousand denats for an insect.

"Pleasant day," Ivan says cordially as we make our way to the door.

He sounds just a touch too giddy. I narrow my eyes, but he only smiles.

I'll be glad to be away.

Sebastian reaches the door first, and he pauses when he touches the handle. He stares at it intently, not moving a muscle.

"What's the matter?" I ask, concerned. I touch his shoulder, and a jolt goes through me, stiffening my muscles, rendering me like stone. I try to move, try to scream, but nothing happens. I'm frozen here, a statue with my hand on Sebastian's jacket, and the terrible aftertaste of bitter magic coats my tongue.

"Lucia?" Avery asks, perplexed.

I want to cry out for him to keep his distance, but I cannot.

The fool brushes my arm. From the corner of my eye, I watch as the magic washes over him, freezing him in place.

Ivan put an enchantment on the door.

Ivan put an *enchantment* on the *door*.

Behind us, I hear the man's footsteps as he draws closer, taking his time. He hums under his breath, delighted with himself. Calm as you please, he takes the butterfly cage right out of Avery's hand. He then proceeds to go through Avery's jacket—taking even more money and several personal belongings. After he's quite sure he's found anything of value, he moves on to Sebastian.

I know my partner is livid—know he's seething. But there's nothing he can do. The thief not only takes the coin pouch he carries under his jacket, but the pocket watch his grandfather gave him as well.

Then Ivan moves to me. He smiles knowingly. "You're probably wondering what I've done to you. Fear not—it's only a harmless earth charm—my own little variation that has an interesting effect on living matter. It is quite obnoxious to be frozen in place though, isn't it? Your legs begin to fall asleep, and your mouth gets quite dry. Several hours in, you begin to wonder if you'll ever move again. Well, I am not without heart. Rest assured, lovely, foolish young adventuress, the spell is a temporary one." He smiles. "In twenty-four hours, you'll be yourself again."

Twenty-four hours? My mind rails against my body, demanding it moves. But, alas, the spell is a sound one.

Ivan turns his eyes on my cloak, and he frowns.

Not the dagger... I have nothing else of value, not really. But losing Avery's gift—the thought makes me ill.

Finally, he shakes his head. "I am afraid even I am above searching a woman. Keep your secrets, my lady. Hopefully, you're carrying the lion's share of the money because otherwise, I'm afraid you'll be stuck in sunny Fermall for quite some time."

Apparently finished with us, he turns to the door only to pause before he reaches the knob.

"Try not to feel too badly about the purchase," Ivan says to Avery. "I would have taken your money on the way out even if you hadn't agreed to buy the larkwing."

He has the audacity to pat Avery's cheek before he opens the door, and then he disappears into the softly-falling snow.

CHAPTER NINETEEN
Have a Cat

Light from the window creeps closer and closer to the toe of my boot, which means we must be nearing twenty-four hours. Yesterday, I distinctly remember the slice of sunshine making its way across my frozen form until that ever-so uncomfortable hour when it shone directly in my eyes. In normal circumstances, that's unpleasant. When you cannot shield your eyes, blink, or move...that's downright torture.

I've spent the last twenty-four hours trapped in my head—which, I've discovered, is a rather unpleasant place to be. With nothing left to occupy myself, and my limbs heavy like lead, I pondered the strange goings-on in Teirn—of larkwings and masquerades and the odd rantings of the beggar in the street.

And I've thought about my relationship, or lack

thereof, with Avery a bit.

Maybe more than a bit.

Maybe that's all I've thought about if I'm truthful.

You'd think with all this lovely time I've had, I would have come to some sort of conclusion. But the only idea that holds any merit is that I need to kiss him again, see that he's not that wonderful. I've built him up on a pedestal in my mind. There is no way there's as much of a spark between us as I remember. I've simply dwelt on it too long.

Yes, my choice is clear.

I must corner the captain, kiss him again—prove once and for all that it was the magic of the hidden island, the exotic wedding that should have never taken place, the adventure of the sea, that stole my heart. Not the captain.

Surely not.

As I'm pondering these thoughts, my nose itches. Not thinking, I wiggle it, hoping to quell the sensation.

I moved my nose.

Concentrating hard, I try to shift my hand. My finger twitches ever so slightly, and I suck in a deep breath—that too is a good sign. For the last day, my breathing has been stilted, the spell allowing my lungs to move just enough to take slow, shallow breaths.

Slowly—and I do mean *slowly*—feeling returns to my limbs. It's like fire in my veins, but any sensation is welcome, even the stabbing pain of my extremities awakening. Beside me, Avery and Sebastian fight the last remnants of the spell as well.

Finally, my legs give, and I crash to the floor. Groaning, I stretch my toes, and then my arms, and soon after that, my shoulders. Avery and Sebastian handle the spell's release a little more gracefully than I do, but that's nothing new. Avery bends over, keeping his balance, crying out in relief. Sebastian lets himself fall against the wall, and he rolls his head from side to side, stretching his neck.

"Now what?" I ask from the floor. The gray and white cat, who found our frozen state extremely amusing, sniffs me and then leaps on my chest. He then proceeds to flick me in the face with his tail.

Avery's eyes flash. "We find Ivan."

"No," Sebastian argues, now stretching his arms. "We must find a way into these masquerades, see what's going on."

I glance at Avery. "Perhaps that's where we'll find Ivan as well."

The captain doesn't look convinced, but he gives in. "Yes, all right. First, we need to assure Adeline we're not dead."

Sebastian winces. I think we all know we're in for it.

Because no one cares about the emotional state

of my dragon, I don't mention that Flink, too, is likely upset by our extended absence. Poor thing was probably worried sick.

After rolling his shoulders several times, Avery offers me his hand. The cat, disgruntled that I'm moving, hops off my chest and stares at me as I rise.

I frown at the little furry beast and then scoop him into my arms and head to the door.

"Lucia," Sebastian says, sounding exhausted. "What are you doing?"

I give my business partner a pointed look over my shoulder. "He deserves a better owner than Ivan."

Avery clears his throat, trying not to smile. "Don't you think a dragon is enough pet for one girl?"

He has a point—a good one. After thinking about it for a moment, I say, "I'll give him to Adeline."

Sebastian mutters under his breath, but I'm already out the door with the cat tucked under my cloak.

There is no sign of Adeline or Flink at the inn. They're not in any of the restaurants, shoppes, or local guilds. I highly doubt they went for a pleasure stroll through the inch of late winter snow that now blankets the ground, as neither of them seems the type to enjoy that sort of thing.

"You're sure you haven't seen her?" Sebastian asks the woman at the front desk of the inn again.

The woman, who fancied Sebastian a few days ago, now looks at him as if he's a nuisance. "No, Lord Thane. As I *already* said, I haven't seen her since yesterday."

Exasperated, Sebastian steps away from the counter—much to the woman's relief. He rubs his face as he asks us, "What are we going to do? She's out there, somewhere, possibly lost, helpless—"

"She's a grown woman, Sebastian, not a puppy," I interrupt. "Besides, she has Flink."

He levels me with a green-eyed stare. "Yes, and a lot of good he'll do her."

I'm about to snarl back because I'm worried about them too, when Avery steps between us. "We'll go to the constable, file a missing person notification." He pauses when he sees my expression and gives me a placating look. "*Missing dragon, too.* If we must, we'll post it on every board from here to Teirn."

We're about to leave the inn when the woman behind the desk calls to us, "Don't forget your things— we left them in the hall. I need your keys as well." She holds out her hands, expectant. "And the money for last night's rent."

"We didn't use our rooms last night," Avery points out.

"Yes, but you had the keys, didn't you?" The woman is not quite as charming as she was when we first arrived.

Avery rolls his eyes and reaches into his inner pocket only to go still as the realization dawns on him. He has no money. Ivan took it.

Sebastian, too, looks a little ill. The cousins exchange a long look, and then they turn to me in one slow, synchronized motion.

I stare at them, confused for half a moment, and then I step back. "After paying Serena for her gown, I hardly have any left!"

"Get on with it, Lucia," Sebastian says, exasperated.

I glance at the woman, frowning.

After several moments, I plop the furry feline I've been carrying for half the day in her arms. "Here. Have a cat."

"Wait!" she calls out, but we're already stepping onto the street.

With that settled, sort of, we make our way through the snowy city to the stone building near the docks that doubles as the local law office and jail.

Our fears are immediately relieved, because as soon as we're inside, we find both the auburn-haired girl and the ornery copper-colored dragon. Adeline looks fit to be tied with her cheeks ablaze, hair a mess, and eyes flashing yet noticeably puffy as if she's been crying.

"You listen to me, you sorry excuse for a man," she snarls, her hands on the constable's desk, leaning over as far as possible to look him in the eyes. "You *will* take me seriously, and *you will* find my companions! They have been missing for over a full day now!"

Flink notices us before Adeline. He lifts his head from the floor and lets out a welcome sort of growl.

"Flink!" Adeline exclaims, whipping around. "For the last time, leave that plant—"

Her eyes go wide when she sees us in the doorway, and she lets out a long breath of relief. Then her expression morphs to livid—a look not unlike my mother's when I've done something less than brilliant. "Where have you been!"

"I found them," the constable says dryly, feeling the need to interrupt. He then promptly holds up his hands in surrender when Adeline whips back to him, ready to rip him to shreds.

"Adeline," Sebastian begins, setting his hands gently on her shoulders to keep her from maiming the leader of the local law authority.

She turns on him. "I haven't even started with you yet! Do you have any idea..."

Avery leans close and murmurs in my ear as Adeline carries on, "What do you think? Should we sneak out while they aren't looking?"

The nearness makes my nerves sing, and my brilliant plan floats into the forefront of my mind. *I'm going to kiss him*. Not here—not now. Probably not even today.

But soon.

I give him a subtle nod and collect Flink while Adeline hollers at both the constable and Sebastian. We slip out the front entrance, closing the door behind us. Flink lets out a horrified squeal when I force him to step into the snow.

"Really?" I ask him, growing exasperated with this whole day.

He stares back at me, his topaz eyes wide, and then collapses against me, just like he used to do when he was young and lovable.

"Oh," I murmur as I stroke his head, right between his two little horns. "I missed you, too."

"I missed him as well," Avery unexpectedly chimes in.

I look at him, incredulous. "You did?"

"If he'd been with us, he could have nullified Ivan's lovely spell."

"Are you very upset about the money?" I ask the captain, knowing how perturbed he was when he found out about Mueller charging both him and Sebastian for my dragon.

Under his cloak, Avery slips his hands into his jacket pockets. "I am...irritated...with myself because

I didn't sense it." His eyes wander to me, locking on mine in a way that makes my breath catch in my throat. "But it could have been worse. You are far more precious than money, and you seem well enough."

In love with the captain? No, not me.

My heart's all warm and squishy, but that could mean all kinds of things. Like I contracted a malignant disease at Ivan's humble abode, and now I'm dying. Yes, that's it. Dying is preferable to love, isn't it?

I gulp, hoping my thoughts aren't displayed for him to see, and then I show him my hand. "Well. My finger's a little tingly."

His lips quirk to the side in a half-smile. Very serious, he says, "Is that so?"

He inches closer in the snowy, not-so-scenic Fermall street and grazes his fingers over my palm, making my senses spark.

I cannot help it; I stare at our hands, barely breathing.

He slowly traces my fingers with his, making my skin tingle. In a husky whisper, he asks, "Better?"

"Hmmm?" I look up, distracted. There's a smile in his eyes, a rotten smugness that betrays that he knows exactly what he does to me. I snatch my hand away. "Oh, I suppose. A little."

Before he can answer, the door flies open, and Adeline storms out, a vision with her curls flying. She tugs on her soft kidskin gloves, glaring at the snow as if it floated from the sky just to ruin her afternoon.

Sebastian trails after her, looking vexed. "I've had about enough of Fermall. I think it's high time we return to Teirn."

We all agree and make the short walk to the stables. Unfortunately, once we arrive, we find a few things missing.

Namely, our carriage, driver, and horses.

Avery, who's quite livid at this point, finds the stable boy. "*Where* is my carriage?"

The boy's eyes go large, and he looks from Avery to the rest of our party. "You...you came for it yesterday," he stammers, clearly terrified.

Slowly—too slowly—Avery takes a careful step back, probably trying to calm the anger flashing in his eyes. "What do you mean *I* collected it yesterday?"

"You, My Lord...you came for it?" The boy shakes his head, probably fearing a beating is in his future. "You were in a hurry, and you had that birdcage—"

"No," I groan as I let my head fall back. Staring at the pigeon family in the rafters, I say, "Ivan."

"*Ivan*," Avery repeats, his tone murderous. He clenches his fist, takes a long, deep breath, and then, with considerable control, exhales. "Fine. It's fine."

The captain clears his throat, but he still looks like he wants to punch something. Adeline watches him with wide eyes. We've never seen him like this.

Without looking at me, Avery says, "Lucia, seeing as how you have no more cats to barter, do you suppose you could pay for carriage fare? It looks as if we'll be taking public transport back to Teirn."

"Mmmhmmm," I say brightly, hoping to diffuse the situation even if only a little. "I sure can."

"Good." He takes another deep breath. "Perfect."

He then turns on his heel and strides out of the stables.

"I think he handled that rather well," Adeline says, and then she and I promptly burst into quiet, horrified laughter.

The man next to me smells like week-old bread. It's a curious fragrance for a human instead of, say, a bakery. And though it's intriguing, as I would like to know *why* he carries that particular fragrance, it's odd enough I am slightly repulsed.

Adeline, the lucky goose, has the good seat, right between Avery and Sebastian, while I'm squished between Sir Smells-Like-Old-Baguettes and a vertically-challenged man who, I swear, scoots closer to me with every bump we hit. And this road is a bit rutted. Public transportation isn't all it's cracked up to be.

Note to self: purchase a horse.

The carriage begins to slow as we near our destination, and I almost fall to my knees with relief. It's been a long week of various forms of transport. Between Elmnare Ridge and Ponta, we even rode in the back of a hay wagon. Sebastian, of course, was put out, and Adeline shivered under her cloak—scowling the entire time, but Avery sat there, happy as you please, content to watch the chilly world go by. The captain baffles me.

To many, of the two cousins, Sebastian is the mystery, a closed book—but I've read every page. I can anticipate his every mood, his every expression. Half the time, I even know what words he will choose. No, it's Avery I still find an enigma. There are layers under his quick, cocky smiles.

He was born into a world I cannot fathom, and yet he relishes even the simple things—embraces them wholeheartedly. Doesn't care if they're considered to be beneath him.

If I were in love with him—*if*—then maybe, *perhaps*, there might be a chance for us to work. *If* he were to love me as well. Which he'd have to admit first.

Not, mind you, that I plan on admitting anything myself. The thought is entirely hypothetical.

The captain catches me watching him, and a ghost of a smile slides across his face, lighting his eyes before it reaches his lips. He boldly meets my gaze, his expression saying he knows he's wearing me down.

I press my lips together to keep from smiling and pull my eyes away from his to look out the window, which is a much safer view.

We're finally back to Teirn, and the air is warm. The storm that blew in last week is a memory, and spring is in the air. In as little as a month, the city will be hot and humid, but right now, it's perfect.

After several more long minutes of winding through the crowded streets, our carriage stops at the stables. Even before the driver can hop down and open the door, I leap up.

Murmuring "pardon me," I shove my way out of the carriage, tripping over Bread-man's feet as I dart. I then stumble to the ground, delighted to be free.

Our driver looks at me as if I am an unmannered kildibeast from the western deserts, shakes his head, and then offers his hand to Adeline, who of course, is standing demurely at the entrance, waiting patiently for assistance.

If I'd been sandwiched between Avery and Sebastian, I wouldn't have been in a hurry either. Then I think of how uncomfortable the reality of that situation would be and decide I would have probably darted just as quickly, perhaps faster.

Avery ambles out after Adeline, the picture of masculine, long-legged perfection. We stashed our cloaks in our packs as soon as we traveled far enough south the weather warmed, and he's now wearing a light-weight, brown leather jacket over a loose ivory shirt. His belt hangs haphazardly from his hips, boasting his dagger and sword. He looks like an adventurer instead of a sea captain—a well-to-do one, of course, and he carries an air of roguish nonchalance about him.

"Yes?" he asks with bright eyes when he catches me, yet again, staring at him.

I gesture to his clothing, attempting to play it cool. "That's a good look for you, Captain."

He clears his throat in a coy way, giving me a wicked half-smile, and leans close so only I will hear his next words. "You are welcome to take a closer look, *Adventuress.*"

Unable to help myself—which is not at all my fault considering he smells dark and delicious and entirely too enticing—I turn my head so my lips brush his ear. Lowering my voice, purposely a touch breathy, I say, "I thought we decided you were to call me Lucia."

Desired effect achieved.

Avery shivers involuntarily and steps away, biting back a grin and shaking his head. He flashes me a look that tells me I'm playing with fire, and I raise an innocent, questioning eyebrow even as my stomach flutters.

Sebastian is the last one out of the carriage, and

he scowls at Avery and me, probably irritated that Adeline is still being short with him. I'm not entirely sure what's going on between them, but it's certainly tense.

Flink growls out a groan as I pull him from the luggage rack. Because it's a public carriage, there was simply no way he could ride at our feet, as he did on the way to Fermall. But he seems to have fared well enough.

He stretches his wings, which are too small to be of actual use, and each scaly leg. Then he rolls his head, leans down in a bowing dog stretch, and then scratches an itch on his flank.

"Are you ready?" I ask him wryly once I'm quite sure he's finished.

The dragon yawns once, letting out a cloud of sparkling flame, and then stands, ready to walk. We make our way down the streets of Teirn, enjoying the warm weather. And we are not the only ones. The walkways are packed today with people strolling about the shoppes.

Delicious smells waft from nearby restaurants, and Flink constantly stops to stick his snout in the air. I'm just giving him another tug when I notice an especially tight knot of people ahead of us.

"What is it, do you think?" Adeline asks, standing on her toes in an attempt to see over the crowd.

Avery pushes his way forward, through the

throng. Sebastian stays with us, frowning at the pan-demonium. Avery returns in a few moments, shaking his head. "There's been another robbery."

I glance ahead. "Another supply shoppe?"

Avery nods, and I charge forward, shoving Flink's lead into Adeline's hands.

"Lucia, no. Wait—" The captain tries to pull me back, but I slip from his grasp.

I push through people, needing to see it myself. When I reach the front of the crowd, I nudge a man aside and then come to an abrupt stop.

It's Dante's shoppe, just as I feared. The windows are broken, and inside, items of varying value are strewn about and trampled. Thousands and thousands of denat's worth of ingredients are ruined. It's obvious the thieves were looking for something in particular, and I am willing to bet good money I know what it was.

I'm just shaking my head, sickened by the amount of waste, when several somber-looking guards emerge from the doorway, carrying a large bundle between them. But it's not a bundle under that thin white cloth.

It's a man.

Sebastian reaches me before Avery, and he sets a hand on my shoulder as soon as he sees the source of my distress. "Oh, Lucia."

"It's Dante," I whisper. "Isn't it?"

Avery comes up from behind me and wraps his

arm around my back, pulling me close.

Still in shock, Sebastian nods. "I'm afraid so."

My stomach writhes, making me feel as if I'm going to be sick. Numb, I let Avery lead me away.

CHAPTER TWENTY
Three Seconds Should Be Enough

We arrive back to find the castle in a tizzy. News of Dante's death has spread like wildfire, and there is no escaping the gossip. People, no matter their station—courtiers, maids, serving men—speak of the increasing danger in Teirn.

And though I didn't know Dante well, I am ill. Who could do this? And why?

A knock sounds on my door, startling me from my thoughts. I open it, fully expecting Avery. Much to my surprise, I find Sebastian instead.

He stands in the hall, pressed and polished in his long black jacket. His hair is just a touch wet, and his eyes are startlingly green in the dim light of the setting sun that shines in through a western window down the way.

My heart does a fleeting extra thump in memory, and that familiar sadness cloaks my shoulders. There was a time when I would have done anything for this man.

"I think we should go home," he says instead of a greeting.

I lean against the door frame and cross my arms, startled. "To Reginae? But we haven't finished the job."

"This is more than a scouting job, Lucia. There's a snake's nest at the center of it, and the more I think about it, the more I believe we are in over our heads. We're not sleuths or guards—we don't work for the king. We're scouts, and right now, you're a little too popular around here for my liking."

I open my mouth to argue, but he cuts me off, continuing, "*The Adventuress, The Siren Slayer*—that's what they're calling you. They don't even use your name. And the truth has morphed into myth. People speak of you as if you're some sort of witch, capable of finding anything, able to take on any creature without harm. Harold mentioned there was a man asking about you while we were gone. Lucia, whoever is stealing these butterflies—eventually, they're going to want you, just like Serena wanted you. And if you don't go with them freely..."

Almost smiling—but not quite because I'm actually a little spooked—I say, "Sebastian, are you trying to say you're afraid I'm going to be kidnapped? Held hostage like a truffle-sniffing pig and let out of my cage only on occasion to magically track down elemental butterflies?"

He shifts, obviously thinking it's a bit ridiculous as well. "I know it sounds—"

"No, I do see your logic, mad as it might be." I've seen the way people look at me, even if it's beyond bizarre. "I'm just having trouble wrapping my head around the fact that *I'm* the woman you're speaking of. I'm not a myth—I'm just...me."

"Yes, I agree. You're not nearly as wonderful as they say," he says, flashing me a quick, unexpected grin.

Oh, I've missed that smile. Every single one you get is special because they are so rare, and you usually have to work hard for them.

I raise an eyebrow. "Feel better? Been trapping that inside for months, have you?"

He steps closer, a bit too close considering I decided to keep things platonic between us, and leans close to my ear. "You have no idea."

I wait for the butterflies, wait for my pulse to quicken. For a moment, I *will* it to. Sebastian's already broken my heart. It would be easy to admire him in a resentful sort of way, licking my wounds in silence. It's better than getting rejected twice, by two different men, in under one year.

But nothing.

"We need to talk, Lucia," he says, his voice low.

I meet his dark green eyes. His gaze is intent and serious, and it takes me by surprise. "Sebastian..."

"I need to tell you something, something important. After the soirée, Grandfather said—"

"Nothing good ever starts with those words, remember? We've discussed this."

He smiles. "He gave us his blessing. Granted, it was given grudgingly, but it happened all the same."

My chest tightens. "What do you mean?"

"We can be together, Lucia. Nothing is keeping us apart."

How I would have rejoiced at this news at the beginning of autumn. It would have changed my world, made my dreams come true. But now...

I can't look at him, so I stare at the buttons on his doublet.

"But you love the captain." His voice is surprisingly even—only a trace of bitterness laces the words.

"Love is...let's not say love." I wrinkle my nose. "Besides, what about Adeline?"

Sebastian's jaw twitches, so I know I've hit a nerve. "What about Adeline?"

"Don't be obtuse—you like her. Just admit it."

"Everyone likes Adeline." His eyes shine. "She's far

less prickly than you."

He won't tell me, but it's there. I know it is. Though he's still clinging to a future we both thought might eventually come to pass, he's ready to move on. He just needs a shove.

I poke him in the stomach for the comment, making him groan. As he doubles over, putting a little more emphasis into it than I think is necessary, his forehead brushes mine, and his short hair tickles my skin. The strands are cool, still the slightest bit damp. I laugh, about to push him away, when a familiar someone clears his throat from the hall.

Sebastian, who's still entirely too close, steps nearer, almost pressing himself flush against me. "Do you need something, Captain? We're a bit busy right now. Perhaps you could come back. Or not—that's entirely up to you."

Startled by the wicked look on Sebastian's face, I shove him away. He backs off, chuckling under his breath, quite happy to have ruffled Avery's feathers. "No matter. Lucia and I are finished, and I was about to leave anyway." He turns back to me, his face suddenly serious. "We're all right, aren't we?"

I smile and nod. We're probably better than we've been in a long time.

He squeezes my shoulder, and then he strolls from the hall, donning a smug look just to rile up his cousin. Avery watches him go with a half amused, half irritated expression.

"Did I interrupt something?" Avery asks in a droll voice once Sebastian's footfalls fade.

I should feel guilty, but there's something delightful about the slightly jealous look on the captain's face. I'm sure that deep down he knows nothing happened between Sebastian and me just now, but he looks irked just from the thought of it.

And I can work with that.

"No." I pat my hair as if I'm hoping to lay it back into place. The captain's light brown eyes narrow with suspicion as he watches my hand go through the strands. "Why do you ask?"

Avery shrugs, feigning disinterest. "I was only mildly curious since I found you tangled up in your business partner's arms and all."

I let my hand drop and slowly saunter toward him, locking my eyes on his. I tilt my head ever so slightly. "What's wrong, Captain? Jealous?"

The corner of his mouth twitches, and he takes a step in. "Not particularly. Should I be?"

I give him a one-shouldered shrug and casually let my hand slide down the side of my neck. "I can't say I would know."

"Are you going to invite me in?" His voice has gone deeper, and a lovely shiver travels all the way from the base of my neck to my toes. He smells as if he just bathed as well, washing away that horrible carriage ride, and the slightly-stronger-than-usual scent of his cologne mingles with the clean tang of soap and something that is uniquely Avery. It's a dangerous combination, one that makes my mind fuzzy and my inhibitions slip into the back of my conscious thoughts.

"I'm not sure that's a good idea," I lie through my teeth. Even as I say it, my hand strays to his loose shirt.

Oh, it's a good idea all right. I'm going to kiss him, be done with it, and move on with my life. Yes, that's why I'm fisting my hands in the fabric of his shirt, tugging him over the threshold...kicking the door shut behind us.

His eyes darken and dart to my lips, making me almost forget this is for closure purposes. It's not about pleasure—no. It's to prove to myself once and for all that Avery isn't the catnip I've convinced myself he is.

I lick my lips. His chest muscles tighten under my palm, and then his hands find my waist.

Startled by how good the contact feels, I let out an involuntary sigh—which isn't the best sign, honestly. In fact, I probably should just get on with it. Three seconds should be long enough. I'll count and then pull away.

"Lucia," he growls into my ear.

"Stop talking," I snarl, on the edge of losing real control. Then I kiss him.

And I mean I *kiss* him. My lips crush to his, and he yanks me close, responding immediately. He's not gentle, but neither am I.

One...two...oh, forget it.

We bump into the wall, crash into a table. He yanks the pins from my hair and then winds his fingers through the messy strands as they fall down my back. I pull him closer and completely lose myself in the sensation.

It's just like the island all over again. Memory washes over me, making me feel everything I've tried so hard to suppress. He's everything.

Everything.

"No!" I jerk out of the captain's arms, leaving him looking thoroughly bewildered. I whirl around and turn my back to him, overwhelmed. I fist my hands in my hair, so mad at myself I can't even think straight.

"Lucia—" he starts, his voice husky and delicious and *infuriating* beyond reason.

"It wasn't supposed to be like this!" I holler as I turn back.

He watches me, wearing a slight smile on his face even though he looks a tiny bit concerned for my sanity.

"You weren't supposed to be...and I wasn't supposed to. And this—" I shake, more terrified than mad. "You need to leave."

With bright eyes, Avery holds up his hands in a surrender even as he stalks closer. "Let me see if I got the gist of that."

"Go," I demand, pointing at the door as I step back.

As usual, the captain doesn't listen. "You have feelings for me—but you're upset about it."

"No," I scoff, my voice rising.

"You might even *love* me," he continues, mock-whispering that dreadful word as he raises his eyebrows in a teasing way. He doesn't bother to hide his grin now.

I bump into my dressing table. "So help me, Avery, if you don't leave right this moment..."

With me trapped, he closes in, setting a hand on either side of the table as he cages me in. "You..."

His words drop off when his gaze drifts to something behind us. His manner changes so abruptly, I blink at him, startled. I twist around, wondering what could possibly cause him to lose his train of thought at this of all moments.

A single blood red rose lies across a crisp white envelope. With a flick of his wrist, Avery snatches the envelope from the dressing table. My name is written on the front in curly, formal writing, and a shiny, thick black ribbon is tied around it, ending in a bow on the front.

I pick up the rose and breathe in its rich, floral fragrance. "What is it?"

Avery hands me the envelope, still frowning at it. "It's yours. You open it."

I slide off the ribbon and break the black seal. There's no crest or initials, just a simple scalloped-edge circle pressed into the wax.

Your attendance is cordially requested tonight.
If you choose to attend, your escort will meet you at
The Stag of the Forest at half past midnight.
Bring one guest; tell no others.
Formal attire required.

I hand the invitation to Avery and let him read it for himself. He raises his eyebrows and looks up. "Well, Lady Adventuress, I think you just got an invitation to one of the underground masquerades."

I have a terrible feeling about this, but I already know I'm going to go. And I cannot go alone. I peer at him, already questioning my decision. "What do you think, Captain? Care to join me?"

We won't tell Sebastian or Adeline, especially not after my conversation with Sebastian earlier. He'd try to keep me from going, and we'd just get into another argument. I don't want that, not when we're doing so well.

Avery gives me a wicked grin. "Middle of the night? Illicit? Mysterious? Sounds like my kind of party."

"Do you know where The Stag of the Forest is located?"

"I do. Meet me at the fountain in the back gardens at midnight, and I'll take you there." He moves in. "Now that we've settled that, where were we?"

I shove him toward the door. "Absolutely not. You're leaving now."

Laughing, he lets me usher him to the hall, but he turns back before he's through the door and snatches my hand, raising it to his lips. Just when I think he's going to brush a kiss over my knuckles, he flips my hand over and presses a soft, lingering kiss to my wrist.

My mouth goes dry, and my knees go wobbly.

"Until tonight," the captain promises, and then he's out the door.

CHAPTER TWENTY-ONE
Underground Masquerade

It was easy slipping from the castle, far simpler than I expected. But now that I'm stepping into the night-time shadows of the garden, I begin to wonder if this is a mistake. Sebastian warned me, and yet here I am, running into the villain's arms as soon as I get an invitation.

Just as I'm losing my nerve, I spot Avery lounging against a wall in that casual way of his, as if he doesn't have a care in the world. His golden-brown hair looks black in the night, and his clothes are dark as well. He looks forbidden.

A thrill runs through me, one I'm ashamed to say is from anticipation and not reservations about the evening. Let's be honest, by this point, my common sense has given up on me and gone on holiday.

I pass the enchanted fountain. It bubbles in several different colors, magically lit from within. It glows in the night, letting off an ethereal light. The captain waits just beyond it. I watch where I'm walking so I don't trip on a stray cobblestone and land on my face, but I can feel his eyes on me.

Clouds approach from the sea, and a cold breeze blows through the gardens, moving tree limbs that are now heavy with buds. It lifts my cloak and toys at my braided hair, which I've pinned in a coil at the top of my head. It would have been easier if I could have asked Adeline for help, but she would have run right to Sebastian and ratted me out.

The weather feels ominous, but there's promise in the air, something exhilarating. One way or another, bad or good, I am confident this night won't be boring.

As soon as I reach him, Avery steps forward to greet me. He steps into my personal space, entirely too close, but doesn't touch me. "Are you warm enough?"

I nod, not trusting my voice.

"And you're sure about this?" His voice seems somehow darker in the night, a bit more dangerous. At some point, Avery became comfortable—everything about him instills confidence, but now I'm reminded that this man is anything but safe.

"I am," I whisper.

Gently, he brushes a finger against my cheek, and

my pulse jumps. "Then let's hurry so we're not late."

Instead of offering his arm, he slides his palm against mine. Our fingers twine together, and he expertly leads me through the castle garden, navigating the maze with ease. I grow nervous as we leave through a gate in the back wall, slipping into a small grove behind the castle. We follow a winding dirt trail, delving deeper and deeper into the woods. Our path is lit with a sliver of a moon, but soon even that's covered by the thickening clouds.

Just when it's too dark to continue without a lantern or charm, I see something through the trees. "Avery, there's a carriage."

Avery nods. "Right on time."

"You're armed, aren't you?" Perhaps I'm not as confident as I was in the light of day, safe in my room in the castle, but I'd like to think I'm simply cautious.

The captain pats the sword that's currently hidden under his cloak. "Always."

I, too, have my dagger under my skirts. It feels foreign—lighter, perhaps a bit deadlier. But I wish it were on my waist, a little easier to access.

As we press forward, something winged and nearly-silent sweeps in front of us, diving to the ground. A tiny creature squeals, and then its cries are silenced as the owl disappears into the trees. Avery and I glance at each other. I wince, slightly unnerved. I know it's the natural way of things, but it's still hard to witness.

"I'm sure that's a good sign," Avery says, his voice heavy with amused sarcasm. Though it's too dark to see his facial expressions, I know the look on his face, the way he raises his eyebrows and the wry smile that makes his eyes seem to light—can see it in my mind as clearly as I know my own name.

I stagger, more startled by the thought than the owl. I know that about Avery—and a dozen other little things as well. I know the way he laughs, the way he cares for his crew with a tenacious passion, the way he looked at me the night we repeated unknown vows on that island a world away. Know that out of all the people in Kalae, he's the one I want to spend time with most, the one I feel completely at ease with, the one who cares for me exactly as I am, never demanding I change, never asking for anything more than I can offer.

"Lucia?" Avery asks after I stand here for a moment too long. "Are you all right? We can still turn back. It's not too late."

"Yes, it is," I whisper, but I'm not talking about the carriage or the masquerade or the elemental butterflies that have turned the royal city upside down.

I love him.

Oblivious to my thoughts, he cocks his head to the side. "You sure?"

"Quite."

After a few more moments, he chuckles and asks, "Then do you think we should continue? Or perhaps we'll wait here and see if they can find us?"

Forcing a laugh because I'm actually terrified, I swat his arm. "Come on."

Before he can say anything else, I yank him the rest of the way. Our narrow trail ends in a wooded lane. The carriage waits by the stag statue in the trees. The pedestal at the base has been charmed with a light spell. After soaking up the rays of the sun all day, it now glows in the night.

The carriage is sleek and black, pulled by four glossy midnight horses. There's no crest, no identifying decor. Our driver and footman are also cloaked in black, and they wear half-masks over their eyes, hiding their identities.

The footman steps forward as soon as we break from the trees, and he gives us an exaggerated bow. "My lady, you and your Captain are most welcome."

I glance at Avery, but the captain's expression gives nothing away. He's watchful, but there's nothing about the set of his jaw or shoulders that makes me think he's tense. If anything, he looks amused by the show.

"To protect your identities, the masquerade master requires all guests wear masks." The man comes forward, offering us each a silken masquerade mask, exactly like his own. They are simple and black, not showy like some of the festival creations I've seen before.

Avery fastens mine for me, tying the ribbon at the back of my head, then he quickly secures his as well. The fabric is cool against my face. On a warmer night, it would likely feel stifling, but now it's exotic and exciting. Anticipation flutters in my stomach, making me almost giddy.

The footman opens the door and helps me into the carriage. It's no surprise that the upholstery is black as well. Avery settles next to me, a little too close for my sanity.

Before the footman closes the door, he says, "We have two more stops, and then we'll be on our way."

As soon as the carriage starts rolling, Avery turns his head so his lips are near my ear. "They're dedicated to their theme."

"What's that?" I ask, trying not to focus on the soft tickle of his words on my skin or the way he looks, half hidden.

"Secrets, mystery..." He pauses, and I turn to him, meeting his eyes in the dark. He lowers his voice and moves in a smidgen closer. "Intrigue."

I gulp and pull my eyes from his.

Soon the soft dirt lane turns to hard cobblestones,

and the horses' hooves clack against them as they trot toward our next stop. Soon, the horses slow. I hear our footman's voice, but when I push aside the heavy black curtain, the windows are too dark to see through.

"They've been charmed," Avery says. "Best not let them catch you trying to see out."

A twinge of apprehension makes me rethink our decision to come tonight. I lean close to Avery. "Do you think this is safe?"

He shrugs, not looking terribly concerned. "Safer than sirens, I imagine."

I suppose that must be true.

In a few moments, the door opens, and the footman assists a woman in a dark red gown into the carriage. The cut is scandalously low, and the color is contrary to what is so popular in the city's daylight hours. After the woman chooses a seat on the opposite side of the carriage, a man enters and sits beside her. Avery nods a greeting to them, but we all stay quiet. They speak to each other in hushed whispers, but I cannot hear what they are saying.

We travel through the city, though in what direction, I have no idea. We pick up another couple, and the ample woman sits next to me, making me scoot even closer to Avery to give her room. I try not to think of how my leg is pressed against his, about how I am close enough to hear every soft breath. He shifts, and our shoulders bump together.

The carriage begins to move again, but this time, it picks up speed. We sit for quite a while, and I grow more anxious when we leave the cobblestone streets again, setting out on a soft dirt road. My mind wanders to Sebastian's words. When it seems we've gone far enough to surely be well-clear of the city, the carriage comes to a stop. The other couples buzz with excitement, though no one speaks to anyone other than their companion, and they all wear masks.

Avery is uncharacteristically quiet, and I wonder if it's because he wants to ensure his identity is kept under wraps or if he's trying to ascertain those of our fellow passengers.

The footman finally opens the door, and we filter out, ladies first. I gape at the quiet, overgrown courtyard we've arrived in. It's a ruin, ancient and crumbling. There's a dry fountain in the middle, and a few benches covered in dormant vines. Tall, thick evergreen bushes surround the tiny courtyard, and with the help of the dark night, they obscure our surroundings.

"A few rules," the footman says as soon as we're clear of the carriage. "Do not share your identity, and do not ask anyone for theirs. The tunnels past the ballroom are forbidden. Do not lose your mask, or you will not be permitted entry again. Also, show it to no one—tell no one. Repeat after me: I will tell no one."

The woman who sat next to me in the carriage looks as if this is all old news, but the couple who got in right after us nods as they say the words, both quite serious. The somber tone, mixed with my nerves, makes me want to laugh. What is this place that they take themselves quite so seriously?

Avery and I both repeat the oath, slightly less enthusiastic than the rest, and then a cold chill runs down my spine.

It was a binding spell—we've been charmed.

I glance at Avery, concerned, but he subtly shakes his head, telling me not to worry myself over it. But that's easier said than done.

After the charm is complete, the footman holds out a hand, casting a type of matter manipulation spell, and a large stone bench slowly inches over the stone courtyard, creating a horrible screeching noise that makes me want to cover my ears. Once the bench is clear, he pulls back a door, revealing a stairway built into the ground. With a flick of his wrist, a flame blooms in the palm of our escort's hand, lighting the dark night. "Follow me."

He leads us down the stairs, into the tunnel. It grows warmer the farther we go, as if the cold night air cannot penetrate the thick layers of stone and earth. We take so many turns, I lose count, and I fear I'll never find my way on my own if we should return.

Instead of tracking our progress, I study the stone walls. The tunnel is very much like the one that led from the caretaker's cottage to the scholars' guild headquarters. In fact, I wouldn't be surprised if it connected somewhere, though I don't remember a doorway off the path we took with Sam that night.

After we've walked for a good ten minutes, the footman takes a right, into a tunnel with a huge ceiling, and stops in front of a double door. Two urns burn on either side, and our escort lets the flame in his palm fade. He knocks on one of the doors. Almost immediately, the knock is answered by another man dressed in black. He too wears a mask. The guard's eyes wander over us, and then he turns to the footman and holds out his hand. "Their entrance fees?"

"All except for theirs." The footman gestures to Avery and me as he hands over a heavy leather satchel. "But they are the masquerade master's personal guests."

We are? That can't be good.

The guard turns to us and nods. If he recognizes us, he doesn't let it show.

Strains of dark, stringed music drift to us through the cracked door. It's alluring and melancholy, and it calls to me, begging me to push past the two men. I grow impatient, wanting them to let us be so we can go in.

Finally, the guard opens the doors wide, allowing us entrance.

The larger woman pushes past me, followed closely by her companion, but the other couple is slightly more hesitant. Avery turns to me, silently offering his arm. I slip my hand through the crook of his elbow, and we step into the dark room.

But it's not black, just dim. A spiderweb of spelled lights glows above us, just bright enough a person can see, but low to give the room a bit of ambiance. What our hosts call a ballroom is a massive cavernous room and very, very old. I gape at the architecture, dumbfounded. Statues and tapestries line the wall, depicting history from a time long ago. If I were a thief, which I'm not, I could tuck a dozen things under my cloak and make a fortune.

I glance at Avery and poke him in the side. "No collecting souvenirs."

His lips twitch, but he doesn't bother to grace that with an answer.

The crowd is larger than I expect, a hundred people give or take. Most are dancing, but even those speaking in intimate clusters move with the haunting music that lilts from a quartet orchestra in the corner.

We stand here for a moment, marveling at it all. Even Avery seems impressed by the display. The air is heavy, almost thick. Dozens of massive urns overflow with sumptuous red roses, just like the one that came with the invitation. They scent the air with their rich perfume. It smells like excitement—sharp and floral and heady, but there's mystery here too, subtle notes of citrus and spice. It muddles my head, makes it hard to think. It's not an unpleasant sensation, and it appears the people around us revel in it, letting go of their inhibitions. There are too many dark corners, too much freedom in concealing one's identity.

The waitstaff, all masked just as the guests, wind their way through the room. Many offer refreshments, but some perform tricks with light and smoke. A squeal of excitement followed by laughter drifts to us from a nearby group, where a man casts a sparking light spell into the air. It bursts into a multitude of colors then snakes through the charmed lights, a dragon of magic—much like the fireworks the caravans sell, but far grander.

As much as my heart is telling me to lose myself in the crowd, draw Avery into the madness, my brain tells me there is something very strange afoot. We need to find the man in charge, see how the larkwing is connected, and then get out of here.

Before I can ask Avery what he thinks our first move should be, a serving man stops in front of us, carrying a tray of crystal flutes holding a clear, bubbling liquid.

We each take one, hoping to hurry the man along.

"Champagne," the man explains in a bored, cultured voice. "From Iaselhall. I understand it's exceptional this evening."

"You haven't tried it?" I ask.

"I'm on duty." He raises an eyebrow, looking at me as if I'm a bit daft, but he is obviously reluctant to leave until I've tried it.

"Right. Thank you," I say pointedly, subtly nodding him along.

He only stands there, staring at me.

"Fine." I take a big gulp though I much prefer cider. The bubbles burn my throat; the concoction is far stronger than champagne should ever be. It reminds me of sweet, bitter grapefruit. I blink, trying not to cough, and a curious sensation settles over me, almost like a charm. Ignoring it, I hold up the flute, mock-toasting the man. "Wonderful. Thank you."

Now go away.

The man nods. "Very good, my lady. Enjoy your evening."

I scowl at him as he leaves. The drink hits my stomach like lead, making me feel slightly ill. I turn to Avery, about to tell him not to drink it, but find him studying his own flute, eyes narrowed. "You probably shouldn't have tried it."

"I don't think one sip will do me in." The room spins, and I grab hold of the captain's arm to support myself.

Looking a little worried for my liking, Avery steadies me. "Probably not...if it were champagne—"

"What do you mean it's not champagne?" I demand, focusing on his eyes and not the spinning room.

"Well," the captain says, growing more concerned, "champagne generally does not *glow*."

CHAPTER TWENTY-TWO
Lark & Song

"The first sip can be a bit rough," a man says from behind me.

I turn in Avery's arms, startled. Somehow, everything is warmer, more vivid, more sumptuous. Nearly everyone sips from their own drinks, and all seem to relish them.

The owner of the voice is handsome as far as I can tell behind his mask. His clothing is expensive and his eyes oddly familiar. Though I've met far too many people in the last week to remember them all, I am certain I know this man.

In one smooth motion, Avery jerks me to his side and draws a hidden dagger, pointing it at the man. "What did she drink?"

The man holds up his hands in surrender, smiling

in a confident way that I find alarming. I mean, I think I do anyway. I'm not sure what I feel. The unpleasant sensation in my stomach begins to subside, and I find myself disinterested in the conversation. All I want to do is pull Avery into the middle of the chaos and forget anyone else exists for the rest of the night.

"Put your dagger away," I whisper near his ear. "Leave the man be and dance with me instead."

"Lucia," he says in a patient voice, not even bothering to look at me.

"*Avery*," I answer, purposely making my voice breathy as I move in closer. "I said leave him be. *Dance with me.*"

The captain stiffens at my side, but he doesn't lower the dagger. He glances down, meeting my gaze, incredulous.

"The lady wants to dance, Captain Greybrow," the masked man says, lowering his hands, a satisfied smile in his eyes. "What gentleman would turn down that offer? I'll leave you be, but do not worry—I'll find you before the evening is over." His easy smile drops. "We have business to discuss."

Avery clenches his jaw as the man turns and disappears into the crowd. He looks like he's about to charge after him but has no idea what to do with me.

Which is ridiculous, because I'm fine.

"Is it warm in here?" I ask, touching the side of

my neck.

"Are you all right?" Avery tightens his arms around me even as his eyes follow my fingers.

He smells amazing. Like the air before a storm.

"I smell like the air...before a storm?" he asks, growing concerned.

"What?" I blink at him.

Surely, I didn't say that out loud. I mean, I do have control over my mouth.

A hint of a crooked smile graces his face. "Not apparently."

Realizing I'm saying everything that comes to mind, I yank away from him. He certainly does not need to hear everything I've been dwelling on lately.

"Lucia..." He pulls me back, not letting me have a chance to breathe.

"No!" I fight him. Putting out the effort makes the room spin faster, and my stomach lurches. "I just need to sit down," I insist.

My vision blurs with smudges of darkness, and my knees start to buckle. Feeling trapped inside a body I can no longer control, I begin to panic. I reach out for him, grasping his arm when I find it. "Avery...what's wrong with me...?"

The captain steps forward and catches me around my waist. Softly, he says, "Lucia, you'll be all right. You have to let the elixir run its course, but you'll be fine."

"Elixir?" The word means something, something bad, but for the life of me, I cannot remember what. Without a lot of conviction, I push against his chest. "Leave me on a bench or something."

Almost laughing, though he sounds far less confident than usual, he whispers, "Not a chance."

My knees start to buckle, and I let myself rest against him. "Avery, no. I'm going to do something stupid, say something stupid."

He pulls us into a corner of the room, a place less populated. "Then don't talk. You want to dance, right? Let's dance."

Gently, he presses on my back, drawing me even closer. We sway back and forth, moving as if rocked by a soft breeze. Feeling a little better, I rest my cheek against him.

"Have you always felt this safe?" I murmur.

"I can't honestly say." There's a smile in his voice, and it calms my nerves further. His hand finds my hair, and he massages the base of my neck. It feels amazing.

"Careful, I'm going to melt on the floor," I say against the soft material of his doublet.

I can feel the vibrations from his answering chuckle on my cheek, and the thought makes me smile. I might tell him that too. I'm not sure.

After a long while, the panic has finally ebbed,

and I'm as content and loose-limbed as a house cat in the sun. "You know what's funny?" I ask him quietly. I have no idea how long we've been like this, but I'm starting to feel like myself again—but better. Warmer and happier and far less conflicted—that same feeling you get right before you fall asleep.

"Hmmm?"

"I was so concerned I was going to admit how I feel about you." I toy with a button on his doublet. "But why would I worry about that?"

He freezes...goes completely motionless.

"What I mean is," I say, realizing I'm saying it all wrong, "*why* wouldn't I want to tell you that I love you? Because of course I do. More than anything, I wanted those vows we exchanged to be binding." Feeling brave, I go on, focusing on the embossed threads in the doublet because it helps with the vertigo. "And I know I shouldn't feel this way, because you're a well-to-do pirate who should have married the queen and I'm only the daughter of a chicken farmer—but I can't help myself."

I'm not sure any of that made a lot of sense. I pull my eyes away from the fabric, wondering why he hasn't answered. The captain looks as if I've slapped him, and a trickle of apprehension runs through my veins. I take an abrupt step back, right out of his arms. Suddenly, it's as if I've fallen headfirst into a frigid lake, and I'm as lucid now as I've ever been.

What have I done?

What have I done?

Overcome, completely mortified, I abruptly turn on my heel. But before I can run away and hide for the rest of my life, the world lurches yet again. Then it goes pitch black, and I feel myself fall.

I wake to raised voices, and I sit up too quickly. Stars flash before my eyes, and my head feels as if someone bashed it with a rock.

"She had a bad reaction, that's all," someone insists. "I assure you, the concoction is usually harmless."

"You're about to have a bad reaction to my blade," Avery snarls.

"*Ow*," I groan as I press my fingers to my temples.

The voices stop abruptly, and the two men in the room turn to me. They're both masked, but as soon as Avery's eyes meet mine, he rips the mask from his face and kneels by my side.

"What happened?" I demand, but I regret it as soon as the words are out because my head *hurts*.

Avery flashes a murderous look over his shoulder—one I wouldn't want to be on the receiving end of. "The shopkeeper drugged you."

"Shopkeeper?" I whisper because it doesn't make my head pound quite as much.

The masked man simultaneously bows and pulls off his mask. I scream and scramble back on the padded bench. Temporarily forgetting my headache, I stare at him, horrified. "It's not possible."

Something is very wrong with me.

"Avery, I need to see Gregory," I say, feeling myself drift toward hysterics. "Take me to him."

The captain scowls at our companion. "You're not seeing ghosts, Lucia."

The man who I last saw covered in a sheet smirks. "I'm afraid Lark and Song isn't quite that potent."

Still holding my head, I stand, reaching out to Avery for assistance. "You're dead," I say to Dante, still unable to wrap my mind around it.

I saw him with my own eyes. He was *gray*.

"Not yet." He winks, and I swear Avery is a heartbeat from lunging at him—which I'm fine with, but first I want answers.

"I don't understand. Did you ambush our carriage on the way to the masquerade? Rise from the dead so you could pursue the life of a highwayman? *What happened?*"

Avery gapes at me.

"That happens sometimes," Dante explains to the captain.

I'm about to swipe Avery's blade and skewer the man myself. "Someone tell me what's going on!"

I wince as my head pounds again, and I close my eyes until the moment passes.

The captain takes me by the shoulders and stares into my eyes. Despite the clatter in my brain, I can't help but notice how good he smells.

I feel a twinge of memory—something fleeting—but it wisps away before I can grasp hold of it. I narrow my eyes, feeling a bit irked with Avery as well. "Why are you looking at me like that?" I glance around the ornate room. It's old—ancient in fact, built of tan stone and decorated with priceless antiques. "And where are we?"

"What's the last thing you remember?" Avery softly demands.

He's acting odd—shifty and a bit desperate. It's strange.

I eye him. "Stepping into the carriage."

The captain curses under his breath and turns from me, running a frustrated hand through his hair. Then he whips back to Dante. "Will her memory return?"

"*What* am I supposed to remember?" Of course, neither of them answer me, even when I snarl under my breath.

Dante purses his lips and stares at me as if I'm an alchemy experiment. "It's hard to say. Perhaps with time."

Avery rolls his shoulders, looking as if it's taking everything in his power not to run the man through with his blade. "Is there anything we can give her to help the process along?"

I point to Avery. "We will deal with this madness in a moment, but for now" —I turn my finger on Dante— "I want to know how you're alive."

The shopkeeper shrugs. "Isn't it obvious? I faked my death."

"But I saw you! You were...*dead*." I whisper the last word.

Not terribly concerned, Dante shrugs. "Looks can be deceiving, and alchemy's come a long way in the last fifty years. You'd be amazed at what we can do."

"So, you staged your own death, made it look as if you were robbed. What about the other shoppes? Are they in on it? Are there goblins in Teirn at all or was that something you concocted as well?"

"I cannot say about the goblins, but I will admit that a few of my ambitious workers might have caused a bit of havoc in the city so that when it came time to take my exit, it would look believable. Eventually, we knew the king would begin to suspect something, and I needed an escape."

"King Harold knows about the tunnels?"

"Of course he does—it's his city." Dante almost smiles. "But he doesn't know how to access this one."

247

"Why?" I demand. "Why would you do all this?"

With a smile, Dante strides across the room and opens a door. There's music in the dark hall beyond, something a little too familiar. He motions for me to join him.

I gape into the ballroom, and déjà vu washes over me, making me feel disoriented.

"Do you see them out there?" Dante whispers near my ear. "They pay the fee, drink my Lark and Song elixir, and suddenly their inhibitions are gone, leaving them happier, joyful, unhindered by the daily stress of life. They pay dearly for it, Lucia. Not everyone has an adverse reaction to it as you did."

Softly, he clicks the door shut. A wave of dizziness washes over me, and I stumble on the bed. "You drugged me?"

Dante wrinkles his nose. "That's a crude way to put it."

I hold up a hand. "Wait. You're an alchemist? An actual one? Not just an herbologist dabbling with magic?"

"College trained." He grins. "Before the mages' college booted me out, anyway."

"Why did they expel you?" Avery asks, narrowing his eyes. I might be wrong, but I don't think the captain cares for the not-quite-deceased shopkeeper. "What did you do?"

Dante chuckles. "They didn't like my particular brand of magic. Said my concoctions were destructive to society, and they sent me on my way."

"You're not even certified!" I growl. "You could kill people."

"Most people would kill for a taste of what I have to offer." His eyes darken. "Some have."

"How can you—"

Before I can finish, Dante takes a step forward, a dark, excited light in his eyes. "But that's not my fault. I haven't hurt anyone, wouldn't hurt anyone. All I'm doing is offering people a chance to escape—add a bit of excitement to their dull lives."

Avery stands silent, his face expressionless, but I shake my head. "But it's wrong!"

"Is it?" Dante insists, and he motions toward a door that leads to the ballroom. "Is it wrong to step out of your ordinary life, experience something magical? Is it wrong of me to want to make a little money along the way?"

I frown at him, feeling too off to argue with him. Lamely, I add, "Elixirs are illegal, and breaking into people's shoppes—destroying their livelihood—is as well."

"Laws are living, breathing things, Lucia. They change with every new king." Dante waves the argument away. "I'm offering you both the chance to be a part of it—take a share in the proceeds. I assure you, the business is far more lucrative than you can imagine. All I need is more larkwings."

Sebastian was right. Of course he was—he always is. Wretched man.

Dante turns to Avery. "I think we all know you've been known to dabble a bit on the wrong side of the law. Surely, as a business man, you can see the available profit—you saw them out there. Most of them come to every masquerade, paying more each time just for a taste of mystery."

"How much did you charge tonight?" Avery asks, a little too curious for my liking.

"Two thousand denats a head."

The air whooshes from my lungs. With that crowd, Dante easily made several hundred thousand denats in one evening.

"From what we understand, the larkwings are almost extinct," Avery says.

Dante makes his way to a bottle on a side table and pours himself a drink. "That is unfortunately true. We were not careful in the beginning, should have focused more on sustaining the growth of the species."

"We?" I ask.

"You haven't figured that out yet?" Dante points to me with his glass. "I'm working with the head of the scholars' guild—Serena's husband. For the last week, you and your two companions have been chasing your tails." His eyes shift about the room. "The foolish woman has no idea what she almost did when she sold the butterfly to that collector in Fermall. I bought it back, but it will come out of her husband's share."

"You have it now? Here?" Avery asks, and I try not to look too interested in the answer.

As if he doesn't quite trust us, Dante narrows his eyes. "It's well protected. And you can consider your agreement with Serena fulfilled. The larkwing is back with its rightful owner."

I glance at Avery, unsure what to think of that. But the real question is what is Serena's husband going to do when he finds out what she's done. Just the thought makes me nervous, and I know we have to find her as soon as we're able.

"So, what do you say, Captain Greybrow? Do you want in?"

Just as I'm saying, "Absolutely not," Avery says, "We will consider it."

"Avery!" I hiss.

He flashes me a look, a stern one that begs me to be quiet—one very much like Sebastian's. I glare at him but reluctantly hold my tongue.

Dante studies us. "You realize I've confided quite a lot of confidential information to you. We don't usually let people leave knowing what you know if they're not open to our proposition."

The captain flashes him a lazy smile. "I think we both know it's only a matter of convincing Lucia it's a sound business deal. We'll be in touch with you by the end of the week."

Dante watches Avery for several moments, probably trying to decide if the captain speaks the truth, and then he nods, apparently satisfied. "We'll be in contact, and for now, I ask that you speak to no one about our... meeting. And please, enjoy the rest of your evening."

Without further ado, he opens the door and motions us into the ballroom. The men nod to each other as we pass Dante, and I chomp at the bit, ready to corner Avery and ask him if he's lost his fool mind.

"Wait," Dante calls. We turn back and find him holding our masks. "Don't want to forget these, now do you?"

My eyes lock on Dante's as I accept the mask. He smiles. "Have a pleasant evening."

Once we're in the ballroom, my headache begins to subside. Bits and pieces of the evening float back to me in brief flashes of color and conversation. Some of it makes no sense, probably bits of a dream I had while I was unconscious, but other parts must be memories.

I scowl at the drinks a man carries on a tray. I remember the feel of the bubbling liquid on my tongue and its overly sweet yet slightly bitter flavor, but I do not believe the crowd was this wild earlier. It's too loud; the laughter sounds like the high-pitched keen of a cackling night animal, and most people speak gibberish. Lots of couples have broken off, doing who-knows-what in the shadows.

"Take me home," I say to Avery, pulling away as he tugs me into his arms so we might dance.

His eyes are on the crowd. "Not yet. They're watching us. Pretend to enjoy yourself."

Knowing he must have some purpose, I sigh and give in, going through the motions but not particularly happy about it. I lower my voice and lean close. "You wouldn't actually consider partnering with that jackal, would you?"

"No." He wears an easy smile, but it's a show for our masked audience. "But we need them to think we are."

"Why?"

He finally lowers his gaze. "You haven't dealt much with this sort of society before, have you?"

"I've barely dealt with the regular sort. Chickens don't generally throw elixir parties under their henhouses."

That earns me a real smile. "No, I suppose they don't. Well, let me explain how this sort of thing works. We were invited into their nest of vipers. If we'd up and refused their offer, as you were so quick to do, we would likely be dead."

I scoff. "I've seen you fight. I highly doubt Dante could have bested you."

A grin flashes across his face, making him go from handsome to devastating. "While I'm flattered by your confidence in me, it's not Dante I was concerned about."

"Then what?"

"Them."

He jerks his chin toward the darkened walls. Sure enough, there are mercenary-like guards standing in groups, watching the party. I am certain there are more where the shadows grow too dark to see.

"Why so many?" I ask.

A new voice joins ours, nearly a whisper in my ear. "Because there are goblins attempting to infiltrate the tunnels."

Avery and I both jerk around. It doesn't matter that the man's identity is concealed—I would know him anywhere.

Sebastian, who's beyond striking with his black mask and teak hair, looks murderous. "*Lucia.* You just couldn't stay away, could you?"

CHAPTER TWENTY-THREE
Air Before a Storm

"What are you doing here?" I demand.

"I could ask you the same thing."

I step out of Avery's arms. "I received an invitation."

Sebastian rolls his eyes. "I did too, but I wasn't going to be foolish enough to go until Adeline said she couldn't find you."

"Why was she looking for me in the middle of the night?"

Avery clears his throat and glances around the room, wearing a rigid, neutral expression. "Now is not the time."

"And what do you mean goblins are trying to break into the tunnels?" I demand, choosing to ignore Avery.

"Do you ever listen to anything—"

"Enough." Avery pulls us apart. "We'll discuss it tomorrow."

I glance around. "Where do you think we are?"

Avery catches my eye and smirks. "Underground."

I give him a withering look as Sebastian clears his throat. "We're just under the botanical gardens."

Slowly, I turn my eyes on my business partner. "How do you know that?"

Looking rather sheepish, he rubs the back of his neck. "I didn't take a carriage. I rode here and sneaked in."

It takes me several minutes to process his words. "How did you know where to find us?"

Sebastian scrunches his nose and looks away. Even Avery looks guilty.

"What aren't you telling me?" I demand.

"You have to understand." Sebastian steps a hair closer. "We were concerned. Overnight, you became some sort of legend in Teirn. Everywhere we went, people were speaking about you—you had a stalker, Lucia."

"Actually, I had a dressmaker's steward," I point out.

The music pauses as the quartet prepares for their next set, and someone hollers, heckling them. One of the guards steps into the light, looking menacing enough the man backs off.

I turn back to Avery and Sebastian and get back to the point. "What did the two of you do?"

Avery crosses his arms, smirking in a wicked way. "What do you think we did?"

Groaning, I drop my forehead into my hands. "You put another tracking spell on me."

"On your new dagger, actually," Sebastian corrects. "What did you expect us to do after you chase dark strangers through the castle and corner them in supply cubbies?"

I look at them through my fingers. "The two of you came up with this?"

The men glance at each other and then shrug. I drop my hands, my irritation changing to amused satisfaction. "Look at you both, working together."

Avery snorts, but Sebastian only shakes his head.

"We'll deal with your subterfuge later." I glance around, taking particular note of the guards. "But for now, how do we get out of here?"

We end up leaving the masquerade with all the other guests. Anytime we'd venture too close to the exit, the burly guards would magically appear. And by magically, I mean they would lumber over and glare at us.

Sebastian slips into the night as soon as we're in the courtyard, and Avery and I find our carriage. The first light of dawn stains the eastern horizon pink by the time we make it back to the castle grounds.

Though there are surely people awake in the kitchens, the gardens are still fast asleep. Birds have returned in the warming weather, and they sing and twitter from the trees as we make our way through the maze of shrubs and sleeping flowers.

"Lucia," Avery says, tugging me back before we reach the main entrance.

I turn and find him directly behind me. "Your mask."

Before I can remove it myself, his fingers deftly untie the knot, and the soft fabric slips from my face. The morning air is cold without it, and the breeze caresses my skin. He must have removed his moments ago.

Without another word, the captain offers me the silken fabric. I stare at it for a moment before I slip it into a pocket in my cloak. Hiding a yawn behind my hand, I turn to continue our walk back. Again, Avery stops me. This time, he steps close. Our hands brush, but he doesn't attempt to take mine.

"I have to ask you a question." His voice is quiet in the early morning, barely loud enough to compete with the birds. His expression is curious, maybe a bit hopeful, but he looks like he's trying to quell the emotion.

Nervous, I worry my lip and nod for him to continue.

"Do you remember anything that happened after you sipped the potion? Any of our...conversation?"

Worry coils in my stomach, smothering any flutters I might have been feeling a moment ago. What did my mind block out?

I shake my head. "Only tiny bits—memories that are more like paintings than life."

Covering what appears to be disappointment with an easy smile, he nods.

Terrified to ask, but knowing I must, I focus on his doublet. "Why?"

A bright and carefree expression slides over his features, loosening his limbs, tugging at his lips in a roguish manner. "It just so happens you confessed your undying love for me. You might have mentioned how handsome I am...smart...cunning. Dashing was likely in there as well."

Slowly, my muscles relax, and I let out a breathy laugh. He's teasing, but there's something he's not telling me. I attempt a flirty grin. "Well, if that's all."

His expression becomes thoughtful, and he's so close, his chin brushes my jaw. So softly I wouldn't hear him if we were any farther apart, he says, "You also said I smelled like the *air before a storm*. Rather poetic, don't you think?"

Slowly, I draw back until I can see his eyes. He does smell like the air before a storm—I said that. I almost remember it. I gulp, overwhelmed. What else did I say?

"Avery?" I whisper.

"Hmmm?" His eyes have dropped to my lips, and he's looking far too serious for my liking.

"Please—tell me the truth. Did I say anything else?"

He pulls his eyes from my lips and meets my gaze. "Yes," he breathes.

My chest clenches. I have a strong desire to flee, run away before I learn more, but my feet are rooted to the garden soil.

A hint of a teasing smile crosses his face, taking my breath away. "But you went and passed out before I could reply."

"It was the elixir," I whisper. Though I'm still not sure what I said, from the way he's looking at me, I have a pretty good idea.

"I know."

He's waiting for more, but I turn and continue toward the castle. He falls into step next to me. When I glance at him, he looks over, raising his eyebrows in question.

"I made a fool of myself, didn't I?" I blurt out, my throat growing thick.

Stopping me, he takes me by the shoulders and boldly meets my gaze. "I swear to you, Lucia, nothing you said was foolish."

I think he's going to say something else. He even opens his mouth briefly, but then he shakes his head and begins walking again. I follow, befuddled. Without looking at me, he slips his hand into mine, and we continue the rest of the way together in silence.

CHAPTER TWENTY-FOUR
The Lower Entrance

I haven't set foot on the Greybrow Serpent for over two weeks, and a visit was long overdue. I had Mason and Jeb come to the castle a few days ago to collect Flink so Avery and I could go to the masquerade. The dragon was restless anyway, tired of his lead and harness. I only hope he behaved himself.

Though the sun has not quite risen, the crew is awake. The salty smell of the sea surrounds me, makes me nostalgic for something I never thought I'd miss. But I'm not sure if it's the ocean I long for or the time I spent on the water, trapped with the ship's captain. Gulls cry overhead, and I feel as if they're mocking me.

After sleeping a good part of yesterday, I feel rejuvenated this morning. Avery's crew calls out their greetings, many of them teasing me, asking how life is in the castle. I smile and wave as I track down the ship's boys.

Finally, I find them tossing pieces of fish to Flink, just to see if the dragon can catch them. Flink appears to be delighted with the game, and he races about the deck, leaping to catch each piece.

I lean against the rail and watch them for several minutes before I finally make myself known. "It seems he was better this time?"

Startled, the boys glance over at me, and then they stand a little straighter. When they see that it's only me—more specifically, that Adeline didn't accompany me—they relax. Jeb grins. "He got into the captain's cabin again."

Groaning, I bury my face in my hands. "Did he break anything?"

"Not this time. He seemed happier in there, so we let him sleep on a shield he pulled from the wall."

Avery's not going to love that.

"We baited him out with food, just like you did last time." Mason holds up a dead mackerel as a visual aid. "It worked like a charm."

With a full belly and a peaceful night's sleep, Flink happily trots to me. I kneel in front of him to give him a good scratch. "I hear you had a good night."

He wrinkles his snout and lets out a long, lazy yawn. Shaking my head, I clip his lead to his harness.

Before I leave, I thank the boys for watching him.

But I do not leave the Serpent quite yet.

"Good morning, Gregory," I say to the mage once I find him.

Before he can answer, there is a loud explosion, followed by a billowing cloud of dark black smoke. Coughing, I blindly search for my way into the light.

"Sorry about that," the mage says brightly once the smoke clears. "I didn't see you there."

"Another spell gone wrong?" I ask, eying the pewter charm in his hand.

Gregory grins. "No, that one worked."

I almost ask him what purpose something like that would serve, but I have something else on my mind. "Where's Yancey?"

Gregory frowns, thinking hard as he runs a hand through his dark hair. His nose and cheeks are tinged with soot, and it's hard to take him seriously. "I don't think I've seen him for several days, and I haven't left the ship."

"Several days?" I ask, incredulous.

"I'm not his keeper, *Lady* Siren Slayer." He raises an eyebrow, teasing me.

"Apparently, you've left the Serpent a few times."

"No need." He flashes me an uncharacteristic grin. "The gossip is happy to find us here."

I roll my eyes. "Do me a favor. Send a courier my

way when Yancey returns."

"Is everything all right?"

"Yes, I just have a few questions for him."

Though the duke's son has never formally studied alchemy, he might be able to help me. I'm looking for a concoction I can take that will revive my memory, and I don't trust any of the local apothecaries in the city—not now.

I pause before I leave the ship and turn back. Hesitant due to the lingering smoke and the memory of the snowstorm, I say, "Gregory, perhaps you could help me."

"I'll do what I can."

"I know alchemy's not in your usual line of expertise, but I drank something I shouldn't have, and now it seems I have a bit of memory loss. Is there anything you can whip up for that?"

"Drank something you shouldn't have?" Gregory laughs and shakes his head. "I'm afraid you'll just have to hope for the best. Perhaps eat more fish."

"Eat...fish?" I cross my arms, skeptical.

Chuckling, he taps his head and wanders away, calling over his shoulder, "It's good for the brain."

"Very helpful, Master Gregory!" I laugh, shaking my head. "Thank you so much!"

"I cannot believe you went to one of the masquerades,

and you didn't take me!"

Adeline's not exactly happy with us. She knew something was amiss when we were all absent yesterday, sleeping our night off, but apparently, she didn't expect it to be *this*.

"I thought you all ate something off!" She glares at Sebastian, Avery, and me all in turn. Sebastian, however, gets the brunt of her ire.

"To be fair," I say, defending myself, "I didn't tell Sebastian either. He just crashed the party."

The four of us sit in the small tea room off Adeline's quarters, trying to decide what to do. Sebastian, who took no oath before he sneaked into the masquerade, was able to tell Adeline where we'd been and what we'd seen. Avery and I are mute on the subject, no matter how we try to be clever with our words. We can, however speak of Dante and his elixir, since we swore no oath to stay mum about that.

"First things first—we have to warn Serena," Sebastian says.

I groan just thinking about it. Something tells me the dressmaker won't take the news well.

Sebastian shoots me a look. "She should be made aware that her husband is in on this."

We all agree, though Avery and Adeline look uncomfortable as well. There's nothing fun about announcing to a woman that her husband is a villain.

"After that," Sebastian continues, "I believe we should leave Teirn. There's no reason for us to linger. In a roundabout way, the larkwing has been returned to its owner. The job is finished, and there is nothing left for us here."

My gaze drifts to Avery. The captain stayed in Teirn to heal, but he's well now. When we first arrived, he tired easily, but he showed no signs of extreme exhaustion at the masquerade, and we were out until morning. Does that mean he'll go back to the sea? Take his ship and sail into the sunset, leaving me on the shore, pining over something that never came to be?

"But what about Dante and his Lark and Song?" I shift, uncomfortable with where my thoughts have traveled. "Shouldn't we do something?"

Avery and Adeline stay silent, but Sebastian thinks about it. "I believe it's our duty as citizens of Kalae to inform the king of what we learned last night. But this is a job for the royal guards. We're not warriors, Lucia. There's not really anything we can do."

"I don't believe Dante will allow us to walk away at this point," Avery says. "We know too much—we're a liability now."

Adeline bites her bottom lip, and her eyes dart between us. Sebastian thinks about it, not immediately protesting Avery's words. If nothing else, I am happy to say the two are learning to get along.

The room goes quiet, all of us lost in our own thoughts. Flink, who's fast asleep on the rug in the middle of the floor, snuffles loudly, and then rolls onto his back, legs up in the air. His front foot twitches as if he's dreaming, and he makes tiny grunting noises. With every breath, he puffs out a small sparkling cloud of elemental glitter.

"He's cold." Adeline promptly snatches a throw blanket from the back of Sebastian's chair, yanking him forward as she pulls it free, and then drapes it over the dragon. Flink immediately goes still, and he cuddles farther into the soft fabric.

Sebastian shakes his head, bewildered, and then gets back to the issue at hand. "We'll speak with the king, see what he says on the matter. For now, do not give Dante an answer either way."

Avery relaxes against the back of my chair, at ease. "And if I want to invest in their business?"

I can tell from his tone he's only trying to get a rise out of Sebastian—and it works. My business partner turns an interesting shade of red and opens his mouth to argue with the captain.

"He's not serious, Sebastian," I say.

Sebastian doesn't look entirely convinced, but it doesn't affect him anyway. Though it's beginning to feel like it, what with the two of us searching for the sea fire ruby and all, Avery's not part of our business.

He can do whatever he likes—even invest in Dante's illegal potions venture.

I, however, believe the captain's moral compass is stronger than he'd like us to give him credit for.

"All right," I say, standing. "First, we must speak to Serena."

"With all her demands for confidentiality, I'm not sure she'd like the four of us barging into her shoppe," Avery points out.

"Then Adeline and I will go," I say, motioning to the seamstress. "Addy, you'll have to do the talking. I'm afraid my tongue's tied."

Sebastian turns to Adeline. "Do you think you know the situation well enough to explain?"

Adeline gives him a withering look, about fed up with his coddling. "Yes, Sebastian, I think I can handle it."

"Then I'll set up an audience with the king," Avery says. Set with all our tasks, we split up. Before Adeline and I are out the door, Avery sets his hand on my arm. "Take Flink with you, all right?"

I give him an incredulous look. "You don't think Serena will mind an unruly lesser dragon in her shoppe?"

"It would make me feel better," he says quietly, real concern in his expression.

And my foolish heart gets all mushy. I know I can

protect myself, and Adeline, should it come down to it, but it's nice to know he cares.

"Come on, Flink," I call to the dragon.

Jolted from slumber, the beast snorts, sneezes once, and then stumbles to his feet. He lets me clip on his lead, and then we're out the door.

Because it's such a nice day, and because it's not as easy as you might think to convince a carriage driver to accept a two hundred pound "munchkin," Adeline and I decide to walk to Serena's shoppe. Trying to look casual, we stop for lunch at an open-air restaurant that boasts herb-rubbed, blackened fish (all for the memory cause), so we don't arrive at the dressmaker's until nearly two in the afternoon.

Just like last time, the doors are locked. But the shutters are closed as well, and the building has a strange feel to it. No one answers when Adeline knocks.

"I don't understand," Adeline says, frowning. "It's the middle of the week. Someone should be here."

A bad feeling settles in my chest, and I knock on the door, louder this time. "It's Lucia and Adeline," I call, hoping if someone is inside, they'll let us in.

To my surprise, the lock softly clicks, and the door barely cracks open.

"Are you alone?" Serena's assistant whispers.

I stand closer to the door and turn casually as if I'm still waiting for an answer, just in case we're being watched. "We are."

"Go to the milliner's. He's three businesses down. Ask to speak to Georgie. Tell him you need to access the lower entrance of Serena's shoppe."

I frown as I listen to the instruction. "Sorry, Adeline," I say loudly. "It doesn't look as if anyone is here after all."

Adeline looks thoroughly bewildered, but she catches on and nods. Then loudly, in a stilted voice, she says, "Oh...well. Hmmm. Too bad."

She's as good a performer as my mother.

"Come on." I give Flink's lead a tug.

Instead of heading straight to the milliner's, we casually stop in at the cobbler's shoppe across the street, and then Adeline buys a soft blue scarf from the tailor next door. Finally, we step into the milliner's shoppe. The air is a touch too warm, and it smells like leather and the curing liquids used to form the hats.

A plump, friendly-looking man looks up from a form. "May I help you?" Then he sees my dragon, and his eyes light up. "Hello, there! That's the largest munchkin I've seen in my life!"

I give him a one-shouldered shrug. "He ate a strange mushroom when he was a hatchling. Say, are you Georgie?"

"I am."

I settle against his desk. "Are you a friend of Serena's?"

Looking a tad bit concerned at my blunt tone, he sets his glue aside, wipes his hands on a cloth, and stands. "She's my cousin, on my mother's side. Is something the matter?"

"Possibly." I frown out the window, watching for suspicious-looking characters. The problem is, I'm not sure what "suspicious-looking" *looks* like exactly. "We think her shoppe is being watched. Her assistant has locked herself inside, and she whispered instructions that we were to ask you about a back entrance."

"Ah." The shopkeeper nods, his jolly expression fading. "She's been acting strange these last few weeks." He stands and motions us toward the back. "And it's not a back entrance, but a lower one."

We follow Georgie into what looks like a storage room to the rear of the shoppe. I expect him to lead us out a back door, but there isn't one. I flash Adeline a look. These people are all crazy. I think Sebastian's right—it's about time we get out of Teirn. But I can't leave until I know Serena and her assistant are all right.

As soon as the shopkeeper begins moving boxes, I realize what he's about. Sure enough, he reveals a trap door in the floor. "You have a candle?"

"I've got it," Adeline says, and then, like it's as easy as breathing, she conjures a light charm in the palm of her hand.

I grin at her. "You're handy to have around. Have I told you that?"

Sighing, looking as if she feels quite under-appreciated, Adeline shakes her head. "Not nearly enough."

"I'll work on that."

Flink insists on going first down the stairs, and I have no reason to argue with him, so I let him lead. Adeline's right behind me, and before we're out of sight, Georgie says, "Be careful, and come right on up when you're done. I'll keep the door unlocked for you."

"Thank you so much, sir." Adeline says the words sincerely, flashing him a smile that's sure to make him melt.

As expected, his cheeks go pink, and he stutters. Luckily, I'm already in the tunnel, because I can't help a tiny eye roll.

"What's with all these secret tunnels?" Adeline asks, sticking close.

"The whole city's riddled with them."

"But Gerard said the king's guards have searched all of Teirn and never found any."

I glance over my shoulder. "Well, they're lying. We've been here a month and found an entire network."

Serena's shoppe is close, so we don't have to walk far. Surprisingly, this tunnel is another direct one, like the cottage to the scholar's guild. There are no offshoots, no doors to other shoppes. Very strange.

We climb the stairs and then quietly knock on the trapdoor that should lead into Serena's shoppe. I turn to Adeline as we wait. It's taking Serena's assistant a long time to answer.

"Do you think she's all right?" Adeline whispers.

"I'm sure they're fine," I say, though I'm not convinced. Hoping to ease Adeline's fears, I change the subject while we wait. "Did you notice that the confections shoppe we passed had macaroons? I wouldn't mind buying—"

I stop short when the trapdoor opens, but it's not Serena's assistant on the other side.

"Hello, Lucia," Dante says cordially.

Startled, I take a step back. "Dante! What are...I mean. *Hello.*"

What is he doing here?

Trying to act as if he didn't catch us sneaking into the dressmaker's shoppe through a secret tunnel in the ground, I smile. "So, Dante, I don't suppose Serena is in?"

"She's gone." He casually crosses his arms and leans against the stone wall. "So, tell me, what business did you have with Serena?"

Gone. *Gone?* What does that mean?

I meet his eyes, trying not to look nervous. Flink's with us after all. He might be worthless most of the time, but he's useful in a scuffle. "We came to inform her that we weren't able to track down the larkwing."

Lies, more lies. Will they ever end?

"Really?" He smiles. "Are you sure you weren't here to warn her that her husband is involved with a group of elixir-making alchemists, and that it would be best if she were to flee before he arrives back in Teirn? I hope not—because I think I mentioned that I didn't want you speaking of the masquerades or our meeting." His eyes flash to Adeline. "Not to anyone."

Well, this isn't going as well as I had hoped. I nudge Adeline back.

"How could I do that?" I say, mock offended. "I was charmed into secrecy. In fact, if my friend here knows about your involvement, perhaps it's because you just admitted it yourself."

He chuckles. "That is a valid argument, but she doesn't look nearly startled enough to see I'm alive, now does she?"

I elbow Adeline in the side. "Act surprised, Adeline."

She gasps in a most unconvincing way, which earns another smile from Dante.

"Funny." He takes a step down. "Pretty and amusing, Lucia. What a deadly combination that is."

Picking up on my anxiousness, Flink growls as Dante approaches. The man pauses to look at the beast.

"Stay where you are," I say, my tone far bolder than I feel. "He's barely trained, and I have no idea what he might do if you get too close."

That, unfortunately, is not a lie.

"We were going to work *together*, Lucia," he says, pulling his eyes from my dragon. He looks truly disappointed. "I so hoped you'd come to me willingly. I like you. I really do."

We walk backward as he talks, but Flink's eyes stay trained on Dante. If we can just make it to Georgie's shoppe...

"You know I'm not going to let you leave, right?"

"I figured you were going to try, but I honestly think I can take you." Dante's not a small man, but what I lack in size I make up for in spunk.

"You are Kalae's siren slayer—I have no doubt. But I don't like to get my hands dirty, so I don't exactly fight fair."

To my surprise, and Adeline's great horror, he pulls a bottle from his pocket and splashes us with a blue liquid that smells an awful lot like rotten fruit.

Nothing happens.

I gape at him. "What was the point of that?"

Dante holds up a hand. "Give it a minute."

But we don't because that would be insane. I turn around and give Adeline a shove. It's all the boost she needs. We run toward Georgie's door, but Dante doesn't even bother to chase us.

"I liked this dress!" Adeline pants. Then she looks over her shoulder and hollers at Dante, "You better hope this washes out, or I will be sending you a bill!"

"Run, Adeline!" I gasp, giving her a hefty push. I don't know what this stuff does, but I have a feeling we don't want to be trapped in the tunnel with Dante when it takes effect.

We rush up the stairs, and I fling the trap door open. "Move—I have to lock it!" I yell, shoving Adeline aside.

Georgie rushes into the back, horrified. He wrings his hands at his waist. "What happened? Where's Serena?"

"We don't know!" I pant. "Lock your door when we leave. Better yet—go home for the day."

"But I..."

I have no idea what he says because I'm dragging Adeline into the street. Flink runs beside us, unsure whether this is a fun game or if something's wrong. But something is *very* wrong, because as soon as we're in the open, a dragonfly lands on my arm. Then a butterfly, and a moth, and another dragonfly.

"LUCIA!" Adeline shrieks, flailing.

They're everywhere, swarming us from all different directions. Flink panics and roars out his sparkling flame, but he doesn't manage to hit us with it.

"Flink! On US!" I scream as I spin in circles, frantically trying to free myself of the insects. They're all over me, crawling with their tiny feet, tickling my skin with their horrible wings.

Adeline faints dead away.

Men come at us from Serena's shoppe, and I start to panic. "FLINK!"

He roars out another flame in the wrong direction, but this time I jump right into it. The effect is almost instantaneous. Suddenly, the insects flee—right onto Adeline.

Oh well. She's unconscious anyway.

I tug on Flink's lead, trying to get him to face her. "Again, Flink! Do it again!"

He looks at me, cocking his scaled head to the side, confused and overwhelmed. It's still not something he does on command—yet another thing I need to work on.

Fortunately, he feels threatened by Dante's men, and he roars out a flame in their direction. I grasp hold of Adeline's arm—trying not to think of how many winged creatures I just crushed, and manage to drag her into the cloud of magic. Like smoke leaving an extinguished flame, the insects fly away from Adeline, no longer interested.

The men gape at us on the street, along with dozens of spectators. I'm not sure how well Dante thought through his plan because there are witnesses aplenty.

I step over Adeline's still-unconscious form and pull my dark dagger from the sheath at my side. Already, shopkeepers are gathering around me, offering protection from Dante's two burly men.

"Leave us," I say, growing far more confident now that I have backup.

The men hold up their hands, and one acts all innocent as he says, "We were just trying to help you, my lady. Never seen anything like it before."

I narrow my eyes, seeing right through his lies. "We're fine now."

They nod and turn down the street. I'm swarmed with questions, but my eyes are on Serena's shoppe. I can just make out a figure in the window—Dante. He watches us intently. Slowly, my eyes drop to Flink. It's the dragon he's focused on, but why? After several more heartbeats, the drape falls closed.

Hoping we're safe for the moment, I sheath my dagger. The silversmith's son pulls Adeline into his arms, ready to carry her to safety. Too bad she's not awake to enjoy it—he's quite handsome.

"She's breathing, and her pulse is normal," Adeline's knight in shining armor says.

"Thank goodness." I was worried she might have hit her head on the cobblestones when she fell...or when I dragged her over to Flink.

The well-meaning crowd presses closer. I try to answer the people's questions as best as I am able, but I don't quite know what happened myself. Obviously, the potion was a bait—likely for the larkwings. Perhaps it's what Serena's husband is using right now as he searches for another butterfly. I sniff my arm and grimace.

Though the magic is gone, we still reek.

"You should take her home," the tailor says, turning to Adeline.

Of all days to leave the carriage behind.

"Do you mind carrying her to the stable?" I say to the handsome man holding my friend. "I hate to ask."

He glances at her and gives her a dimpled smile. "Not in the least, but why don't you take my family's carriage?"

Oh, wait until I tell her about this.

"We would be so appreciative," I tell him.

In just a few minutes, the man who I learn is named Curtis deposits Adeline into the waiting carriage. After he sets her on the velveteen seat, he brushes a few stray curls away from her face, seeming reluctant to leave her.

"You should come with us," I say, my voice dry. "It's your carriage after all."

Curtis glances at me, looking a bit embarrassed.

But not embarrassed enough to decline. "You'll need someone to carry her out when you reach your destination."

"Naturally."

He sits next to the seamstress. Weary, knowing Sebastian is going to yell at me, I boot Flink into the carriage and crawl over him to the bench opposite Adeline and her new admirer.

I realize as soon as we're going down the road that I might have made a great error in judgment—what if the silversmith was in on the ruse? We would have been trapped with no way to escape.

Fortunately, Curtis is simply a helpful bystander. We roll over the drawbridge, under the portcullis, and make our way through the buildings to the castle's main courtyard.

I'm growing concerned, though. I fully expected Adeline to wake by now, but she's still unconscious.

"Do you mind carrying her in?" I ask Curtis, though I already know the answer.

He once again pulls Adeline into his arms with relish. He doesn't even seem to mind the sickly-sweet stink of Dante's concoction.

Courtiers and the castle staff all gasp when they see us exit the carriage, and the commotion is just enough to finally bring Adeline to her senses. She blinks, groans softly, and then freezes when she meets

Curtis's gaze.

"Hello," he murmurs.

All she can manage is a tiny peep.

Then she shudders, probably remembering why she passed out. "Lucia," she says and then frantically turns her head, looking for me.

"I'm here," I assure her as we make our way inside the massive double doors.

"What was it he covered us in?"

"I don't really want to talk about it," I say, shuddering.

She thinks about it a moment, shivers herself, and then nods.

We finally reach the main foyer, pressing our way through dozens of people—they just keep gathering. News travels quickly for such a large castle, and in only moments, Avery and Sebastian come running from the throne room, throwing open the doors like dashing heroes of old.

Sebastian takes one look at Curtis, and his expression goes to stone. But Avery only has eyes for me. He pushes people aside without as much as an "excuse me," and then he roughly takes me by the shoulders, scowling as he looks me over. "What *happened* to you?"

"Dante."

The captain's eyes go hard, and his eyebrows draw low. "Did he hurt you?"

I give him a small, cocky smile. "*Please*—he never caught us."

That breaks through his stormy exterior, and he shakes his head, laughing under his breath.

Shortly after Sebastian and Avery's grand entrance, the king and queen walk through the doors. The crowds part, giving them room to pass.

Harold looks shocked, but Minerva wears a repulsed look on her face. She motions her hand over my stained outfit. "What is *that*?"

"Some sort of butterfly bait," I tell her.

"But why...?" She looks at me as if I purposely doused myself in the stuff.

I am happy to say I am smart enough to keep my mouth shut. Even I know it's a bad idea to sass the queen.

"Take Adeline to the infirmary," Harold says, and then he frowns at me. "Lady Lucia, do you need medical attention as well?"

"I'm fine."

"Then come with me, all of you." With that, His Majesty turns on his heel and returns to his throne room.

CHAPTER TWENTY-FIVE
Disappearing Dragon

I shove another dress in my trunk and then sit on it when it won't latch. I huff out a breath, feeling rather melancholy.

Our audience with King Harold didn't go quite the way I expected. We were thanked for the information, and then politely told to leave the mess to the royal guards, asked to travel into one of the other provinces where it's safe. Apparently, the king is concerned about the man who visited him while we were in Fermall—one of Dante's lackeys, no doubt. He's been back several times, but Harold refused to give him any information on my whereabouts.

Queen Minerva told Avery that he, of course, was welcome to stay. I have no idea what he'll do. Probably head back to sea.

After fully laying on the trunk, sprawled out on my belly like a cat in the sun, I'm finally able to snap the latch closed. I lie here, legs dangling, feet and calves resting on the floor, feeling melancholy.

We've never left a job feeling so unfinished. What happens now? Is Serena safe? Will Dante come after us anyway? Surely, he won't let us go—we know too much.

Flink shuffles around the room, copper-scaled tail dragging on the floor, sniffing about like a pig. He's bored of Teirn, and I don't blame him. I wouldn't want a lead snapped on me every time I left my room either. He needs to stretch his legs and tiny flightless wings, get some fresh air.

Maybe that's what I need too. I let my head dangle toward the floor, not bothering to move even when a knock sounds on my door.

"It's open," I call from my precarious perch on the trunk.

Adeline pokes her head in the room. Knowing me as she does, she doesn't even give me a strange look when she spots me. "Sebastian says a boy will be up for the trunks in a few minutes. Have you packed everything?"

"Mmmhmm," I hum.

She waits a moment and then steps into the room, shutting the door behind her. "Are you all right?"

"Mmmhmm."

Kneeling in front of me, letting her long golden-rod skirts pool on the floor around her, she meets my eyes. "Have you talked to him?"

"Dante? No, I think we've had plenty of closure."

Adeline gives me a wry smile. "Avery."

Just his name makes my stomach churn.

"About what?" I ask, purposely being obtuse.

"You know what." She frowns. "Will you sit up? I feel like I'm having a conversation with a squirrel. And isn't all the blood rushing to your head? That can't be comfortable."

I puff out my cheeks and slowly exhale as I slide off the trunk and plop onto the floor, crossing my legs like a child. Adeline shakes her head. "You're a mess over him, aren't you?"

"No," I lie.

"So, it won't bother you at all that King Harold is going to send him to Marlane to retrieve a shipment of gold from the island mine?"

My jaw twitches, and the air whooshes from my lungs, making me feel as if the wind was knocked right out of me.

Gently, she says, "The king just asked him to go. I was there, speaking with Minerva, so I'm afraid I over-heard."

"What was his answer?"

Adeline's face softened. "He sent a courier with a message to prepare his crew."

The news is a blow to my heart, and it takes me a moment to process it.

"He's scared, Lucia," she insists, refusing to leave me alone. "And so are you. It's the most ridiculous thing—both of you are big, brave adventurers, and yet you cannot admit that you love each other."

She looks like she wants to go on—try to make me talk about my feelings of all things, but the captain himself knocks once and then walks in the room.

Trying to keep things light though I feel like I'm floundering, I raise an eyebrow. "What if I'd been indecent?"

A swift smile flashes across his face. "I would have forgiven you."

Adeline stands quickly, giving me a stern look as she makes her way to the door. "Captain Greybrow, Lucia was just telling me she needed to speak with you."

Once again, my companions had all better be glad I don't know magic, because Adeline would get a taste of it right now. I give her a hard smile as I imagine a little black rain cloud sprouting up over her head, raining all over her silk and velvet gown, making her perfect curls frizzy.

She frowns at me from behind Avery and hurries

into the hall. I stare at the closed door for several moments before I finally let my eyes stray to the captain.

He settles against the wall, crossing his arms and boot-clad feet, watching me expectantly. My heart goes a few degrees cooler when I notice he's wearing his captain's jacket.

"You seem to have healed well." I don't quite meet his eyes, and I busy myself with a few remaining trinkets on the dressing table—which is a mistake, because the last of them is Flink's gold ball. There are so many memories there. I fumble it, and the ball falls to the floor, much to Flink's delight.

It's the strangest thing; when Sebastian rejected me, I felt intense sadness. I hurt for days. But the thought of Avery leaving—it's not the same. Instead of a sharp, painful moment that heals after the initial shock, this is a burning sensation in my core—a slow, gnawing wound that feels as if it will consume me before it dies out.

"I feel fine," he answers.

I nod. "Good."

Silence.

"Lucia..."

That's all he says, just my name. I ignore him for a moment, and then I look back. "What?"

"Sebastian says you are headed back to Reginae to get Adeline settled in Uncle Selden's shoppe."

And here I am, nodding again. I wait for Avery to volunteer something, but he's unusually tight-lipped.

"And I understand you are sailing to Marlane?" I finally say, unable to stop myself. And, oh, the words come out very bitter.

He glances at the door Adeline just exited through. "I—"

"I'm sure the pay is good." I turn away, but I look at him over my shoulder. "Perhaps even better than the illegal Lark and Song business."

"You said you loved me," he says bluntly. When I whip back to him, he crosses his arms. His eyes are guarded, but he holds his ground. "At the masquerade. Did you mean it? Or was it the elixir?"

Fear—real, true fear slices right through. Things still aren't the same between Sebastian and me—they most likely never will be, and we have years and years of history knitting us together. What if I admit my feelings, hand Avery my heart, and he doesn't want it? I know that he said he did, but how much was real? How much was the magic of the island, making him think he felt things he didn't actually feel?

I wait too long to answer, or perhaps he misinterprets the panic on my face. He pushes away from the wall and walks right for me. But what breaks my heart is the way he hides away anything he might be feeling behind his roguish smile. It's fake; I know it is. Know

289

it like I know my own heart.

"Tell me the truth—how much will you miss me when I'm gone?" he asks, pretending he never spoke his last words. "Will you pine for me, perhaps write poetry in your journal, count the days until I return?"

He's making light of the moment, sweeping it under the rug...trying to take it back. I have no idea how to decipher his actions.

The simple truth is, whatever happened between us was real on the island. *Real.* But that was a different a time, a different life.

What does location matter? a desperate voice whispers in my head. *Love is love.*

But love ruins everything. It makes things awkward and painful and sad—just look at Sebastian and me.

Yet, something deep down tells me it can be brilliant—blindingly beautiful. And maybe, just maybe, Avery and I have a chance at that. But if one of us doesn't fess up...then it dies—becomes a regret, a painful "what if."

A sad little trinket in the jewelry box of your memory that's too painful to take out, but sometimes you do anyway, just because you cannot let yourself forget.

And I can't have that. I will be brave.

I open my mouth to confess how I feel, my skin

all prickly with nerves, when yet another knock sounds at the door. "Lady Lucia?" a boy calls through the thick wood. "We're here to collect your trunk."

And then it happens so fast. Avery moves aside, opening the door for the group of boys who have come for my things, and steps into the hall. With a cocky jerk of his chin and crooked grin, he turns back to look at me from the doorway. "Keep out of trouble while I'm away, Lady Adventuress."

Exasperated, I shake my head, trying to see past the young men hauling about my things. "Avery—"

"That's a girl—no more of this 'captain' nonsense."

The boys seem to be everywhere, all at once. And when did I collect this much *stuff*? It takes several moments, but finally, they leave. Luckily, Avery's still at the door. Maybe he's not quite so eager to go after all.

"Don't leave like this," I say.

His facade flickers for a moment, and his next words sound sincere. "Go with your business partner, Lucia. Take care of Adeline. I'll give you some breathing room, but I will find you again—and that's a promise. This isn't over."

I cross my arms, growing angry. "Are you really doing this? Isn't it a bit dramatic, even for you?"

"Possibly. But I like it when you chase after me." With a wink and that awful grin I've come to love so much, he closes the door, making his grand exit.

I groan, irritated with him—irritated with myself. What's wrong with us? My gut tells me he loves me... well, I'm almost eighty-percent certain. Adeline was right—the captain is *scared*. He's just as pathetic as I am.

And it is insane—completely mad—that two reasonably logical adults can act this way.

But can I run after him? Oh, no. Not after he said that!

I growl into my hands and then smack the door. I can be the bigger person—I will not let my pride be our undoing. "Fine!" I yell at the door. "You win!"

With the full intention of running after the captain, just like he wants, I turn to grab Flink's lead. But then I stop. I twirl in a full circle, growing nervous.

"Flink?" I call. "Flink!" I rip apart the room, even checking in places that are too small for him to disappear into.

The dragon's gone. Where did he go? When did he leave? He must have slipped out with my trunks.

But discarded, on the ground, lies his golden ball. He never gives it up, not unless I trade him for food. Dread builds in my belly, and the sensation becomes full-out fear. *He'd never leave without the ball, not unless someone baited him.*

Someone took Flink.

I go tearing into the hall, praying I'm wrong. If I

am, the copper-colored reptile is about to get a very strongly-worded lecture about wandering off. But I don't find the dragon. Instead, I spot a man who looks like a respectable captain but swaggers like a pirate.

"Avery!"

The captain turns back, grinning. "To tell you the truth, I thought it would take a little longer."

CHAPTER TWENTY-SIX
Breaking and Entering

"He's gone!" I holler to Avery, nearly tripping on a rug as I jog after him.

"Who's gone?"

"Flink." Breathless, I come to a stop in front of him, my insides knotting with apprehension. "Dante took him, I'm sure of it."

The captain looks bewildered, and he cocks his head ever so slightly to the side. "Dante...took your dragon?"

I don't like the incredulous look he's giving me. "Yes!"

"Why would he do that?"

"I don't know—but you should have seen how he looked at Flink when he saw him neutralize his potion. He wants him."

Avery frowns, looking a bit like a person would before they're about to patronize a small child with a vivid imagination. "Lucia, Flink hasn't exactly been a model pet—"

"Are you trying to tell me he took himself on a walk? Clipped his lead to his harness?"

The captain's certainty flickers, but he's still not swayed. "Maybe you misplaced—"

Growling in frustration, I stalk away from him.

"Where are you going?" Avery calls to me.

I look over my shoulder and pin him with my glare. "To find Sebastian. *He'll* believe me."

It's a low blow, and I almost feel guilty about the wicked satisfaction I get from the irritation that crosses his face. Almost.

"Lucia, stop."

Ignoring him, I continue down the hall.

"I'll help you look for him." He has to jog to catch up with me.

I shoot him another venomous look. "Don't you have a ship to captain?"

He stops me with a soft hand on my shoulder, forcing me to stop. When I refuse to look at him, he takes my chin and tilts it toward him, making me meet his eyes. "Now listen—though I don't think Dante stole Flink, I know the dragon is important to you. Therefore, the dragon is important to me. I will help you

295

find him."

"I thought you were leaving."

"And I thought you were going back to Reginae."

We stare at each other for several moments, neither of us yielding...but neither of us walking away either.

"Perhaps we should check your ship first," I finally say, giving in. "Just in case he wandered that way again."

"Let's find Sebastian and Adeline, let them know he's missing. They can look for him as well."

I nod, and to my horror, my eyes begin to sting.

Avery makes a soft, slightly amused noise, and yanks me to him, crushing me to his chest. "Look at you, hardened Lady Siren Slayer, all weepy over a missing dragon."

Because he's being sweet, and because it feels so very good to be in his arms, I soften against him and let him hold me for just a moment before we begin our search.

"All right," I say as I pull away. "I'm fine. Let's find Flink."

I was wrong—Sebastian doesn't believe me. Adeline looks like she wants to, but her gaze keeps darting back to my business partner as if she doesn't want to say the wrong thing in front of him.

"There is no way Dante, or anyone else for that matter, wants your dragon, Lucia. He is a menace to society. You are truly the only person with the patience for him."

Well.

I set my hands on my hips and stare him down. "But you'll help look for him."

Sebastian doesn't flinch under my gaze. "Of course."

The relief is instantaneous. "Perhaps you and Adeline can search the castle? We're going to start on Avery's ship, see if there's some chance he wandered there again."

Though I'm only going there so I can convince Avery to go with me to the botanical gardens. I know Dante has Flink, just like I know we don't have much time to get him back. The thought of my poor dragon in the clutches of the insane alchemist makes my stomach churn. My mind wanders to all the ingredients in Dante's shoppe—of the dragon hide and scales and worse, but I shake my head and force myself not to dwell on it.

Avery's crew is already loading the Greybrow Serpent for their next voyage. The sight makes me ill, but I try not to look at the cargo and supplies making their way up the gangplank. It doesn't escape my notice that

Avery tries to ignore it too.

"Gregory!" I holler as soon as I spot the mage.

He glances over, smiling. "I knew you'd come with us, Lucia." Then his eyebrows scrunch together when he sees the look on my face. "What's the matter?"

I explain Flink's disappearance, but unlike Avery and Sebastian, he doesn't immediately push my theory aside. "He left his ball?"

Biting my bottom lip, I nod.

"You might be right."

I shoot Avery a victorious look, but there's no joy in it.

"Given what you've told me, I think there is a chance the alchemist took him."

Avery scratches his ear, probably hoping the mage was going to talk some sense into me—not further convince me. "And why exactly do we think that?"

"A dragon's elemental essence encompasses every part of them. Every scale, every tooth, every drop of blood—" Gregory stops short when he sees the look on my face. Then he clears his throat. "It can all be used in concoctions, and if it's carefully balanced with ingredients with similar characteristics, you can make a powerful potion indeed. A neutralizing concoction would be worth a fortune."

Dante's going to kill Flink.

Without wasting any time, I grasp Avery's arm

and yank him toward the gangplank.

"Wait, Lucia!" Gregory yells.

I look over my shoulder, but I don't slow my pace.

"Yancey hasn't returned," he says. "I just thought you'd like to know."

Fabulous. Now I'm worried about my dragon and the big brute.

"Oh, and Lucia?"

"What?"

"I have some things that might help you if you're going to break into the tunnels."

The last thing we need is a bagful of Gregory's experiments. "There's no time."

"But..."

The mage goes on, but I block him out and drag the captain down the plank. Avery turns back to Gregory, not looking terribly concerned. "If we're not back by sundown, you might send someone to find us."

We've been all over these wretched gardens, but have we found the courtyard with the passage that leads to the tunnels? No.

The day is warm, more spring than late winter. Tinslefoil, one of the earliest flowers of the season, is ablaze with hundreds of tiny orange-red blooms, and the garden is full-to-bursting with them. Because of that, we are far from alone. Couples wander down the flower-lined walkways, heads bent together, not a care in the world. Families enjoy the sunshine as well, and we're never far from the excited squeals of children.

"Why didn't I ask Sebastian where the entrance was?" I say, nearly defeated as we circle the area yet again. We find ourselves at the amphitheater where Madam Lavinia assaulted our ears.

Not ready to give up, Avery scans the perimeter. "It's here somewhere."

"But where?"

Avery frowns as he watches the crowd. After several minutes, his lips tip in a satisfied smile. "Looks like we found ourselves a guide."

"What are you talking..." My words fade as I turn to see who captured the captain's attention.

There, looking as shifty as always, is our dear friend Ivan. He weaves past the crowd, his eyes darting this way and that before he squeezes past two close hedges in a flowerbed.

Without a word, we follow him, pretending we are both very stealthy. To Avery's credit, he actually is stealthy. Me? Not as much. Yet somehow, we still manage to sneak behind the thief without drawing his attention. Twigs catch my hair and scratch my exposed skin as we push through thick brush in this forgotten and untended area of the gardens.

"This must not be the way we traveled in the carriage," I quietly gripe as I struggle with an overgrown evergreen bough.

Avery holds the branch instead of answering, reminding me with his eyes that I need to keep quiet.

Ivan stops just once, standing perfectly still as if he senses something is amiss. Avery pulls me into the safety of another tall hedgerow, and we peer at him through the dense evergreen foliage. Barely breathing, I watch as he scans the path behind him, looking as if he's about to bolt.

Much to my relief, he nods to himself and then continues. Even more careful this time, we continue trailing him. Just when I start to wonder if he's led us on a wild goose chase, we turn a corner, and the courtyard lies in front of us, beckoning us onto its ancient cobblestones. Without so much as a glance behind him, Ivan moves the bench aside, opens the hidden door, and disappears into the black interior.

We wait a minute more, making sure he's not going to pop back out, and cautiously make our way to the entrance. The trail the carriage must have taken goes off into the trees, into the dense forest, off to the left.

Avery studies the road. "It would probably take hours to reach the entrance by foot if you were to go that way."

I eye Avery. "Can you wait to maim Ivan until after I've found Flink?"

A quick grin creases the edges of the captain's handsome eyes. "What makes you think I plan to go after him?"

"Because I know you."

If he wonders why my voice has gone soft, he doesn't mention it. He nods toward the door that leads to the tunnels. "Shall we?"

A tremor of apprehension runs through me. The first time we went down those stairs, we were invited, but that is far from the case now. What will Dante do if he finds us?

But we have no choice, because I will not leave Flink in the hands of a madman.

Avery pulls on the door, but it sticks. "It's locked."

Frustrated, I kneel next to him to study it. Then I angle my head toward him. "Can you pick locks?"

"What do you think?"

Without a word, I slide my dagger from its sheath and hand it to him.

Grinning, he declines the blade and rummages through the deep inside pocket of his jacket.

"Please tell me that's not an actual lockpick kit," I say, covering my eyes with my hand when he unties a leather pouch with an assortment of steel picks.

"I could smash the lock if you'd rather," he says, but he's already gotten to work.

"Pirate," I mutter, but unlike the few times I used the word before, I'm only teasing. Mostly.

It takes a few minutes. I peer over my shoulder the whole time, terrified we're going to be discovered.

Finally, the beautiful sound of a lock clicking open meets my ears, and Avery sits back on his heels, satisfied. After quickly stashing the pouch in his pocket, he opens the door. "After you, Lady Lucia."

I turn to him before I step inside. "Thank you… for coming with me."

"I'd go anywhere with you," he says flippantly. Then his expression changes, and he lowers his voice. "You simply have to *ask*."

There's so much unspoken meaning in those words. The knot in my stomach loosens, and my chest begins to tingle. I find myself leaning forward, close…

And then something crashes through the brush behind us. Instantly, we leap to our feet, both of us reaching for our blades.

The grouse stares at us for several moments and then lets out a squawk before she lowers her head to the ground in search for fallen seeds. I let out an exaggerated breath and grab my chest.

Avery brushes off his embarrassment at being startled by a wild chicken and gestures toward the door once more. "We should probably…"

"Right."

I slip in first, wishing for the lights our previous guide created. Before, the tunnels were mysterious, exciting. But now I find their dark, musty smell unsettling, and a premonition of trouble passes through me, eating at my confidence.

Quietly, Avery closes the door. He's about to reset the lock when I set my hand on his, stopping him. "What if we need to leave in a hurry? Wouldn't it be best not to fumble with locks?"

"Good point."

We make our way forward, and I trail my fingers along the walls to ensure we don't miss a turn. Hints of sunlight shine down from a few cracks in the ceiling, and dust motes wink in the dim rays. The light does little to illuminate the tunnel, but it keeps it from being as black as night, and I'm grateful for it.

I think we're just about to the large cavern when voices drift to us from farther down the tunnel, echoing off the ancient stone walls. We creep forward until we reach a doorway.

The ballroom doesn't look as grand right now. Utilitarian torches burn along the walls, brightening the space with flickering light. Dante stands in the middle of the room, speaking with Ivan. Oddly—or not so oddly now that I think about it—Serena's assistant stands with them.

"Did you use the attractant?" Dante demands.

Ivan crosses his arms. "Yes, and we caught a mess of all kinds of insects—but no larkwings. You've hunted them out. They're gone."

Dante rubs his brow and stares at the ceiling. "Then we move onto the next project."

"I don't care what you do—I want payment for the butterfly, and then I need to get out of the city before the Captain of the Greybrow Serpent tracks me down."

I glance at Avery, but his eyes are still on the exchange. Dante jerks his head toward the left, and Serena's assistant hurries out of sight, perhaps off to collect Ivan's money.

Once she's gone, Dante steps closer, lowering his voice to the point that I almost can't hear him. "We had a good run with the Lark and Song, but I think I'm onto something that will make us richer than the king himself."

Ivan stares at him for a moment. "I'm listening."

"I'm working on a concoction that neutralizes magic."

Avery tenses next to me, possibly believing me for the first time.

"Neutralizes?" Ivan says, incredulous. "Or lessens the effects?"

"Neutralizes."

The thief looks impressed. "What do you need from me?"

"Nothing too difficult to find. Dendrill root, a bag of fresh silverwart. My stocks are low, and I need to experiment."

"Do I look like a common scout?"

"I'll pay you a thousand denats."

If I didn't know what those ingredients were for, I'd run out there myself, begging for the job.

Ivan thinks about it for a moment and then sighs as if put out. "Fine—but you pay me for the larkwing now."

Dante nods, and the woman returns with Ivan's payment. Afraid Ivan's about to leave, I look around for a spot to hide. Unfortunately, the walls are smooth and offer no protection.

"Oh," Dante says, turning back to Ivan just as he was about to leave the cavern. "I need some kind of descaling tool. Think you can find me something? It's such an inconvenience I had to leave everything be-hind when I ransacked my shoppe."

A descaling tool? I nearly pass out at the thought.

"For what?" Ivan asks.

Dante flashes him a lazy grin. "Dragon hide."

"Not a problem," Ivan says, and then he starts to walk our way.

Avery leans close to my ear. "I don't suppose you have an invisibility charm at your disposal?"

"Not on me," I say, truly hoping it wasn't one of

306

the things Gregory had been trying to offer.

"All right, here's what we're going to—"

But I'll never know what Avery is about to say because Dante hollers, "And a few glass beakers, too. I need something that's sturdy enough it can take prolonged heat while I distill an element from blood."

And with those words, I temporarily lose access to my common sense and self-control. It's simply gone, wisped into the air.

Before Avery can stop me, overcome with rage, I charge into the cavern, ripping my dagger from its sheath. "If you have touched so much as one scale on my dragon's body, I will descale *you*."

CHAPTER TWENTY-SEVEN
Uninvited Guests

Avery mutters a curse behind me, and then he follows, slightly less enthusiastic.

Dante turns my way, only looking mildly surprised. "I wondered when you'd get here. With your reputation, I would have been sorely disappointed if you hadn't shown."

"Where is Flink?" I demand, holding my blade in front of me. Though it's an impressive dagger, I must say it looks a bit puny now that Dante's brute guards are drawing their swords and slowly making their way toward me. I extend my blade, warning them to stay back.

"Hello to you as well, Captain." Dante waves down his guards, less than impressed with my entrance, and then turns to me. "He's fine, for now." He frowns and makes a clucking noise as if he's thinking very hard. "I'm afraid I wasn't ready for entertaining. I have just a bit of Lark and Song left, but something tells me you won't be interested in that. Talia—you know how to make tea, don't you, love?"

Serena's assistant frowns.

"What am I saying? Of course you do. Run off and fetch us some—oh, and a few of those little biscuits too—the ones with icing."

He's not taking my ambush seriously, and that's very irritating. What's the point of charging into someone's secret lair if they don't even bother to attack you when they notice your arrival?

"This is not a tea party." I slide my dagger back into its sheath, beyond put out.

Ivan looks a wee bit nervous now that he and the captain are in the same room. Trying to stay as small as possible, like a rat, he inches toward the room off this one, probably not daring to cross Avery to make his way to the exit. Avery watches him, his expression nothing less than menacing, but he does not leave me to chase after the man.

Dante walks toward us, but he doesn't look threatening—more like he wants to do business. "How long were you lurking in the hall? Did you hear the part where Ivan said there were no more butterflies for my lovely concoction, or do I need to fill you in from the beginning?"

I shake my head, ready to throttle him, but Avery takes over, volunteering to do the talking. "We heard."

"Oh good," Dante says, looking genuinely relieved he doesn't have to go over it again. "Let me be forthright with you. I believe there are larkwings left, and I think that if anyone can find them, it's you. So, I'm going to make you a deal. If you want your dragon back, all you have to do is find me a few more butterflies. Nothing to it." He smiles in the friendliest way. "If you can't do that, I'm afraid I need your Flink for my next business venture. You understand, I'm sure. I'll pay you for him, of course, if it comes to that. How much do you think he's worth?"

Avery holds me back, which is probably a good idea, because I'm beginning to see red.

"You listen carefully you pig-goat of a man, I will slice you from your navel to—"

"Lucia," Avery says, half-amused. "When in the enemies' lair, we usually refrain from detailing how you're envisioning their murder."

Dante makes a scoffing noise. "I'm not the enemy."

Before I can answer, Serena's assistant walks back into the ballroom with a silver tray in hand. And there's a tea pot—an actual tea pot.

"This is insane," I mutter under my breath.

"Are you telling me that no matter what, you

won't be willing to do a few side scouting jobs for me then?" Dante says, looking quite disappointed. "And you won't sell me the dragon?"

"That's exactly what I'm telling you." I give him my sweetest smile, one I reserve for times just like this.

Dante exhales slowly and then nods. "Oh, well. Share some tea, let me try to persuade you just a bit longer, and if you still have no interest, I suppose I'll take you to your dragon."

Avery narrows his eyes. "And why would you do that?"

"Do you really have to ask? She is a siren slayer, and you are known to be ruthless in certain circles—a force to be reckoned with. What chance do I have of winning against the likes of you two? Do you think I'm ignorant of your achievements?"

All very valid points. I suppose one cup of tea won't hurt—and those biscuits do look tasty. Hesitant, Avery and I join Dante at the table.

Talia pours our tea, and Dante leaps into the finer points of his business strategy. Neither Avery or I drink until Dante takes his first sip—which he does with gusto. After several minutes, I figure it's safe.

Dante prattles on so long, I begin to get very, very sleepy.

"So," he says, folding his hands on the table before us. "As you can see, you'd only have to work for maybe a year, and then you could retire anywhere you want—leave Kalae. Buy yourself an island."

I blink at him. "What island?"

Dante leans forward, a satisfied smile on his face. "Any island you want."

Covering a yawn, I shake my head. Next to me, Avery does the same.

Dante pulls a pocket watch out of his jacket—*Sebastian's* watch. The one Ivan stole. "If my calculations are correct, you have about thirty seconds."

"Until what?" Avery demands, his voice tired but slightly more coherent than I feel.

"Until the sleeping concoction takes full effect." He leans forward, giving us a grim smile. "For future reference, it's best not to sit down to tea with an alchemist you do not trust."

"He duped us," I say to Avery as I dangle my legs over the side of our rather ornate cage. I'm not sure what kind of birds the ancient people of Kalae used to house in here, but they must have been huge.

"Hmmm?" Avery's made himself comfortable next to me, with his back against the bars and his legs extended in front of him. Our prison sways gently, which would surely make me ill if I weren't still wearing the anti-nausea charm I purchased on my first sea voyage.

"I've had a lot of time to think about it," I continue. "Dante tricked us by telling us how amazing we are. That should have been our first tip because honestly, we're not all that great."

"Speak for yourself," Avery says with a rotten grin.

I turn to him. "Do you think Flink is all right?"

There's a flicker of uncertainty in his eyes that does nothing for my confidence, but he nods. "It will be fine."

The captain thinks he's clever with his words, but it does not escape my notice that he says "it" and not "Flink." He means the situation—the situation that I will surely get over even if my dragon does not make it. My throat tightens, and I look away.

We're not high off the ground, maybe eight feet, and situated in a corner of the cavernous room. Judging from the singed metal bars, I have a suspicion that we're in a greater phoenix cage, which would have been quite a sight to behold.

Dante's men mill around on the other side of the room, looking rather bored. Ivan hasn't made an appearance again. Apparently, he's hiding in the depths of the tunnels, not brave enough to show his face even though we're caged. No one comes or goes, and time crawls on.

I have no idea what Dante plans to do with us, but I almost wish he'd hurry and get it over with.

With nothing else to do, I stare out at the room, my hands on the bars on either side of my face. Gregory should be coming for us soon—hopefully, with a good dose of that illegal fire magic he's so skilled at.

Disinterested, I watch the men as they while away the hours. I'm half asleep when a weird shuffling noise fills the cavern. It sounds as if it's coming from the entrance tunnel.

Everyone stops what they're doing and glances at each other, waiting for someone to explain what the mystery noise is.

I sit up straighter, dread filling my belly. "Avery... we left the door unlocked."

The captain's eyes are on the doorway. The noise grows, as do the strange grunts and low mutterings that accompany it. "Why does that sound like a bunch of—"

"Goblins," I screech as the beasts come pouring into the hall, half running, half crawling. The creatures have bulbous heads, wrinkled, malformed bodies that are covered in sporadic patches of hair, and they move like apes. They communicate in some sort of language, but all I hear is groans and grunts and squeals.

The guards yell and rush forward, meeting their newest uninvited guests. I gape at the creatures, sorely missing my dagger. A tiny blade is better than no blade at all.

Horrified and completely helpless, we watch as the battle begins. Dante's few guards are vastly outnumbered, and though they slay several of the creatures, they are soon overpowered. The goblins swarm around the men, picking them up and carrying them in great groups, going deeper into the tunnels.

My only consolation is that they won't eat them in front of us. As nightmarish as the goblins might be, they aren't completely uncivilized—they prefer to boil their humans before they consume them.

Realizing that we're hanging in the corner, like a tasty tidbit offering, a group of five lumbers to us, their unnatural yellow eyes bright with hungry greed. They talk amongst themselves—rather, they make noises—and then they start poking the cage with the sticks they brought in with them.

"Watch it!" I yell down, staring at one who just smacked me in the foot. "I've killed more than my share of your nasty type, and I have my sites on *you*."

Avery sits down, letting them do their worst, not looking as concerned as I feel he should be. "They'll get bored in a few minutes."

"You're just going to sit there?"

"What do you want me to do?"

He has a point. Finally, I join him, careful to keep my arms and legs tucked in. After about fifteen minutes, they grow tired and wander after the others.

A heavy silence descends over the cavern.

"All right." Avery sits up and digs his lockpick set from his pocket once more. Now that the coast is clear, he'll be able to use it. "Let's get out of here."

It doesn't take him long to unlock the cage, but I stare at the ground, uncertain. I don't love heights, and though we're not really all that high up, my legs begin to shake at the thought of leaping. "You go first."

Avery flashes me an amused look, but he doesn't tease me. With ease, he flips onto his stomach and lowers himself, finally letting himself drop when his boots hover only a few feet off the ground. The movement makes the cage sway back and forth, and I grasp hold of the bars to keep my footing.

"Your turn," he says, obviously quite proud of himself and his graceful display.

I bite the inside of my cheek. "That's all right. I think I'll just live here."

"Come on. I've got you."

I study the ground again and then meet his eyes. The cage continues to rock, making me dizzy. "Nope. I'm good."

"*Lucia.*" The one word says everything—that he'll catch me, that I shouldn't be afraid, that the goblins could come back at any moment.

It's an irrational fear. I know that—I really do. But that doesn't make it any easier.

"Drop down, just like I did, and I'll grab hold of you."

Okay. All right. Yes.

It's sad that I've been in the belly of a great amphibious beast in the wildlands of Grenalda, and I wasn't anywhere near this scared.

Slowly, taking my dear sweet time even though we don't have it to take, I lower myself to my rump and dangle my legs over the edge. "I'm just going to... leap off."

The captain nods. "All right."

"And you're going to catch me."

"Yes, I am."

I take another deep breath, and then I hear a noise coming from the entrance tunnels. There are more goblins coming, and Avery's on the ground, vulnerable. His sword is on the table across the hall—I can see it from here. But he'll never be able to reach it in time.

"Lucia, sometimes we have to do things, even if we're scared. I need you to be brave."

The ground seems like it's farther away every time I look at it. "Easy for you to say. You're not scared of anything."

The noise grows louder, and I stare at the entry, frozen like a terrified rabbit. Avery's going to be boiled alive if I don't hurry up.

"Look at me, Lucia," Avery says, his voice soft. I

meet his eyes, and he hesitates, almost as if he's deliberating whether or not he should speak what's on his mind. "I fear some things."

"Really? What?" I say, knowing he's just trying to get me down.

He straightens his shoulders, stands a little taller. "You."

"Me?" I laugh, but it comes out as a terrified, flighty sound.

"Of admitting something to you." He pins me with his eyes, ignoring the sound of the goblins as they grow quite near to the tunnel entrance. "If I face my fear, will you leap down?"

My heart's in my throat. What's he saying? Numbly, I nod. Only moments pass, but it seems as if time stills.

"I love you, Lucia." The words are almost a whisper, but then he grows more confident, and his voice rises. "Desperately and completely. Even if you don't love me—even if you won't admit it if you do."

I stare at him, the height and the leap ahead of me forgotten.

"Now it's your turn." He looks like he's the one who just leaped from the cage. "Lucia, *jump*."

CHAPTER TWENTY-EIGHT
No Dragon Left Behind

Before I can change my mind, I leap. And then I'm
in Avery's arms, safe—but only for the moment. Together, we race across the hall toward our weapons,
though we both know we'll never make it in time. Still,
we must try.

The noise grows louder. Avery pulls me behind
him, ready to take the new wave of goblins head on,
even unarmed.

But it's not goblins who come crashing through
the doorway as loud as a group of turkeys in the brush.

"About time you show up," I snarl at Sebastian and
the rest of our group, doubling over in relief. Gregory
and Gerard are with him, but there's a fourth member
of their party as well. I narrow my eyes at the group,
particularly at the auburn-haired girl who's wearing

trousers and brandishing a flimsy rapier. At least she has her hair up. I level my gaze on Sebastian. "You brought Adeline! She's going to be eaten by the goblins!"

"G-goblins," Adeline stutters, not looking quite as brave as she did a moment ago. "Here?"

"She demanded she come with us," Sebastian says, obviously thinking it's ludicrous as well. "What goblins?"

"They broke into the tunnels," Avery says, carefully omitting the part where we basically left the back door open for them. "There are at least a hundred of them—maybe more."

"Why are we standing around? Let's leave before they come back."

"They kidnapped all of Dante's men about thirty minutes ago," Avery says.

My business partner, a man who hates to get his hands dirty, grits his teeth, holding back a curse or two. "There's nothing the six of us can do against a horde of goblins. We need to alert the king."

I stand rooted to the ground, not about to leave. "They have Flink."

Sebastian stares at me, looking as if he's about ready to toss me over his shoulder. "Lucia..."

The men are silent for a moment, and I take the opportunity to retrieve Avery's sword and my dagger.

When I return to the group, I look at the mage. "Are you with us?"

"Captain?" Gregory asks. "It's your decision."

We turn to Avery, waiting to see what he says. "Sebastian, take Adeline back to the castle and inform Harold of the situation."

Sebastian's first instinct is to argue with Avery, but he finally nods.

"The rest of you will come with me. Gregory, do you have a spell to stun the goblins when we find them?"

The mage flashes us a smile, and then he quickly schools it. "I think I can manage something."

After recent events, his words are chilling. As if sensing what I'm thinking, Gregory chuckles under his breath.

"Once we find the group, Gerard and Gregory will escort them out. Lucia and I will find Flink, and then we'll meet Gregory at the entrance of the tunnels."

Everyone nods. The only one who looks uncertain of the plan is Sebastian. "What if Lucia..." He clears his throat, knowing I'm not going to like the next part. "What if she comes with us?"

"*Sebastian,*" I hiss.

Avery doesn't shoot down the idea right away, and I glare at him. He takes me by the shoulders. "I'll find Flink—I'll bring him back to you."

"I'm not going."

"No one would think less of you," he says quietly, assuring me it's all right. What he really means is he wouldn't think less of me. But I already know that.

"I'm going with you."

He studies me for several heartbeats, and then he nods. "All right. It's your choice."

Before he leaves, Sebastian yanks me against his chest and whispers near my ear, "Do not get yourself killed, do you understand? Absolutely no heroics."

I flash him a smile. "When am I anything less than careful?"

A noise from deeper in the tunnel spooks Adeline, and she jumps back, ready to dart.

"Get her out of here," I tell him.

Sebastian nods and takes Adeline by the arm. He leaves without looking back, probably because if he does, he'll change his mind and try to take me with him.

"Are we ready?" Avery asks, rolling his head from side to side, stretching his neck.

Gregory almost looks eager, and Gerard...well, he simply looks pretty, but I'm hoping he can hold his own in a fight.

We make our way through the room that Dante entertained Avery and me in when I passed out at the masquerade. Everything is still and eerie. There's a partially-played game of chess on the table. Half the pieces are on their sides. A goblet of wine rests on a bench near the doorway, forgotten.

There's a female scream from deep in the tunnels, and I shiver. I almost forgot about Serena. Does Dante have her too? Are they holding her—will she be an easy target for the goblins?

None of us speaks as we move through the ancient maze. Any other time, I'd stop and marvel at the carvings and ornate architecture—a wonder from another century, but I barely notice it now. We wind and twist, and I hope one of us has a good memory, because I'm afraid I'm hopelessly turned around.

Avery leads, sword at the ready. The blade glows in the light, almost as if it's as eager for a fight as our mage. I follow directly behind Avery. Gerard is behind me, and Gregory stands at the rear, watching our backs. We enter another room, but this time, we're not alone.

A pair of goblins screech when they spot us, and they leap across the room in several long bounds. Avery rushes forward, finishing off the first almost before we even begin. I duck as the second makes a swipe for me, spin on my heel, and then plunge my blade into the creature, all while reminding myself that if caught, he'd gladly eat me.

Gregory finishes the beast with a quick burst of

fire, and the room goes silent.

Avery doesn't even look winded. He glances at me. "You good?"

I nod. It's not the first time I've gone up against the monsters, but it's never a picnic.

We run into several more goblins, some alone, some in groups as large as ten. The thicker they get, the more I remind myself we must be drawing near the prisoners. A gash in my cheek stings. I'm not even sure when I got it, but I wipe away the blood and cringe at my hand.

Avery has a bite wound on his arm that will need to be tended, and Gerard's walking like he got hit in the side. The only one who's come this far unscathed is our mage, and he's not even out of breath. Without him, I'm certain we'd be dead by now. There are just too many of them.

"Do you hear that?" I whisper to Avery, touching his back to alert him to stop. The sound of someone softly crying filters down the halls. "It's Serena's assistant."

We change course, go back to the last hall and then take another one to the left. I peek my head around a corner to see what we're up against. We've reached another large room. This one isn't as huge as the cavernous ballroom, but it's still plenty large enough for sixty goblins to congregate in. It appears to be a kitchen and cellar of sorts, and there are wine and ale barrels aplenty. The goblins have already tapped into them, and they lounge about the floor, drinking straight from the barrels, baring their teeth and fighting whenever another tries to push them out of the way. It's chaos...but it's controlled in its own way.

In the corner, a fire already crackles in the huge hearth. Five goblins drag a massive cast iron cauldron across the floor, running into their lounging comrades as they go.

To our immediate left is another room, this one smaller—a pantry if you will, because the human dinner course is ready and waiting. Several lazy guards stand watch, but their eager eyes are on the pot and not on their hostages

"Gregory," Avery whispers. "Take care of them— be as quiet as you can."

Our mage nods. He holds up his hand and concentrates on his targets. The goblins immediately press their hands to their overlarge, pointy ears and then fall to the ground.

"You two stay here—keep watch." Avery steps forward. "Lucia, with me."

We wait several moments until none of the goblins seem to be looking our way, and then we dart into the room. Several men begin to yell, but I hold my finger to my lips, reminding them to stay silent. After a quick scan, to my relief, I see Serena isn't here. Talia is the only woman in the group. Tears stain her dirty face, and she's as pale as death.

As quickly as possible, Avery and I start on the rudimentary ties. Fortunately for us, goblins aren't known for their patience, and the knots are sloppy at best. We free Talia first and send her across the hall to Gerard and Gregory. She falls into Gerard's arms, softly sobbing. We send the rest of the men two at a time, until the only ones left are Ivan and Dante.

Before Avery releases Ivan, he goes through his pockets, helping himself to the money and random trinkets he has stashed away. He studies a wicked-looking dagger he pulls from the man's sheath. It appears to be Milindrian-forged, quite old, and the blade glows blue. It's worth a lot of money, and it doesn't appear to be like anything else in the captain's extensive collection.

"How about I keep this and your pocket change," Avery says, eying the man, "and we call it even?"

Ivan glares at him, but he nods.

"Good." Avery loosens his ropes and sends him over to Gregory, silently telling the mage to keep a careful eye on him.

"Well, looks like we're done here," I say to Avery as I turn to leave.

Dante lets out a muffled plea—sounding quite

pathetic and desperate. The goblins gagged him—not something they usually do to their victims. He must have squealed very loudly.

I kneel in front of him. "Here's how this is going to work. I'm going to make a deal with you. You're going to tell me where you're keeping Flink, and if he's well and unharmed, we'll come back for you. If you lie—we leave you. If he's hurt—we leave you. If you irritate me further—we leave you."

He doesn't need to know I won't leave him to the goblins. Unless he's hurt my dragon, and then... Let's just say he better hope Flink is alive.

Avery rips the fabric from the alchemist's mouth and cringes. It's stained with goblin sweat and so filthy it's stiff—I know I wouldn't want it shoved in my mouth. "You heard her," the captain says. "Tell us where the dragon is."

As a nice extra touch, Avery holds the point of his blade to Dante's jugular.

"Search him for Sebastian's pocket watch," I add. It only takes the captain a moment to locate it. He hands it to me and then turns back to the alchemist.

"The dragon?" Avery prompts, nudging the blade closer.

"Two halls from here." Dante gulps, his eyes wild. "Take a right, and then a left, and then another right. We held him in the treasure room to keep him calm."

Satisfied with the man's answer, Avery nods and glances at the wad of fabric. Then he shrugs to himself and shoves it back in Dante's mouth. The man lets out a muffled curse, but we ignore it as we flee across the way, over to where Gregory waits for us.

"Gerard's leading the prisoners to the entrance," the mage says. "I'm going to follow him. Are you sure you'll be all right on your own?"

Avery nods. "Wait for us in the large cavern."

Before he leaves, Gregory turns to me. He takes my hand and shoves a medallion in my palm. "If you find yourself surrounded, throw this into the air."

"What does it do?" I ask, beyond wary.

"You're going to have to trust me—only use it if you absolutely have to."

That doesn't sound ominous at all.

The mage leaves, and we follow Dante's directions deeper into the maze. The tunnels are warmer here, making me wonder if we're near an underground heat source. Beads of sweat trail between my shoulder blades and run down my face. I wipe my forehead with the back of my hand. Goblins, who generally like their climate a bit cooler, don't linger here.

We finally find the door, and I find myself pausing outside.

"What's the matter?" Avery asks.

I turn to him. "What if he's..."

328

Avery nods, understanding. "I'll go in first."

Feeling like a coward, I step back. I clench my eyes shut as Avery opens the door.

"Lucia..." Avery says, sounding a bit off.

Terror runs through me, almost paralyzing me. Unable to help myself, I open my eyes and dart into the room.

Avery crosses his arms and leans against the door frame. "We'll never get him out of here."

A very alive, very healthy-looking Flink sits atop a pile of gold and countless treasures, like a king on a throne. He lets out a happy churring sound of greeting when he sees us, and then he burrows his shining copper self even deeper into his new bed.

CHAPTER TWENTY-NINE
Do We Have a Choice?

"Come on, Flink," I say. "It's time to go."

Does the dragon move? No, he does not.

Knowing that the situation calls for it, I set my hands on my hips and give him my best stern look. I point at the ground by my feet. "Flink. *Now.*"

He stares at me with his adorable dragon eyes, not budging. I'm going to have to get him myself.

Avery follows me into the room, gawking at our new surroundings. I give him a stern look, not unlike what I just used on Flink. "Not you too."

The captain flashes me a grin and begins to poke around in the treasures. He holds up a particularly fine dagger. "Want another one? I just swiped a new toy from Ivan, but I hate to leave this one behind."

Shaking my head, I turn back to the dragon. "We

don't have all day, Flink."

Whoever brought him in here must have removed his lead and harness, but I have no idea what they did with them.

An awful, jarring goblin cry rings out in the vicinity of their banquet room, and I turn to Avery.

"I think they just realized their dinner escaped," Avery says, interested in the treasure no longer. "They'll kill Dante if we don't hurry."

What I wouldn't give for a piece of cheese. Together, the two of us tug at the dragon, trying to get him moving. When we realize that's futile, we give up on that and go behind him to push. He fights us, refusing to budge no matter what we do or say. We need to leave *now*. What am I going to do?

Desperate, I sink to my knees in front of Flink, scratching him on the head just where he likes it. Hoping he will hear logic—hoping he will understand me at all—I say, "We have to go—we don't have a choice. I need you to come with us, but I cannot make you."

Then I stand and give him a lingering look as I walk away. One last time, over my shoulder, I call, "Come on, Flink."

I don't look back, even when my throat feels it's going to close completely. We rush to the room where we left the alchemist, and Avery already prepares for a fight. I suck in a horrified breath and stop short in the hall.

The goblins have Dante, and they're passing him along, tossing him about the room as if he were a leather ball. They're past angry—completely enraged, and they take out their fury on the alchemist. Slowly, with each toss, he gets closer to the now-boiling pot.

"We have to save him," I say as I rush forward. No one, not even Dante, deserves to die that way.

Avery holds me back. "There are too many of them."

I glance at Gregory's medallion, nervous. "What do you think? Do we dare?"

"Do we have a choice?"

Good point.

Before I can talk myself out of it, I heave the medallion into the room, throwing it high above the chaos. It explodes at the apex of its flight, and a green, gas-like mist settles over the room.

It *reeks*. The kind of reek that makes skunks smell pleasant—the kind of reek that's right up there with Moss Forest orchids. The goblins begin to shriek and flail, and they drop Dante. He crashes to the floor with a hard and heavy thud.

Seeing his chance, Avery darts into the fray, leaving me coughing in the hall. He emerges with the alchemist, and tears run down both their faces as they choke and gasp for air. After a moment, Avery straightens, ready to move. There's no time to untie Dante, so Avery slices the ropes around the alchemist's legs so the man can at least run.

I glance over my shoulder, looking for Flink, hoping. My heart nearly shatters, for there is no sign of my dragon.

With no choice, we run through the tunnels as fast as we are able, only taking a few wrong turns in the process. The goblins are behind us, racing through the halls as fast as their gangly legs will carry them. Finally, we reach the room off the cavernous hall. I knock past the chess board, sending the rest of the pieces flying.

Gregory waits for us at the entrance of the hall.

"Can you collapse the entrance tunnel behind us?" Avery yells as we rush toward the mage.

Without a word of question, the mage raises his hands, collecting the magic in the air.

And that's when I hear it—a far off roar.

"Wait!" I yell. "Flink's coming!"

"Lucia," Avery says, pulling me with him when I stop. "They'll kill us this time; we have no choice."

I struggle against him and look over my shoulder. "FLINK!"

There it is again, and this time, I know Avery hears it. Flink listened, he *obeyed*.

He's coming.

Gregory stands with his hands raised, waiting for

his captain's signal. The goblins emerge from the small room. They bare their teeth and brandish sticks in the air like weapons, swarming into the cavern like ants chased from their hill.

Then a copper dragon bursts from the crowd of monsters, snarling and snapping. They shy away from him, some shrieking, terrified of their natural predator, even if he is pint-sized in comparison to the greater dragons they so rightly fear.

"Run, Lucia!" Avery yells. "It's too late!"

"No!"

Avery pulls me out of the cavern, practically carrying me as he runs down the last hall. Gregory is right behind us. The door stands wide open, beckoning us with its promise of safety. Avery shoves me out the door, into the courtyard.

"Now!" he yells just as I cry, "Wait!"

A great rumble shakes the ground, making me gasp. The earth heaves and bucks, but Gregory stands calmly. His hands are raised, and his eyes are dark with intense concentration. Just as I see the silhouettes of the monsters nearing the entrance, just as the stones of the courtyard begin to give way, Flink leaps from the tunnel.

Dust and debris rise, choking me, and the roar is deafening. I reach for Flink as I watch the ground swallow the cavern. The whole time, Gregory controls it all, safely closing the passage, locking the goblins inside.

CHAPTER THIRTY
Did You Mean It?

I stumble to the ground, crawling toward Flink. As if this were nothing more than a fun game, Flink trots to me and plops down at my side. I allow myself a few tears—even mighty siren slayers can cry if the situation calls for it, and bury my face against the dragon's warm, smooth scales. He butts my head, making contented noises not unlike that of a cat.

The dust settles around us, and as the sounds of the tremulous crash cease, I realize we're not alone.

The king and his men must have arrived just before we escaped the tunnels, and guards restrain Dante and his men. We're surrounded by torches, and too many people talk all at once—it's much too loud. Harold demands Avery's attention, and the captain explains the situation in detail.

I'm dizzy from the excitement. My head's too light, and my muscles want to run even though we are now safe.

Gregory kneels next to me. "Besides the cut on your cheek, are you hurt?"

I shake my head, willing my heart to slow its rapid pace.

"Would you like me to heal it?"

I think about it for a moment, wondering if a scar will make people take me more seriously. But vanity wins, and I nod. The wound tingles as Gregory knits the flesh, but it's over in just a moment.

Avery finally breaks from the crowd, and the mage rises to his feet, patting my shoulder as he makes way for the captain. "Don't be too mad at Avery for ordering me to close the tunnels before we knew if your dragon could escape. Like it or not, your safety will always come first."

Gregory pauses as he passes Avery and the two do the manly look of silent acknowledgment. Then, laughing, Avery clasps Gregory's shoulder.

Finally, the captain kneels in front of Flink and looks the dragon right in the eyes, pretending I'm not here. "Tell me, dragon to man, is she angry I almost left you behind?"

Of course, Flink doesn't answer.

Though I don't want to smile, I can't quite help it.

337

"Gregory told me I'm not allowed to be."

Avery looks over and grins. "That's why I let him speak with you first." Leaving Flink's side, he comes to me and pulls me to my feet. His eyes search mine. "Are you all right?"

There are too many people milling around, so I tug him away from the chaos. We find another small courtyard, this one with a sleeping fountain. It's dark and still. Nervous but determined, I face Avery.

"Did you mean it?" I don't have to refer to his confession in the great hall. He knows. "Or did you say it so I would jump?"

My pulse quickens, and I'm terrified of his answer. For a moment, he looks like he might brush the moment we had in the tunnel away, but then his features soften. "I meant it."

"I did too," I whisper in a rush. "When I said it at the masquerade. I mean, I don't actually remember, but—"

I never finish the words because Avery yanks me against him and crushes his lips to mine. He smiles at my surprise, and I laugh and pull him closer. It's sweeter than any kiss we've ever shared, not urgent, not forbidden, not rushed. Slow and perfect, with a slow-smoldering heat that makes my skin tingle.

"Now what?" I murmur when he finally draws back. "Where do we go from here?"

The same old obstacle lies between us, making the moment bittersweet.

He rests his forehead against mine. "Come with me to Marlane."

The sea is not, and I doubt will ever be, my favorite place. But I want to be with Avery—even if that means another month or two on the water.

"Yes, I suppose." I shrug, nonchalant.

Avery shakes his head and kisses me again.

CHAPTER THIRTY-ONE
Can You Catch?

Serena and Sam are gone. No one has seen them in days, and Dante swore to the king that he never touched her. The alchemist is in the dungeons, serving his time along with Ivan and their accomplices.

As for us, we're being heralded as heroes once again, much to Minerva's chagrin. She smiles at me over her delicate tea cup, but the expression doesn't meet her eyes. I don't think we'll be fast friends anytime soon.

We sit in a royal parlor, enjoying a going away party of sorts. Avery's grandmother and sister are here, and so is Lord Thane. It reminds me of my first day in the castle, but I don't feel nearly as out of place.

"Yes, we leave this afternoon," Avery tells Harold.

His Majesty nods, pleased. But then he turns to

Sebastian. "So, if Lady Lucia goes with Avery, is this the end of your scouting partnership?"

Sebastian and I share a look. We haven't talked about it, in fact, we've avoided the subject completely.

"Only temporarily," Sebastian finally answers. "While Lucia assists Avery in his expedition, I will see that Adeline is properly settled in Reshire. I'm certain we'll meet again soon afterward."

But he doesn't sound certain. And I'm not either.

Before the king can press further, a guard bursts into the room. "Your Majesty, Bib Hanhaust has been apprehended, and his wife and their steward are with him. We've held him for questioning."

"Who?" I ask Avery.

The captain sits back. "Serena's husband."

Harold nods, resolute. "Bring them in."

In just a few minutes, Serena sweeps into the room, a lovely vision in pale pink silk and flowing blond hair. "I don't care if you are the king—how dare you accuse my husband of—" she stops short when she sees the rest of us. Confusion, and then fear, mars her lovely features.

But she's nowhere as confused as I am, because Bib Hanhaust himself is right behind her. Together, the couple is a human oxymoron. Where Serena is a goddess in the flesh, Bib is short, a bit paunchy, almost completely bald, and has a rather red nose.

SHARI L. TAPSCOTT

"Please forgive my wife, Your Majesty, but with all due respect," Bib says when Serena is struck dumb, "these charges are ridiculous. Connected to alchemists concocting elixirs? I haven't even been in Teirn!"

"Bib," Harold says, sounding very tired, "we already know you were involved with Dante—he admitted it. Not only were you providing the alchemist with the larkwings needed to make his illegal concoction, but you were using royal grant money to do so."

Bib's eyebrows scrunch with genuine confusion. "I wasn't selling larkwings to an alchemist! Why would I do that? They're almost extinct! I have been working feverishly to preserve their species." He's worked himself up and is now quite indignant. "Why else do you think I was traipsing around in the forest, looking for a mate for the specimen I brought back several months ago?"

King Harold looks rightly confused. Either Bib is an excellent actor, or he's telling the truth. "Then why would Dante link you? What purpose could that possibly serve? It's not like he was able to use you as a scapegoat—he's in the dungeons as we speak."

"Who is *Dante*?" Bib demands, then he turns to his wife. "Isn't that the shopkeeper fellow your assistant is sweet on?"

"Oh, no," I murmur to myself, and everyone turns.

"What?" Sebastian asks.

I swallow and look right at Serena, asking for permission to speak of our agreement. She very subtly—but very insistently—shakes her head.

Fine. I'll see if I can work around it.

I turn to Bib. "While you were away, your larkwing *disappeared* from your office—"

Before I can finish the words, Bib gasps, overcome with horror.

"Serena, desperate for its return," I continue, looking right at her as I ignore him, "hired us to find it, and we...well..."

Sebastian, sensing I'm struggling due to the lingering effects of the silencing charm, jumps in, "We tracked the butterfly back to Dante and his web of alchemists. When Lucia and Avery attended one of the masquerades to *investigate*" —he flashes us a wry look— "they learned that you were working with Dante, and that your scholars' guild search was a cover-up. You were actually collecting the larkwings for Dante's concoction."

Bib turns red. "I wasn't—"

"But we didn't know that Dante was in a romantic relationship with Talia," I interrupt. "She would have known where you were, and it would have been simple for Dante to say you were working together, when you, in fact, were not."

Serena goes pale, and she slowly raises a hand to her mouth, looking like she's going to be ill. We all turn to her, but her gaze is locked on mine. Softly, she says, "It was Talia who convinced me to sell the butterfly."

"You *what*?" Bib exclaims, aghast.

"She was the one who said you were having an affair—she said she *saw* you! And I—I was out of my mind with jealousy when you left that night, and when she said it would serve you right if I sold your larkwing..."

Bib takes his wife by the shoulders—which is difficult since she is taller than he—and gives her a look of such genuine love, it makes me uncomfortable. "Serena, I told you then, and I will tell you now, you are my *everything*."

He goes on, but I don't have the stomach to listen.

King Harold holds up his hand, tired of the whole ordeal. "I believe you're innocent, Bib. Let's put this whole thing behind us."

"What about the goblins?" Adeline asks, speaking up for the first time. "Why were they so interested in the tunnels? They never wander this far south."

Bib extends his hands in front of him like no one ever listens to him. "That was the whole point of the expedition! Goblins eat larkwings. Apparently, they are quite the delicacy. Once a year, when the larkwings are plentiful, they hunt them. Addicted to the creature's drug-like element, they've been in a tizzy since the larkwings have become scarce. Now they're causing all kinds of havoc, traipsing all over the provinces, hoping to track them. They are simple, but there is some thought process there."

"What will they do now that the butterfly is extinct?" I ask.

Bib turns to me, his eyes lighting for the first time. "Ah—but they are not extinct. I've returned with a pair, and I plan to begin a breeding program immediately, carefully rebuilding their species."

Butterfly breeding program? Disturbing.

Sebastian stands and shakes Bib's hand and nods to Serena. "Though I am glad it worked out, I'm sorry we were unable to retrieve your wildwood larkwing."

The dressmaker sighs. "It's all right. I'm sorry I involved you."

We say our goodbyes, and finally, it is my turn to face the queen. I'm not sure there's much to say.

"I'm sorry I never replaced your vase."

Minerva studies me for several long moments, and then she leans forward, silently asking me to do the same. I raise my eyebrows, waiting for her to say whatever it is she deems to be so secretive.

"I broke the real one a year ago. That was a fake."

"*No,*" I say, astounded. "It was very well done."

She raises her eyebrows and shrugs.

After another moment, she says, "Take care of Avery."

Well, this conversation just went awkward.

"No...hard feelings?" I ask, truly curious.

Minerva laughs—truly laughs. "Please, Lucia. I'm married to a *king*."

Right.

Though she might be sad to see Avery leave, and though she's certainly not going to shed any tears over my departure, I think we've made a breakthrough.

I move to Lady Claire and Elizabetta. Avery's grandmother gives me an appraising look. "When you return, we're going to get to know each other better."

Even though that statement terrifies me, I manage to smile.

Elizabetta hugs me before I move on. She's tall for her age, very nearly my height. Before she lets me go, she whispers, "Convince Avery to take me with him next time, all right?"

She gives me a pointed look when she releases me, and I promise I will try.

Before we leave, Harold takes my hands. "You are welcome anytime, Lady Lucia."

"Thank you for everything, Your Majesty."

We finally leave the castle. My trunks have already been sent to the Serpent. Adeline and Sebastian are going to drop Avery and me off at the pier, and then we'll go our separate ways.

The ride is quiet. Occasionally, my eyes meet Adeline's, and she smiles encouragingly. But the mood is a little sad.

Avery assists me from the carriage, and I take in a great gulp of the salty air. The day is so warm, it borders on hot. Spring has arrived in all its balmy glory. Flink bounds onto the pier, basking in the warmth.

The Greybrow Serpent waits, ready for its next adventure. Gregory waves from the ship. There's no sign of Yancey—no one's seen him in weeks. I hope that wherever he is, he is well and safe.

I turn to my friends, preparing myself for good-byes.

Adeline hugs me first, wrapping me in her sweet-pea scented arms. "I'll miss you. Be careful, all right?"

I smile against her hair. "I will."

We pull apart, and Sebastian steps forward. Adeline slides her arm through Avery's and pulls him aside, asking him about the sea birds, giving us a moment of privacy.

"Your parents aren't going to like this," Sebastian says, not quite smiling but not scowling either.

"Tell them I swear I'll behave myself. And don't forget to give Mother the orchids." Somehow the plants I brought from the whirlpool island are still alive.

The air is heavy between us, and it crushes against

my lungs. Not quite looking at him, I say, "I'm going to miss you."

He growls and then reluctantly admits, "I'm going to miss you too."

I look back, trying to laugh. "It's only for a few months."

He pulls me close and sets his chin on my head. "Take care of yourself, Lucia."

I close my eyes, for the last time letting a few fleeting "what-ifs" pass through my mind. But it wasn't right for us. I love Sebastian, but I'm in love with Avery. And I know now there is a vast difference between the two.

Before I step back, I breathe in Sebastian's familiar, comfortable scent. Goodbyes hurt, and this one feels substantial.

Blinking quickly, I hide my tears with a smile and pull away. It's finished.

Avery walks back, a sympathetic smile on his face. He knows this is hard, and though he's probably a little jealous, he's very sweet about it. We say our final goodbyes, and Avery leads me toward the Greybrow Serpent with a soft hand on the small of my back.

But before we start up the gangplank, a man yells from the pier, "Lady Lucia!"

I turn, startled. The owner of the voice hurries forward. He's tall and lean with dark hair and even darker eyes. His skin is caramel, and judging from his clothing, he looks like he belongs to one of the traveling caravans. And oddly, there's something familiar about him.

"You're a hard girl to track down," he says, sucking in a deep breath after the run. "Especially with your king determined to keep you hidden."

This must be the man Harold repeatedly turned away. "Do I know you?"

His eyes shine with good humor. "You don't remember me, but I didn't expect you to."

Avery shifts closer to me.

"My name is Gorin, and we met two years before, on a dark night in Reshire."

Something dances in my memory, just out of grasp.

"At the time, you were the most beautiful girl I'd ever seen. You thoroughly charmed me, and we made a trade—my ice charm for one—"

"Phoenix feather," I breathe, the night coming back to me in a rush.

We were younger then, and he hadn't yet grown out of his gangly, puppy stage. I was right at the time— he grew up to be quite handsome.

Avery stands silently at my side, but I can feel his questions.

"Actually, I sent you after a greater fire hippogriff." Gorin grins. "But that's not the point. I've come to collect, and I don't have a need for the charm or a feather."

That's good. The ice charm now belongs to Prince Kaiu, far away in the whirlpool island, and we sold the feather.

Sebastian and Adeline make their way to us, curious.

"What is it you need?" Avery asks.

Gorin's smile grows—reminding me very much of the boy I met those long two years ago. "Just a flower...a flower that is proving very difficult to track down. Rumor has it Lady Lucia and her partner are the best, and since you owe me..."

Gregory and several members of the crew have come to the edge of the ship, and they're watching the exchange.

I grin at Gregory. "I happen to have a very powerful mage at my disposal. How about he whips you up an ice charm, and we call it even?"

The mage rolls his eyes, amused that I'm so quick to offer his services.

Gorin shakes his head. "I'm afraid that won't do. You see, that ring was my great, great, *great* grandmother's, and nothing will ever replace it. I need *you*."

We stare at each other for several long moments, and then I give in. "What do you need the flower for?"

"I am in love with a girl—a beautiful, vibrant girl. But her father refused to let us marry, so I begged him for a task. I'll do anything, I told him, if he would only give me a chance to prove myself."

Avery's expression eases considerably. "What task did he give you?"

Gorin runs a hand through his hair, exasperated. "He's very ill—aging too quickly. Dying, most likely. He told me to bring him the cure."

"And what does this flower do exactly?" I ask.

The man leans forward, his eyes bright. "It will restore his youth."

It's impossible, but Gorin watches me with such an earnest expression, I don't have the heart to tell him no.

"All right," I say finally. "When we return from Marlane, I will help you find this flower."

"There's no time," he says, looking desperate. "She marries another on the first day of summer. Too many weeks have already passed."

I groan. "Give me a few moments to speak with my party."

Gladly, Gorin strides to the edge of the pier and stares at the birds diving into the water.

Avery looks at me for several moments, and then softly, he says, "You should go."

Sebastian nods. "I'll accompany her."

351

"Well, then I'm going too!" Adeline exclaims.

I stare at Avery. "Come with us."

He shakes his head. "I cannot. I already told Harold I'd fetch his gold. My hands are tied, Lucia. I can't back out now."

"You choose today to become an upstanding citizen?" I cross my arms, exasperated.

Avery closes the distance between us, not caring that we're surrounded by people. "I will bring back the king's gold, and then I will find you—no matter where you are or how far you travel."

"You swear it?"

His lips brush mine as he whispers, "I swear."

"How?"

"Keep the dagger close." He grins an evil smirk, but for the first time, I'm grateful for his love of tracking spells.

"You'll hurry?"

"I will."

The thought of leaving him for even a month makes breathing painful.

"I love you," I murmur against his lips. "And I will miss you."

The captain of the Greybrow Serpent kisses me properly, in front of all of Teirn. People whistle and cheer, but we ignore them.

Sebastian and Adeline come to my side as Avery

walks up the gangplank.

In his captain's jacket and tall, dark boots, he's so handsome. And he's mine. I can wait a month; I can wait forever if it comes down to it.

The crew raises the ship's anchor and adjusts the sails. Adeline wraps her arm around my shoulders as the Greybrow Serpent pulls away from the dock. Suddenly, Avery jogs from the rail and disappears into his cabin only to return moments later.

"Lucia," he hollers when he returns. "Can you catch?"

Laughing, shaking my head at his strange behavior, I hold out my hands. He heaves a small velvet pouch at me, and I almost fumble it into the cove. The ship drifts farther away, and I hurry to open it.

"Hold it for me—keep it safe," he yells, grinning like a fool. "I have a question to ask you when I return!"

My heart catches in my throat, and my fingers tremble as I turn the pouch over in my palm. A sea fire ruby catches the sunlight, taking my breath away. That day, months ago, he must have collected his own after I left the cave. But it's not the ruby that does me in, but the gold that surrounds it.

"What is it?" Adeline asks, unable to quell her curiosity. She gasps the moment she lays eyes on it. "Lucia—that's a ring!"

Yes, it is.

I look up, and my gaze locks on Avery's. He leans on the rail, promises in his eyes. I stand here until I cannot see him any longer, until the Greybrow Serpent disappears into the horizon. Then I thread the ring on the chain I wear at my neck.

After I look at it one last time, I tuck the ring under my bodice, close to my heart.

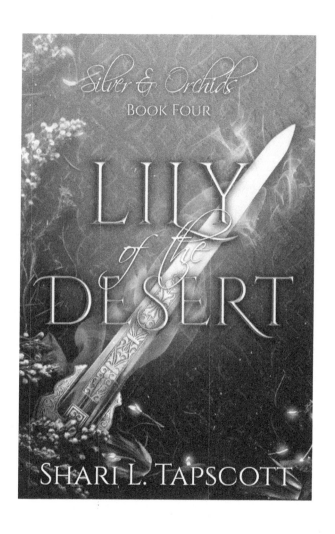

Silver & Orchids
BOOK FOUR

LILY
of the
DESERT

SHARI L. TAPSCOTT

AVAILABLE
NOVEMBER 16, 2017

About the Author

Shari L. Tapscott writes young adult fantasy and humorous contemporary fiction. When she's not writing or reading, she enjoys gardening, making soap, and pretending she can sing. She loves white chocolate mochas, furry animals, spending time with her family, and characters who refuse to behave.

Tapscott lives in western Colorado with her husband, son, daughter, and two very spoiled Saint Bernards.

To learn more about Shari's books, please visit: **shariltapscott.com**

Made in the USA
Las Vegas, NV
20 January 2022

41971496R00215